ESCAPE

by

Jared Austin

Huntsville, Alabama

This is a work of fiction. All of the characters, organizations, and events portrayed in this novel are either products of the author's imagination or are used fictitiously.

ESCAPE

ISBN: 978-1-956834-03-1

Published by Up Past Dawn LLC. Find us at:
https://jareddanielaustin.com

Table of Contents

Dedication

To Rosalie and Sawyer
I hope you see the endless possibilities before you
And seize those that bring you happiness and meaning

Acknowledgments

Book two is complete. Wow! And so many people to thank for helping me get here. My wife, Dana Austin, for her encouragement. Mel Howard, Kay Glover, Troy Farsoun, Darren Gannuch, Heather Montgomery, and Nellie Maulsby, thank you for the careful critiques and discussions of each of these stories, which helped me grow the world first created in *Space City*. Thank you to my Teach to Write and the North Alabama Science Fiction and Cake Appreciation Society (NASFCAS) writing groups, which listened to me read through these stories, sometimes multiple times, and offering insightful critiques.

I'd also like to thank Amy Herring and Bryan Jones for consultation and support in my cover revisions.

Lastly, thank you readers, for taking the time out of your busy lives to spend it with me and the world of *Space City*. I hope you enjoy yourself and consider it time well spent!

Nico's Flying Venice

Chapter 1

"X-ray. X-ray. X-ray. Why didn't you warn me?" Neil Ericson yelled, fleeing the gilded St. Mark's Basilica as if escaping captivity.

"X-ray?" Nico Colombo tensed, waiting for whatever had spooked Neil to emerge from the basilica. The first sign of life in his Venice sim—had to be part of the academy trial sim he'd hacked and merged with his landscape.

Something guarded their first task.

Opulent marble statues of horses and saints crowned the enormous Romanesque cathedral. Within external arches, religious mosaic murals composed from tiny glass squares generated a gleam as if Heaven itself lit St. Marks. Nico's first view of the basilica since his mother's death.

No guard emerged. Nico frowned. Neil wasn't the sort to spook easily. Despite being just sixteen, Neil had thwarted the Dahaka attack upon Space City just a couple months prior. So what caused his alarm now?

Nico used his wrist-comp, strapped over the left arm of his gray explorer suit, to summon his scouts. The dozen firefly-like machines closed in from around the square and zipped around Nico's head as if anxious for a command.

An angel statue crashed to the pavement, crushing a couple of the bots. Nico ducked, sidestepping. The remaining scouts scattered. Nico eyed the basilica's roof, expecting some formidable guard. Only the statues stood waiting, minus the one lying shattered at his feet.

A red warning flashed on Nico's wrist-comp, alerting him that three bots were offline. He bit his lower lip. A quarter of his scouts lost in the first few minutes of exploring the sim.

Had the statue fallen on its own?

Nico shook his head. *Not in a sim. Did someone or something knock it over, then retreat from view? Possibly, but this is a fourth-year sim trial. Think outside the box.*

Neil's prior warning hit. X-ray. Nico blinked, thinking of x-rays, or more accurately, RF-waves, but everyone called them x-ray. His contacts activated, transforming the world into a wall of bright blue, as if he were seeing the world according to their heat signatures. Lines of red symbols appeared on the blue wall, roughly where the front of St. Mark's began. Nico couldn't read them.

He blinked once, deliberately; the contacts snapped a picture of the symbols, which he could send to his wrist-comp for deciphering.

Above the lines a giant red, orange, and yellow exoskeleton appeared on the basilica roof's edge, studying him. As if comprehending it had been spotted, the insect leapt to the ground, sending a massive shiver through the concrete and up Nico's legs. Nico tensed to steady himself.

Standing on the ground, the creature's head was level with the angel statues on the roof. The insect's long neck and head rocked back and forth like an old-fashioned metronome. Or a swinging hypnotist's tool. Two front arms, like scythes, cut the air between them. A couple of swipes from those would cleave him into neatly sliced layers, like a stack of pancakes oozing with jelly.

A small part of Nico's mind screamed, *it's a sim. End it*!

Laser fire struck the bulbous right orb, one of two on the insect's head. As its arms covered the orbs, hands seized Nico's shoulders, pulling him backward.

"Do you want to bathe in stomach acid?" Neil fired a second shot from the weapon system in his suit, the lasers bursting forth from gloved fingertips.

Nico deactivated the contacts so he could run. Neil jerked Nico further along the Piazza.

"No, the clock tower." Nico redirected Neil toward the Torre dell' Orologio.

A marble winged lion, perched on a ledge above the clock tower face, roared in fury at the creature. Right then Nico wished he hadn't rendered the lion immobile.

The boys raced under the arch to the clock tower entrance. Nico looked back instinctively. Empty as a school in the evening. Why was the insect only visible via x-ray?

Nico yanked open the door. He shoved Neil inside and dove in after. The thud of the insect colliding with the rebounding door shook the walls.

This must be what the three little pigs felt like with a wolf at the door, Nico decided.

The clock tower's tiny room, with a tight spiral staircase and a trapdoor in the floor, offered little protection.

Nico lunged for the trapdoor, hauling it open by an iron ring. "This way."

Support braces, interlaced like the underside of a wooden pier, floated over open sky. Below the braces, clouds mimicked cushions as if to break a fall.

Neil backed away. "You go that way. I'm trying the stairs."

"The staircase leads to the clock's machinery. This is our only escape." Not waiting for a reply, Nico scrambled through the floor onto the wooden support braces that connected the entire city from below.

The door splintering behind Neil compelled him down through the hole. They scooted across the support braces until silence enveloped them like a guardian angel.

Despite the hush, Nico shivered. Adrenaline coursed through him. What sort of creature was that guard?

Neil clung to a support beam, casting furtive glances at the sky below. "Ever notice the pull of gravity becomes tangible near a ledge?"

Nico didn't respond, but he was second guessing his decision to make Venice a floating landscape right about now. He could've created secret tunnels instead.

"If I fell, how far does it go?" Neil asked.

"I wouldn't recommend it," Nico replied hastily, reaching out a hand to stop Neil if he tried.

Neil's eyes narrowed. "You didn't."

Nico pulled his hand back and focused on his wrist-comp, summoning his scouts. Neil punched him for an answer.

"I thought a fourth-year trial sim would be great." Nico didn't look up.

"Fourth year? We just completed our first!"

Nico scrunched his nose. He hadn't worked all year on his Venice landscape just to pair it with a petting zoo trial.

"The danger setting is high?" Neil asked.

Nico hesitated, then nodded. With the danger setting on high, everything in the sim operated realistically. If the creature had caught them, it would be enjoying Nico and Neil skewers right about now. Well, the insect wasn't literally real, and their bodies remained inside the metal cages that generated the sim, so they'd be figurative skewers? Either way, the sim operated so realistically that if it had caught them, they'd literally be brain dead. Normally the high danger setting was only used when the Academy needed the fourth-year students on maximum alert while preparing them for special missions. The instructors were always involved and could quickly eliminate the sim in an emergency. In such a sim, emergency personnel were also waiting in the sims facility during the duration of the trial.

Today, they were on their own.

"Well, why did you create an invisible, giant insect for this sim?" Neil's face reddened. "You couldn't create a more reasonable creature for a high danger setting?"

"I didn't. Came with the trial."

Neil huffed. "Fourth year. Right. So where we headed? That trapdoor is probably buried under rubble."

Nico grinned and pulled up the Venice map on his wrist-comp. "There are dozens more."

"Great. How far? I'd prefer not to keep testing my fear of heights."

"That depends. What did you find in St. Mark's?"

"How does that affect where the closest trapdoor is?"

Nico shook his head. "I'm trying to determine which direction we need to go. So?"

Neil's face soured. "A 3D printer and a data drive."

"What was on the data drive?"

"You know; I didn't think to check because that giant insect showed up the moment I found them. Now can we go?"

The trapdoors were marked in red. The closest one was—

Nico mentally leapt, as if he'd just won a free, special edition, signed copy of his favorite comic. Their destination was the Costellazione Palace.

"What are you smiling about?" Neil asked.

"I know where we're headed. Come on." Nico changed the basic settings for the scouts to include scanning x-rays and sent them toward the Palace.

Every couple of minutes, while they moved from brace to brace, Nico felt a twinge in his back, as if they were being watched. Each time he panicked a little and activated his contacts to search for the creature. No red indicators.

Viewing the world as a blue canvas was even more unsettling. He wished that part wasn't necessary. The contacts emitted a low-power RF signal. Everything in the environment reflected those signals, but the contacts used a standard background subtraction algorithm to eliminate static objects, thus the blue screen. Nico wondered how it was possible for the creature to avoid reflecting regular light.

Forty minutes passed while they navigated the braces to the trapdoor leading up into the Costellazione Palace. He'd always called it *the Palace*. A buzz grew and the remaining scouts appeared; a bubble welled up in his chest as he remembered he'd already lost a few.

The scouts ringed the trapdoor, waiting for Nico to open it, before they zoomed into the Palace. Despite his anticipation to see the place, he waited for the scouts to finish surveillance.

They delivered an all-clear notice to his wrist-comp.

Holding his breath, Nico climbed into a childhood love. His re-creation of the Palace stayed faithful to his memory, but with a few embellishments thrown in. The trapdoor led into the old theater's sole screen room. The walls, painted like a medieval version of Venice, had an added glow to mimic the city as it would've looked lit by night fires and lanterns.

In the real Palace, lights on the ceiling depicted the constellations as seen from Venice. Here, Nico took the liberty of making those constellations shimmer in the air, rotating as they would in the night sky as the seasons passed. Occasionally, a constellation light blinked like those on a passing aircraft as one of the scouts passed through it.

The Palace's marble floors, decorated in complex geometric patterns, created the illusion that one always stood on the highpoint, as if the ground shifted as one moved about the room. Few children lived on Torcello island to the northeast of Venice where Nico had grown up, so he had regularly ridden a vaporetto over, telling his father he was visiting his ma. He'd always spent at least some time in St. Mark's Square or here in the Palace. Many times after watching a movie, he'd remained seated, staring up at the constellations on the ceiling and dreaming up his own stories. Never had he anticipated he might one day fashion worlds like this himself.

Neil slammed the trapdoor shut, took a quick glance around the place as if to assure himself they were actually safe, then removed his pack. He fished out the 3D printer and a penny-sized silver data drive.

Annoyed that Neil had taken no more than a cursory glance of the Palace, Nico joined him to inspect the devices. The 3D printer, an obsidian rod, resembled the batons passed in a relay race. It possessed a QC code. Neil opened the cover on the ink slot. Empty.

"Can I see that?" Nico asked.

Neil handed Nico the printer and turned his attention to the data drive.

Nico scanned the QC code. A little message popped up on the wrist-comp screen.

3D printer connected. Ready to print.
This 3D printer was made in Giudecca's Women's Prison.

Nico's heart trembled arrhythmically.

Giudeccas' inmates made simple clothing, sequin-encrusted women's bags, and jewelry. They could never fashion a 3D printer, so the last line was a clue. But why there? The academy couldn't know—

"Weird." Neil didn't look up from his wrist-comp. "Only thing on this data drive is a key diagram. Nothing about where to use it. Find anything?"

Nico debated cutting the sim short right then. Give Neil some excuse for why they had to stop. Nico hadn't returned to the prison after his ma's death, even to visit his adopted aunts.

"Nico, find anything with that QC code?"

Ending the sim abruptly would only invite the unwanted questions, but Nico decided he'd only give Neil what he needed to know. "Yeah, the printer's from a women's prison on La Giudecca Island. It's a short boat ride south of Venice." Nico turned his back on Neil and watched his aerial constellations. They'd drifted into a Fall alignment.

"We need to print this key and unlock something in the prison, then," Neil reasoned.

Nico nodded. Was Giudecca's inclusion in the trial a sign the instructors knew he was the son of a murderer? He'd not shared that information with anyone since moving to Space City.

Alarms on Nico's wrist-comp sounded off. Neil jumped to his feet, Nico a step behind. Several heads bobbed in the front row of chairs like whack-a-mole on an energy drink. Flashes of yellow fur and small buck teeth—combined with hisses and growls—cleared the front row of chairs to the second. New ones replaced the old. The scratching of claws on the floor suggested more out of sight.

Pounding on the door behind them, close to the ground like tiny battering rams, spurred Nico to action. He pivoted toward the trapdoor to retreat, but it had vanished, leaving a gaping hole in the floor. Nico braced his legs and leaned over the hole, peering down. The support braces around the trapdoor had also vanished in a perfect square pattern; those remaining no longer looked secure.

Neil pointed toward the far wall. "Side exit."

Nico slipped the 3D printer into his pack and ran. The little beasts cleared two rows at a time in pursuit. Nico rounded the last row of chairs and halted, Neil beside him. Halfway to the exit loomed a second square hole in the floor.

"Another trapdoor, Nico?"

Light washed down on their heads from a new hole in the ceiling. Sunlight poured in, obscuring one constellation. For a second Nico feared the insect had found them, but a quick check of x-ray indicated that wasn't the case.

The creatures reached the closest chairs and leapt, teeth flashing. Nico thought of rabid gophers. He pointed his fingers at one and fired his suit lasers, knocking it backward. Neil fired at others. A couple landed at Nico's feet and he kicked, knocking one down the hole in the floor. Goal! But now all the chairs in the theater appeared covered in the gophers.

"We can't fight them all. Get going." Neil fired two-handed into the mass of bodies.

A narrow ledge between the hole and the wall was just wide enough that Nico thought he could walk it. He stepped forward, terrified he'd get knocked off balance and tumble down the hole.

The gophers piled onto the floor between them and the door. Nico shot at those closest, trying to clear a path while creeping along the ledge. He reached the far side of the hole. Searing pain in his left leg revealed one gopher he'd missed, and it had bitten his leg. He kicked it loose and charged forward. Little bodies slammed into his legs. One landed on his shoulder and bit into his bicep. Nico howled in pain, but shot it off with his good arm.

At the exit, Nico threw himself into the door, bursting out onto a constricted street. Neil plunged through behind him, along with several of the creatures. Nico shoved the door closed. Neil shot those that had made it out. Across the street, a wood pile was stacked against a building. Neil retrieved a block and jammed it through the door handle until it wedged against the wall.

Nico slumped away from the door. He stepped onto one of the dead creature's bodies then dodged away, half fearing it might reanimate. He checked his shoulder and legs where he'd been bitten, but the suit had absorbed the damage. The bites stung, but that was it.

He activated the contacts to verify no giant insects lurked nearby. Rows of symbols appeared in red on the side of the Palace, similar to what he'd seen on St. Mark's Basilica.

"There's something here in x-ray." Nico reached up and touched the symbols, but felt only the bricks.

"What?" Neil asked.

Nico couldn't read the symbols. He summoned the scouts, which emerged through the hole in the Palace roof. They scanned the symbols and relayed them to his wrist-comp. He set these lines up, as well as the others, in the deciphering program.

No other buildings on the empty street was marked with the red symbols, so Nico deactivated the contacts.

Neil scanned a gopher body with his wrist-comp. "Your scouts suck at giving us a heads-up."

"They gave us an alarm."

"Once the creatures were already there." Neil jabbed a finger at the theater.

"They gave us a few seconds head start. Not much, but we escaped." Nico was puzzled himself as to why the scouts had missed the creatures, but he hadn't spotted them with his contacts either.

Neil shook his head, eyes narrowed. He pointed down the street. "Let's get going before something else shows up."

Nico wanted to defend the scouts further, but he'd just have to prove their value.

Silence haunted the street, penned in by multi-story buildings, with diverse hues, like checkered cliffs. They seemed to press inward, squeezing like a vice, so that Nico picked up his pace. His wrist-comp beeped six hours, causing him to jump.

"No wonder those creatures from the Palace, the Mydaers, were pissed." Neil stared at his wrist-comp. "They're from Gleeson. I'd be a little deranged if I had to smell the Malsain all the time, too."

Nico chuckled. The lizard-like Malsain reeked, like a fraternity bathroom the day after a major party.

"There's some crazy creatures on that planet." Neil's voice sounded excited, like he hoped they'd run into some along the way.

Nico was torn between pulling the information up to learn as much as possible, or ignoring it to avoid freaking himself out. After all, the sim couldn't have all the creatures that lived on Gleeson.

Taps on a window drew Nico's attention. Mydaers swarmed toward them on the ground and walls.

"Neil!"

Nico ran, cutting down the next street toward the Grand Canal, roughly ten feet ahead. His brain registered the clap before a yellow awning crashed to the ground further up the street paralleling the docks. A half dozen scouts circled overhead and Nico realized his wrist-comp flashed red. He had accidentally silenced the alarm during the chaos inside the Palace. Nico activated his contacts in time to see the insect creature rising from beneath the awning. Nico froze, hoping the insect wouldn't notice them.

Retreat was impossible. Too many Mydaers behind.

Deactivating the contacts, Nico spotted several gondolas, propelled by Pegasus-wings, floating on the Grand Canal.

"Try for it?" Nico whispered.

A loud clap, like two sledgehammers clanging against each other.

"Go!" Neil shoved Nico forward and they charged for the closest gondola.

The canal was so close. As Nico leapt, sharp pain sliced his back; a blow sent him flying.

He struck the gondola and clung to its side. His ribs spasmed, while his legs dangled. A wing from the gondola dug into his side.

Neil hauled himself onboard, then hurried over and pulled Nico in. Nico immediately activated his contacts. On the dock's edge, the creature leaned forward. It pawed at the open air in the canal, crouched to leap, then shuffled sideways, keeping pace with the gondola. The Mydaers all stayed a safe distance behind the creature, observing.

The pain from the wound on Nico's back forced him to curl in on himself, breathing through the ache from his ribs. The cut chilled him, as if someone had poured liquid nitrogen into the wound.

"I think that thing poisoned me," Neil said. "It got me and now my arm is numb."

"Got me, too," Nico gasped. He decided the insect wasn't attacking for now and deactivated his contacts.

Neil clutched his shoulder, but his eyes widened as he noticed Nico's back. Neil crouched beside him. "These cuts don't look deep. Suit took most of the damage, but the coloration around the wound is weird. Sort of bluish."

Nico remembered the alarm he'd gotten from the scouts. They'd have scanned the creature this time. "The scouts—" Pain in his ribs cut his words short. He doubled back over. Panting, he forwarded the message to Neil. "We've got details on it from the scouts."

The gondola had drifted deeper into the canal, but not so far the insect couldn't spring across the distance. Yet, it hadn't. Perhaps it feared the gondola would collapse under its weight.

"Wish I had a supersized fly swatter about now," Nico said.

Neil chuckled as he checked the information retrieved from the academy database after the scouts scanned and identified the creature. "When we get out of here, you need to expand the range on the scouts."

Nico started to argue it was *his* fault they missed the scouts' alarm, but he became conscious of missing weight. Pulse quickening, he scanned the gondola. Empty but for them.

"Neil, my pack!"

Neil looked up from his wrist-comp, expression uncomprehending. "What?"

"My pack is gone." Nico checked the docks back the way they'd come. Clinging to the dock's edge about fifty yards back was his pack.

"It's fine. I've still got mine." Neil went back to scrolling. "So listen, this thing is called a Pandirus."

Nico watched helplessly as they drifted further away. "The 3D printer was in my pack. We can't print the key for Giudeccas!"

Neil didn't answer. How could he be so unconcerned? Without the printer, they might not complete their next task. They'd have to give up. But maybe he didn't care.

Nico pursed his lips. He had spent months creating his sim, and less than two hours in they were close to failing.

A few shadows crossed over the gondola. The scouts! Nico jumped to his feet, groaning from the pain in his ribs. Tapping a couple buttons on his wrist-comp, he sent the scouts after the pack. The scouts simultaneously rotated to face the pack, scrunching together as if to consult amongst themselves. After a second, they shot forward in unison.

"Listen to this." Neil ran a finger over the screen. "Pandirus possess tremendous ability to track enemy pheromones from a distance of two or three miles away. Once a Pandirus locates a target, it stalks for hours."

Was Neil trying to convince him to give up?

Nico gritted his teeth, not about to be coerced into dropping out. He *could* complete a fourth year sim.

By this point, the scouts had managed to lift the pack several feet off the ground and drifted out over the canal in pursuit. Nico clenched his fists triumphantly.

"Holy crap, listen to this!" Neil practically bounced in the gondola. He must've found something he thought would sway Nico.

"I'm not ending the sim early." Nico crossed his arms.

"What?" Neil looked up from his reading, frowning. He shook his head. "That's not what I'm saying. Listen. A Pandirus will try to pierce its enemies with its pincer-like arms, then retreat. The arms inject a neurotoxin that sends false signals to the brain telling it that the body is freezing to death. Over hours up to a day, the neurotoxin spreads throughout the body, convincing the brain that everything is shutting down."

Nico closed his eyes, breathing deeply to manage the pain and calm his nerves.

"The Pandirus waits until its enemy is completely immobilized, then moves in and devours it alive."

Neil rotated his wrist-comp toward Nico, showing a picture depicting a Pandirus clutching a bloody, unrecognizable carcass between its lance-arms.

"So how do we heal ourselves?"

Neil resumed reading. "Not sure. Just says seek immediate medical help."

Nico turned his attention back to his scouts. They'd covered half the distance. Did it matter if they got the printer back? The timer on his wrist-comp showed they had six hours remaining to complete their tasks, and they'd presumably need a majority of that time. How long until the neurotoxin made completing the tasks impossible? Ignoring the danger to himself was one thing. He couldn't put Neil's life at risk simply to beat a fourth-year trial for fun.

As if to punctuate this line of thought, Nico's pack slid to the side, perched precariously. His breath caught in his throat. He wanted to shout, to warn the scouts, for all the good it'd do. The pack slipped off and plummeted toward the clouds like a reverse sky dive.

The scouts raced after the pack. Nico grabbed the gondola rail, peering over. His pack rapidly dwindled. Why had he created gondolas with wings? If he'd given them jet engines, he could've retrieved the pack himself.

Minutes later, to his horror, the scouts leveled out, having lost the pack on radar. It had long since disappeared from view. Their only means of completing the next task. The pack shouldn't have fallen faster than the scouts flew, yet somehow they'd lost it. Maybe Neil was right.

Plopping down onto the gondola hull, Nico seized his hair in his hands. Time to drop out before the neurotoxin turned them into ice sculptures.

Escape wasn't a bright red button on Nico's wrist-comp. Nor could he simply reset the sim. Instead, to end the sim prior to trial completion, he had a code word.

Carpe Diem.

He had chosen it as a code word first because though it might be clichéd, he felt he had done just that by creating this sim. More importantly, he chose it to deter himself from quitting just because things got too hard. Quitters and Carpe Diem never fit together. Quitters and cowardice, or lazy, even with impatience or stupidity, but never linked to seize the day.

Nico opened his mouth, but that was as far as he got. He couldn't utter the words. They were his rallying cry. The first time he had hacked into the academy database, he had stumbled in while searching for help in his programming class. He'd been so mortified that for the next three days he had refused to touch a computer. Programming had been overwhelming, yet hacking into the school database had happened effortlessly. Perhaps he was a natural criminal after all, he'd reasoned.

But no punishment had come and the stress of completing his class project had driven him back into the database to study the school sims. Comparing the programming code to what he observed within the sims had made everything click. Instructor Collins had lauded Nico's work after that, and urged him to create his own sims.

Seize the day.

That his success had occurred after hacking into the academy database still bothered him. His mother *had* tainted him. But that knowledge hadn't stopped him.

"Listen to this." Neil tapped Nico's leg with his foot. "The Pandirus' speed enables it to close in and attack swiftly. A light grenade serves as the most effective weapon, particularly when fired from a light launcher or drone. If the Pandirus gets close enough for hand use of a light grenade, it's too late."

Nico closed his eyes and placed two fingers on the bridge of his nose. How many ways could he screw this up?

Neil tapped his shoulder. "Now we know how to fight it."

"But no way to get one."

Neil shook his head.

"My packs gone," Nico said. Neil continued to stare, so Nico added, "3D printer went with it."

Neil bit his lip, then shrugged. "We'll find another way."

Nico laughed, not liking the anxiety he heard there, and switched to x-ray. The Pandirus continued to pace the gondola. "Can we call a temporary truce until we find some weapons? Make it a fair fight."

The Pandirus pounded its front arms.

Nico turned back to Neil. "I don't think he's amenable to an arms race."

"We'll figure out something."

Neil might. He was a team captain and had defeated the Dahaka leader. Nico pushed away the question of whether he'd invited Neil to explore the sim with him for that very reason.

Chapter 2

The Venezia Santa Lucia drifted into view. Nico's first instinct was to cry upon seeing the railway station. What wouldn't go wrong? Was the sim trial toying with him? The gondola had carried them the wrong direction to the canal's western entrance. La Giudecca Island lurked below the Grand Canal's southeast mouth.

The clock tower face crowned the Venezia, causing Nico to do a double-take. The Torre dell' Orologio's top half had been replicated on top of the railway station. Roman numerals from one to twenty-four surrounded the unique clock tower's face to keep time while another hand marked the zodiac cycle. On top of that, the clock tracked the phases of the sun and moon in a center circle. Basically a feat created by engineers to impress girls because they didn't know how to talk to them. Was the clock tower's presence on the railway station roof a reminder of the time left in the trial?

Numerous gondolas and the larger vaporettos plied the waters in front of the railway station and Via Liberta bridge, which connected Venice to the mainland. Half the robust bridge was highway, the other half train tracks.

Their gondola drifted toward simple concrete steps that led to a square in front of the railway station. They had no paddles to steer the gondola away. A few scant minutes remained until it delivered them on a silver platter to the Pandirus.

Gasping from a sudden lack of breath, Nico activated his contacts and searched the station grounds. The Pandirus had vanished. When had it stopped following? Had it actually granted them a truce? It would be the first time an animal in any academy sim acted in such an intelligent manner.

"Neil, did you—"

"See the Pandirus disappear? It's probably lying in wait for the neurotoxin to cripple us."

Nico shook his head. "The RF waves pass through walls. If the Pandirus was close, we'd see it."

The gondola docked. From the outside, the railway station resembled a mall. An abandoned one.

"Is this the place?" Neil asked.

"No." Nico shivered, feeling like something stared at him. Or was he simply paranoid? "The gondola carried us the wrong way."

"What now?"

Nico shrugged. "Hope the gondola takes off again and carries us to La Giudecca?"

An envelope icon and a beep on his wrist-comp alerted him to a new message.

Replacement supplies available inside.
Last chance for restock.

Nico grinned in relief. Most sim trial's had a supply depot. Participants could obtain items necessary to complete tasks. Depots typically provided temporary shelter, too.

"Bet we'll find a replacement printer inside." Neil leapt from the gondola to the dock.

If they were lucky, the depot would have drones to help locate and avoid the Pandirus. Would it be too much to hope for a drone with missiles?

"You coming?" Neil arched an eyebrow.

Nico's stomach grumbled. How could he be hungry with the Pandirus hunting them? Perhaps his hunger offered a sign that they had found safety. A ridiculous idea, but it gave Nico the courage to step off the gondola.

*****

The supply depot was in the far right corner past ticket counters, chairs, and restrooms. The depot held far more than they needed to complete the trial a dozen times. Backup explorer suits and wrist-comps. Printing materials such as thermoplastics, rubber, porcelain, clay, numerous types of metal and titanium alloys, aluminum, metal and ceramic powders, and paper.

And 3D printers!

Nico grabbed one of the small black cylinders. Not a weapon, true, but it would print light grenades.

In addition to the printer, they stocked up on metal and titanium alloys, Nico putting his in a new pack. A quick search of the depot revealed no light grenades, but several light launchers. "How do they have launchers, but no grenades?" He grabbed two of the launchers, which resembled futuristic crossbows.

"No drones either," Neil said from across the room.

Nico huffed. If this were a real mission, they'd be equipped with a drone. Why disallow them in a sim trial? It was like taking a math exam without the use of a calculator. In real world situations he'd have access to both.

Disgruntled by the academy's unfair restrictions, Nico searched through the medical supplies and found salves and bandages for his back and Neil's shoulder. His back had numbed, but his lungs felt raw, as if he'd exercised in frigid weather.

"Neil, will you help me?" Nico held out a rag and pointed over his shoulder.

Neil joined him and took the rag, dousing it in alcohol before dabbing at the wound to clean away the blood. It felt as if Neil had inserted a dry ice knife in his back.

After cleaning the wound, Neil applied a salve, then covered it with a bandage. Nico returned the favor, cleaning up Neil's shoulder.

They replaced their damaged explorer suits with new ones. "I'm going to print out a few light grenades before we leave."

Nico had the light grenade diagram and ingredients list on his wrist-comp, which Neil had given him after the Dahaka encounter on Mars. If this got them safely through the sim trial, he'd load Neil up with candy from his father's store.

"I'll handle the key," Neil replied.

Nico grabbed the ingredients from the shelves and poured them into the printer, then spread a print cloth on the ground. Tingling with excitement—this would be his first ever light grenade—Nico activated the print job.

The black rod rose into the air, floating. A thin red laser from the printer moved back and forth over the print cloth, building the first of six light grenades.

"I found some dried purple melon and jerky." Neil offered Nico bottled water.

The depot also carried candy from his father's store. Nico's stomach rumbled again as he perused the treats. Caramel toffees, rainbow beans, chocolate spacecraft and planets…and coconut cakes! After all they'd endured so far, Nico felt he deserved coconut cakes. In fact, if things went bad, these might be his last.

He devoured six.

Stomach fat and happy as a pig, Nico tossed four more cakes into his pack. He'd have them for a celebration if they finished the trial.

The print job finished. Nico scooped up the grapefruit-sized silver grenades. He wrapped them individually in print cloths for modest protection; three he eased into his pack while the other trio he gave to Neil.

Neil zipped up his pack. "Time to move out. Wasted an hour already."

Nico thought he could stand to waste a few more. Hide out in the station. Let the timer dwindle. But then they might as well end the sim now.

The insults his classmates would hurl at him for such cowardice propelled him to the railway station exit. He paused at the doors, shoulders tensed. Neil raised his arm to leave, but Nico blocked him.

"Let me check if the scouts found anything first." Nico knew full well the scouts hadn't. He'd have heard the alerts. Double-checking gave him a few extra seconds. But with each passing second, he found himself increasingly rooted in place. His stomach gurgled. Was it fear, the effects of the neurotoxin, or simply all those coconut cakes he'd eaten?

Neil raised his light launcher, one grenade loaded and ready to fire. Nico fished out his own weapon and a grenade. It felt good to have something to defend himself with.

"Ready?" Neil asked.

Nico nodded.

They both opened a door and stepped outside, the square empty. At the docks, gondolas and vaporettos waited. Finger beside the trigger, Nico scanned the perimeter, then remembered the Pandirus had last come from the roof of St. Mark's. A jolt of terror ran up his backside. He spun, raising his light launcher. He nearly shot the marble lion on the clock tower ledge before realizing it wasn't the Pandirus.

Neil tapped Nico's shoulder and he spun again. Neil pointed at the docks. "Let's get going."

They rushed down the steps to the square. As Nico ran, he once more fought the urge to activate his contacts. *Trust the scouts.*

A vaporetto was the closest option, so Nico leapt aboard the waterbus. As soon as his feet hit the deck, the vaporetto decamped, shifting out into the canal as he angled for the cabin.

The waterbus pitched.

The impact knocked Nico off his feet. His chin struck the deck as did the light launcher. The grenade fired and soared overboard. Nico grappled for anything to right himself. He activated his contacts. The Pandirus stepped toward him, rocking the vaporetto again.

Arms flailing, chest hollow, Nico slid across the deck toward the Pandirus. He wanted to shout, to scream Carpe Diem. The words came out as a wheeze. In his mind he howled it over and over.

A blinding red light, bursting out from the Pandirus' face, forced Nico to shield his own. A concussive blast followed. Heat singed Nico's face and the vaporetto pitched again. He blinked rapidly, vision clearing enough to reveal the Pandirus was gone.

He sat up, searching for the creature. It was off the boat, some distance away now. Back on the docks, it appeared. He deactivated his contacts to locate his weapon.

Neil reloaded. "Got it."

"Didn't do much damage, though," Nico lamented. His weapon lay wedged near the front of the vaporetto.

"That's a second one on shore. The first fell overboard."

Nico grabbed the cabin wall to pull himself to his feet. "Two?"

Neil nodded, already aiming at the docks, but didn't fire.

Nico re-activated his contacts. The remaining Pandirus marched along the shore, staring down the canal as if searching for its partner, then let out a piercing wail.

Nico and Neil both clapped their hands over their ears.

In his mind, Nico replayed the last—What was it? Thirty seconds or so? Seemed a lot longer. Leaping onto the vaporetto, charging for the cabin, the boat pitching as a Pandirus landed on deck, him falling hard and sliding toward it, and—

"No. No. No." Nico shut off the contacts and pulled up the sim code on his wrist-comp.

"What is it? Neil asked, hands still clasped over his ears.

"Carpe Diem." Nico cycled through the code—he could see but not change it inside the sim—in search of the escape string. Lines of code dwindled away with no sign of it.

"Why is Carpe Diem bad?"

Nico methodically worked line by line through the code for the sim trial and his Venice landscape. It wasn't there. He'd forgotten to include an emergency exit line in the program!

Neil placed his hand on Nico's arm. "What does Carpe Diem mean?"

"Carpe Diem is my emergency exit! Our sole means to end the sim early!"

Neil's face darkened, hand dropping away.

"I would've expected the academy trial to include—" The answer came to Nico before he finished the question. He kicked the gondola's side, screaming his frustration.

All Neil's good humor was gone. "You've trapped us here?"

Nico pointed at the wrist-comp. "The sim trial emergency exit code must've been located within its landscape code."

"The landscape you replaced."

Nico flushed. He had no answer. He studied the tall buildings lining the canal, silent guards keeping them on course.

"What're our options?" Neil asked.

Nico regretted not including some animal life in the sim—seagulls or pigeons—something simple and familiar. In their absence, Venice had mutated until he hardly recognized it. "Without an emergency exit, we finish the trial. There's no turning it off."

Neil threw his hands up in the air. "We're on a countdown. What happens when the timer runs out?"

Nico entered the vaporetto cabin and slumped onto a chair in the front row.

Neil followed him. "Someone outside the sim can turn it off."

"How many students participate in long sims?" Nico stared at the floor, unable to look Neil in the eye.

Neil slammed his free fist down on the back of a chair and remained bent over it. "Anyone who sees us in the sim warehouse will assume we'd end it if we got into trouble."

"Yes," Nico replied weakly.

"So we either complete the tasks before the timer runs out or we may be here a long while?"

"Until the neurotoxin kills us," Nico said. He'd trapped them in a fourth year sim trial with the maximum danger setting and no escape.

Neil dropped into a seat, arms flopped out on the chairs on either side of him. Twenty minutes later, the vaporetto carried them clear of the canal's mouth and closer to St. Mark's square. The marble lion atop the Torre dell' Orologio continued to roar.

*****

They rode the vaporetto to its third stop before debarking onto Spinalonga, an old name for La Giudecca Island due to its resemblance to a fish skeleton. As a child, Nico had listened raptly to bedtime stories from his father of how the island formed from the remains of fish cast away by fisherman. The fish bones had collected into massive piles. Over time, the bones had fused into stone, forming the series of islands known as Spinalonga. Nico had accepted the story the way many children believe in Santa Claus. The story was so fantastic it must be true. A few years later, after a local Bishop had overheard Nico recounting the strange story to other naïve young boys, he had set Nico straight in front of them.

Nico had refused to speak to his father for the next week.

Now, as they trekked toward the prison, Nico remembered the story fondly. His father had always had a knack for telling good stories, and had wished to spark a sense of wonder in his son. That sense of wonder had led Nico to create this sim.

It might also get him killed.

The Casa di Reclusione Femminile had originated as a convent in the thirteenth century before eventually becoming a women's prison. The building resembled a blending of the two. The entrance mirrored most churches with a tall, central structure and a sloped roof that led to a single point with a pole on top, which had likely held a cross in the past. The rest of the prison resembled a typical, uninspiring rectangle building with evenly-spaced rows of windows. No tourist destination.

"Do you hear that?" Neil stared west.

A buzzing, like vibrating insect wings mike'd up, drifted on the island breeze toward them, accompanied by the scent of refuse and citrus. Nico activated the contacts and seconds later, a trio of winged Pandirus flew into view.

Neil raised his weapon to shoot, but Nico pushed it back down. They hadn't been seen.

"Get inside."

Chapter 3

Nico led them along a corridor within the prison. Water stains riddled the old walls, creating chunks that crumbled into piles on the floor. If the Pandirus located them, they'd break those walls as if through wet cardboard. Knowing they needed a refuge, Nico sought his mother's old cell.

Each cell—a common room with individual bedrooms and bathrooms surrounding it—held five or six female inmates. Renovated ten years back, the cells had little in common with the rest of the old building. Cell after cell Nico passed before he burst through a doorway and nearly ploughed into a short, plump woman with hair curled up in a gray bun.

Aunt Agnese.

"Nico, you didn't warn us you were visiting." Aunt Agnese looked over his shoulder, and added, "Who's your friend?"

Nico opened his mouth, but it suddenly felt as if his Adam's apple had expanded to fill his windpipe. Good old Aunt Agnese, who had cooked for them in the cell's kitchenette. Behind her, Aunt Gina sewed, sitting on a couch beside Grumpy Ida who read a book, usually fairy tales.

"Give your Aunt Agnese a hug." She held her arms wide, waiting.

Nico flushed, reluctant to hug her in front of Neil. As Nico hesitated, he noticed her incorporeal nature. Same with Aunt Gina and Grumpy Ida.

"Come now. What're you waiting for?" Aunt Agnese threw her arms around him.

Nico felt only air and a little warmth like a blanket pulled from the dryer.

"It's good to see you, Nico," she said, voice tight from the embrace.

"You, too, Aunt Agnese." The words tumbled from him; he had to force back wetness that swelled within his eyes, and hoped Neil hadn't seen.

When Aunt Agnese stepped back, Grumpy Ida swiped at the scouts circling overhead. "Did you bring these bugs with you?"

Aunt Gina took Agnese's place. Nico quickly hugged her and stepped back. "They're my scouts. Flying machines, not bugs."

Grumpy Ida continued to swat at them. "They're polluting my cell."

"I think they're lovely." Aunt Gina held up her hands. To Nico's surprise, a few scouts landed. Their lights blinked rapidly, making Nico think of excited puppies for some reason.

Aunt Agnese moved over beside Neil, eyeing him with a mischievous grin. "Are you going to introduce me to your friend?"

Neil fidgeted, as if flustered.

"He's my buddy Neil."

"Neil, it's wonderful to meet you," Aunt Agnese greeted, throwing her arms around him. Neil's eyes widened and he tensed, but didn't pull away. She stepped back. "Are you a classmate of Nico's?"

"Yes, Aunt Agnese," Nico answered, floored that he was talking to his aunts. A sim of them anyway. Why were they like ghosts? "We're both second years at the academy."

It felt like returning home after years away. Nico had always hated admitting that he felt safe when visiting his ma and aunts. Whenever anyone back home on Torcello Island had discovered his ma was an inmate at Giudeccas, they had given him pitying smiles. After they learned she had killed her sister, their grimaces and condolences shamed him. Yet his comfort and ease whenever he had visited his ma made him fear what that meant.

"Are you going to stand here wasting all day, or are you going to say hello to your ma?" Aunt Agnese asked, frowning in admonition. Every time he'd visited as a child, she'd insisted he give his ma a hug and an *I love you* first thing, and if he forgot, she'd scold him until he did.

"Ma is here?" Nico's heart leapt.

Aunt Agnese shooed him toward his ma's doorway and Nico rushed through into an empty room. His heart dropped like a thermostat tossed into a freezer. He moved over to her bed and plopped onto the mattress.

Six years. Six years since she'd passed in her sleep.

A bird's song filled the room. The familiar warbling caused Nico to smile, then he jumped up and searched for the bird. A European starling, perched on a high shelf, whistled a greeting. The small black and green bird—covered with white spots and possessing orange highlights on its wings—was Jacque.

A bit of a ghost like his aunts.

Jacque had lived in a nest on that shelf. They'd all loved Jacque, but Nico's ma had held a special fondness for the starling, and he for her. Of all the women at the prison, Jacque landed on her arm alone. No one could touch him but her. When Nico's ma had worked in the garden, Jacque had always perched in the tree overhead, whistling gaily.

How was the little starling here? Or his aunts? He hadn't written code for any of them. They must be a part of the sim trial. A part of the next task.

Neil appeared alone in the doorway. "Your mother's in prison?"

"Was." Nico couldn't manage more.

Jacque landed on the bed, trilling. Neil arched an eyebrow.

"That's Jacque. He belonged to ma." Nico smiled at the little starling. "I never learned why ma killed her sister, so I used to devise stories. I envisioned my aunt like a witch from one of Grumpy Ida's fairy tales, and ma and Jacque had fought her sister to protect me."

"Your aunts, too?" Neil nodded toward the other room.

Nico grinned. "Yes. They were her cellmates. Aunt Agnese was falsely accused by a noble of attempting to poison him with her soup. Grumpy Ida liberated books from old warehouses." He'd reasoned their innocence explained why he felt safe and comfortable with them.

"The only clue we have regarding the second task is the key." Neil fished it out of his pack. "Did your mom possess any sort of a lockbox?"

Nico shook his head. "Not that I know of."

"Would she have kept it secret?"

"Not from me."

"How about your aunts?"

Nico rose from the bed, a twinge of regret at leaving his ma's room so soon, but they had tasks to complete and time vanished.

Returning to the common room, Nico found Aunt Agnese stirring a pot of vegetable stew. "Aunt Agnese, do you recognize this key?"

Aunt Agnese examined the key, then shook her head. "It's been years since I needed one."

"Aunt Gina, Aunt Ida, what about either of you?" Nico carried the key to the couch.

"It's a lovely key," Aunt Gina remarked, but shook her head. "Not mine."

"Mine either," Grumpy Ida added.

The key had to open something, but if they had to search every cell in the prison—

Jacque flew into the common room, landed on Nico's wrists, then pecked at the key. For a half second Nico feared the little starling might eat it. But Jacque launched himself, trilling again, and exited the common room. The scouts followed on their own.

"Who is up for an adventure?" Aunt Gina jumped to her feet and marched for the door.

"No!" Nico rushed to block the way, thinking of the Pandirus somewhere outside. "It's not safe. Neil and I will go."

"I'm staying right here." Grumpy Ida remained on the couch, focused on her book.

"You should all stay here," Nico agreed.

Aunt Gina balled up her fists and stomped forward. Nico tensed, putting out his hands to stop her, but she passed right through him. He inhaled in surprise and turned to find her marching down the hallway.

Before Nico could react, Aunt Agnese had barreled past him as well. "If she's going I better, too."

Nico reached after her, then remembered the futility of that. Why wouldn't they listen?

Neil chuckled and shrugged his shoulders as he passed by, leaving Nico to bring up the rear.

Jacque led them past the central open courtyard to the prison garden where his ma and other inmates had grown vegetables. The starling landed on a tall, bushy Aleppo pine at the center and trilled at them.

Aunt Gina stared around the garden, hands clenched as if expecting some great mystery to materialize for them to solve. Aunt Agnese placed her hands on her hips as if preparing to hand out chores.

Nico activated his contacts. No signs of the Pandirus nearby, but he directed the scouts to scan the garden before patrolling the prison.

Neil shuffled through a row of vegetables. Nico turned off the x-ray and moved to the opposite side of the tree. Tomatoes, eggplant, artichokes, and garlic filled up the rows. The smell of recently tilled earth infused the garden. Little knives and shears waited on a table along a nearby wall. Everything belonged. Nothing stood out.

Usually the sim trials offered a specific clue that made the next step obvious, or it was like 'which of these things is not like the others.'

That's the way a first-year trial worked, Nico amended, then turned to Neil. "Find anything?"

"No." Neil drifted toward the rear of the garden.

Aunt Agnese and Aunt Gina had retrieved tools and started pulling weeds.

Nico tried x-ray, finding it weird to watch his aunts' garden, seeing nothing but their glowing outlines. He slowly completed a circuit of the rows, constantly activating and deactivating the contacts hoping something would stand out. He crossed to the pine and circled it, examining the trunk and branches for clues.

The countdown on his wrist-comp dropped to three and a half hours.

Gritting his teeth, Nico banged his fists against the trunk. "Why did you bring us here?"

He coughed. His entire chest felt like crushed ice. How foolish of him to believe he was ready to complete a fourth-year trial. He, a criminal's son. Why had they allowed him into the academy?

"Son, I've a surprise for you."

Nico turned from the computer. His father stood arm-in-arm with uncle Roberto.

"Uncle Roberto!" Nico cried. "You're home."

He raced to his uncle, who hauled him into a bear hug.

At the time, Nico had thought his father running a candy store was the best thing that could ever happen to him. Discovering the candy shop catered to a secret alliance onboard a space city beyond the moon had floored him. In those first few moments in space, he'd sworn to do whatever the academy asked of him. He'd never go back.

"Have the scouts found anything?" Neil called from the rear fence.

"Not yet." Nothing Nico had done had helped them solve the next task. From inside the sim, he couldn't hack the code and reprogram. Following all the same rules as everyone else, he was failing. All his real accomplishments resulted from breaking the rules. Hacking into the academy database. Running the candy black market.

Who had thought him worth a spot in the academy?

Hands shaking, Nico fumbled to tear it open. Inside he found an acceptance letter. This coming fall, three weeks after his 16th birthday, he'd enroll at the academy! Excitement filled him to bursting.

"I'm so proud of you," his father said.

Nico gritted his teeth. He couldn't quit.

Suddenly remembering the strange red symbols on St. Mark's and the Palace, Nico checked his wrist-comp. The decryption program hadn't decoded the messages yet. Nor had he thought to check the prison exterior for the symbols. If he found any, they might present a clue to solving this task. Assuming he could ever decipher them.

Nico circled the trunk again, examining it a second time with x-ray. He even tapped for a hidden hollow spot. When that failed he dropped to his hands and knees to search its base. Partially covered by vines, Nico found a small bronze lid, no more than six inches long. He brushed away the vines, revealing a keyhole.

Jacque sang triumphantly.

Nico inserted the key into the hole and the lock turned, the lid popping up a fraction. Inside Nico found a piece of paper with a message and a four-digit code.

On thy balcony, thou dost wait.
Death of a rose. My love and hate.
Thou, though bronzed, I seek in all haste
To give back thy stars, now graced.
8284

Nico read through the riddle again, trying to puzzle out the clue.

"May I?" Neil reached for the paper.

Nico handed it to him. The answer slipped away, aggravatingly beyond reach.

Jacque started squawking, wings flapping violently. Nico barely glanced to see what was wrong before his wrist-comp alarms sounded off. The scouts had discovered something. Nico blinked, activating his contacts.

Three Pandirus descended upon the garden. Neil fired a light grenade at the insects, nailing one and sending it crashing beyond the perimeter fence. Nico fired his second as well, but hit the top of the tree instead. Burning branches rained down on them.

His aunts screamed. Nico deactivated his contacts and ran to their sides. He helped them up and ensured they weren't hurt.

"I don't mean to be rude, but move it." Neil loaded his last grenade.

Aunt Gina and Agnese fled, Nico on their heels. He wanted to pick them up and carry them to safety, but couldn't lift sims.

They raced through the courtyard. A bench they passed imploded.

"Hurry," Nico urged. It would be his fault if his aunts were hurt. The Pandirus hunted him.

They re-entered the prison, Neil a step behind. He turned and fired back through the doorway. A Pandirus screamed in pain.

"Nico, your last grenade," Neil shouted.

Nico started to remove the last grenade from his pack. His aunts were halfway down the hall, headed for their cell.

"Not that way," he shouted, but they paid him no mind. He chased after them, loading the light grenade as he ran.

The walls shook, pieces crumbling to the ground. Aunt Gina reached their cell first and darted inside, Aunt Agnese only a couple of steps behind her. He had to get them out of here.

Nico darted into the room to find Grumpy Ida still on the couch with her book, oblivious to the chaos. A memory of her reading to him resurfaced.

"What's Montague? It is nor hand, nor foot, nor arm, nor face, nor any other part belonging to a man. O, be some other name! What's in a name? That which we call a rose by any other word would smell as sweet," she'd read, reciting loudly as though performing on a stage. *The Tragedy of Romeo and Juliet.*

The clue sounded similar, not a quote, but as if it mimicked the language of the play. Still trying to figure it out, but with no time to waste, Nico rushed to lift Grumpy Ida from the couch. His hands passed right through her. "We can't stay here. We're in trouble."

"I'm not going anywhere." Grumpy Ida crossed her arms, brow furrowed.

"Please, Aunt Ida." Nico ran to Aunt Gina's door. She'd ducked behind the bed. He waved for her to come. "I can get you away."

Aunt Gina shook her head, refusing to budge.

"Nico," Neil called from the doorway. "We have to get out of here."

The pounding on the walls continued, like battering rams.

"I can't leave my aunts." Nico couldn't believe Neil would even suggest it.

"They aren't real," Neil said calmly. "This is a test to sidetrack you from the mission."

Nico shook his head. "I can't." The academy couldn't ask that of them, to leave family behind.

"You're not, just the memory of them." Neil insisted. "They're nothing more than a mental distraction. Focus on the mission."

Nico felt a warmth on his wrist. Grumpy Ida. "We're all proud of you, Nico. Your ma, too."

Tears welled up in Nico's eyes and he shifted so Neil couldn't see. Nico knew she was biased. As family, she and the rest of his aunts were programmed to see the best of him. They were blind to his faults.

Grumpy Ida smiled. "Don't hold back. Go."

She let his wrist go. Nico hesitated, so she pushed him toward Neil. Nico wanted to remain, to hide away with his aunts until the danger passed. He followed Neil out because he couldn't reveal his cowardice.

Parts of the ceiling had collapsed, leaving holes in the cloudy hallway. Each attack knocked loose clumps of rubble and grit that nearly crushed the scouts. Nico hesitated, reconsidering hiding out in his aunts' cells. Doing so would only draw the Pandirus upon them. Granted, they weren't real, but this was a test of how he would act in the real world. He would not return shamefaced to his aunts after they proudly watched him exit. Nor put them in danger.

Nico reactivated his contacts. The Pandirus struck through the holes, trying to get at them. To keep moving forward, Nico focused on Neil's red form. Neil knew how to survive an attack like this. All they needed to do was survive.

A wall exploded inward behind Neil, cutting Nico off. He skidded to a halt. A Pandirus arm reached through the hole, swinging wildly. Nico aimed his launcher at the arm—

"Nico, no," Neil hissed. "That's our last grenade."

Neil stepped close to the arm and fired through the hole with his suit lasers. The arm jerked back outside. Nico deactivated his contacts and darted forward. The lasers would annoy the Pandirus more than harm it.

They reached the front entrance. Neil threw the doors wide. Nico hesitated a moment, activating his contacts just long enough to make sure they had a clear path, before racing toward the docks lining the canal. They angled toward the nearest gondola. As Nico leapt for safety, the ground disappeared underneath his feet.

The boys landed in the gondola. Nico dropped to a knee to catch his balance before he spun back. La Giudecca women's prison…the island—Pandirus and all—had vanished.

Chapter 4

Icy shock immobilized Nico. Not even dust remained of La Giudecca Island. It had evaporated from the sim, leaving the scouts hovering over a clear blue sky.

"I've never seen anything like this in a sim," Neil said. "You didn't do this?"

"No." Nico dropped to the floor in the gondola. "If I'd hesitated a second longer, I'd have missed the gondola. I'd still be falling for who knows how long."

The strange red symbols. He hadn't checked for them on the prison walls and now it was too late. He still had no clue as to their purpose.

A single beep on his wrist-comp alerted him to a new message.

From: Caleb Thorton.

Frowning, Nico read out loud.

Found your sim. Well done! A little too perfect for fun, so I improved it. I added in a timer. Every ten minutes, a piece of Venice dissolves. That should add intrigue to the simple challenge of completing tasks. If you fail to finish within the eight-hour limit, you fall.

You're welcome,
Caleb

"I'll kill him." Neil looked ready to spit in a Pandirus' eye.

Nico reviewed his map. Three quarters of Venice had disappeared along with all of La Giudecca. Instead of a time limit for completing the trial tasks, as they'd thought, the timer tracked the removal of Venice.

Nico supposed it amounted to the same thing. If they failed to finish the final task within the remaining time, they'd fall until someone rescued them or the rush of adrenaline killed them. Or the neurotoxin did.

Bile rose up in Nico's throat. He turned and emptied his stomach overboard, his body screaming at the partial exposure to the endless sky below.

"If Caleb were here," Nico wiped his mouth clean, "I'd shove him overboard. See how he likes his improvements."

How much of the city would remain by the time they crossed the canal?

"Any idea what the riddle meant?" Neil asked, taking a seat beside him.

Nico considered the riddle for a minute, comparing it with Shakespeare's play. The answer came to him. "It refers to Casa de Giullietta, the fictional home of Juliet Capulet."

"Oh, that's in Venice?"

"Verona."

Neil's eyes widened. "Wow! How big did you make this sim?"

Nico opened his mouth to reply that he hadn't created anything beyond Venice, but closed it again. Part of the map extended beyond the wrist-comp screen. Frowning, he re-sized the map. Venice shrunk and in the screen's upper left-hand corner materialized Italy's mainland all the way to Verona.

The final task took place outside the scope of his original landscape. Something in the academy trial code allowed it to automatically expand to meet requirements. That would come in handy. He'd need to search for that code string later.

"Can we get to Verona in this gondola?" Neil asked.

"Never get there in time."

"What other options are there? Cars? Planes?"

Nico flushed. "It's not like we use cars in Space City."

"What about the railway station?" Neil pulled up the city map on his own wrist-comp. "Any trains?"

Nico shook himself, trying to clear his head. Joints and muscles protested. His entire back and now his shoulders were numb. He pulled up the scouts' scan data from their earlier visit. He half-shouted as a feed from a scout confirmed it. A single black locomotive on the tracks behind the railway station.

Nico flashed the scout footage at Neil. "They came through."

Neil half-smiled.

Chapter 5

Additional sections of the city had disappeared, leaving a Venetian Swiss cheese. The Palace was among the missing. Nico slumped against the side of the gondola, mind seeming to spin wildly and sluggishly at the same time like a revving engine of a car in neutral. His eyelids grew heavy, exhaustion burying him like a heavy rug.

"No. It's gone," Neil said.

The gondola pulled up to the docks and another huge blank hole where the railway station had been.

Neil seized his hair with both hands. "Just the one grenade left."

A chill washed through Nico, but not from the revelation. He shivered all over. He clenched shaking, pale hands, but the tremors didn't abate. His fingertips prickled as if mini electrical charges slithered beneath the skin.

Despite the loss of control, Nico hauled himself to his feet. "Come on. We don't have time to waste."

The black locomotive remained. No cars attached. The sight boosted Nico like a sugar rush from downing a soda. Driving a locomotive seemed to trump everything else for the moment.

Nico leapt over the gondola rail and raced toward the train. Reaching it, he hopped up the steps. "Dibs on driving."

Neil shoved past him. "As team captain, I'll hand out orders."

The locomotive rolled forward on its own, the growing chug of its engines a symphony breaking the city's silence.

Neil's shoulders slumped and he kicked the co-engineer's seat. "I really wanted to drive it."

Nico contented himself with leaning out the window to enjoy as they traveled onto the vast bridge leading to the mainland of Italy.

Chapter 6

Roofs caved in. Pink-hued rubble strewn across cobblestone streets. Checkered areas where parts of Verona had vanished. The city looked like it had endured heavy military bombardment. Nico had half-hoped Caleb's destruction was confined to Venice, but it had surged past them.

"Where's the house?" Neil hopped off the locomotive as it pulled to a stop in the Verona Porta Nuova railway station.

The tracks ended at a hole one hundred yards ahead. As Nico exited the locomotive, he tried to push away the thought of the train diving through the hole, carrying them with it.

"Nico?" Neil paused atop a knee-high wall, waiting for direction.

Explosions rocked the city to the North, and both boys dropped to a crouch.

"Pandirus?" Nico whispered. None registered on x-ray.

When nothing moved into view, Neil started to climb over a low pile of stones. "Could be. Or something new."

What else could this trial throw at us? Nico wondered.

It took what remained of his ebbing resolve to move forward. Less than forty-five minutes remained before all this disappeared, yet each step brought a greater desire to lie down and not worry about it. How easy would it be to go to sleep?

Nico shook his head, trying to fight off the effects of the neurotoxin.

Neil paused, leaning against a lonely archway, the rest of the building collapsed. His left arm hung at his side and he blinked, as if having trouble keeping his eyes open. "Almost… there?"

Nico placed his hands on his hips and nodded.

His wrist-comp lit up with warnings from the scouts. Nico grabbed Neil's shoulder, halting him. He showed the warnings to Neil and pointed to the street they were about to turn onto.

"Can we detour?" Neil whispered.

Nico shook his head. "It's the only access to the house."

They crept forward, rounding the corner onto Via Capello. Mydaers climbed the walls ahead or hung from balconies. Flying brown beasts with soccer ball-like bodies and long wings darted overhead. Dozens of other strange creatures filled the street. Checking his x-ray vision, Nico discovered they were dwarfed by a half dozen Pandirus roaming the narrow street in single file. No path to sneak over to Juliet's fabled home.

Two of the Pandirus rose up on powerful hind legs and pounded the walls of a neighboring building with their front paws. Each blow shook the medieval home.

Nico deactivated his contacts and ducked into a doorway.

Neil slumped against the door frame. "Any ideas?"

"With one grenade to take on that?" Nico waved at the occupation. He offered Neil his launcher with the last grenade. He doubted he even had the strength to aim. "Take this. Maybe you can—"

Neil pushed the weapon back. "I need your help. Like on Mars."

Nico laughed, which became a series of muffled coughs. "I retreated while you faced the Dahaka."

"You saved lives." Neil looked about ready to tip over onto the ground. "Got the survivors back to the ship. If you hadn't, they would've died."

"I should've fought with you, not run away."

Neil's chin jutted out. "If you hadn't followed orders we'd have died."

"You admit I couldn't have helped?"

Neil doubled over, body tensing. He gasped then straightened, mostly. "After defeating the Dahaka, we had to stop the CME from destroying Space City. We shifted it enough to shoot the wall of the building we were in and save our ship. During our escape, it fired. We wouldn't have escaped on our own. The general materialized. He got us out of there. If you hadn't followed orders, he wouldn't have rescued us. You did what was needed. Now do it again."

Nico nodded. He doubted Neil's reasoning, but he could follow orders. He climbed to his feet, gritting his teeth to stifle a groan. As he tried to puzzle out a way through, his wrist-comp alerted him that the decryption program had finally deciphered the strange symbols on St. Mark's, as well as the Palace. The messages for both translated the same.

Welcome in peace.

Raising an eyebrow, Nico showed the message to Neil.

"Wait." Neil's eyes darted all over the place, his expression brightening with each passing second. "I don't believe it."

Nico tried to figure out what Neil had seen, but the effort sapped his strength. "What?"

"They're intelligent." Neil patted his arm. "Look at the Pandirus."

Nico activated the contacts.

Neil's voice, though drained, had a twinge of excitement. "The two in the middle are guards. The other four are patrolling."

Two Pandirus stood on either side of the entrance to Casa de Giulietta, but every few seconds they pounded on the walls, seemingly trying to knock them down. Nico told Neil so.

"No." Neil shook his head. "Watch them. They're synchronized." Sure enough, after a couple of breaths, the Pandirus guards struck the walls again in unison. "It's an alert system."

Nico cringed at the possibility of reinforcements.

"Check out the flying creatures." Neil pointed them out. "They're actually gatherers, running a complex supply chain."

Nico turned off the x-ray. The little round fliers all winged into or out from the courtyard that made up Juliet's home. Nico zoomed in with the contacts. Each flier entering the courtyard held something clutched in its sharp beak.

Nico's wrist-comp flashed. Five minutes remained. "None of this helps us get through."

"Maybe we can communicate?"

The possibility of communicating with the creatures made Nico blink. How could they even begin to talk to the creatures? Would the Pandirus or Mydaers even give them the chance, or attack first as the others had done?

Nico's shivering stopped. It would be so easy to close his eyes and forget about everything.

A foot kicked his shin, drawing his head upright. He hadn't realized he'd lowered it. The neurotoxin had almost run its course.

"Don't drift—" Neil's own head bobbed, but he remained standing, if stooped. "I want to get home."

Home. The word made Nico think of both St. Mark's and the Palace at the same time. They were homes of a sort to him as a child. But that meant nothing. They'd encountered these creatures in St. Mark's, the Palace, the railway station, and in Giudecca prison. *Except* they hadn't encountered anything in the railway station. Only after they'd departed. And the Pandirus had invaded the prison, hunting them. But the Pandirus in St. Marks and the Mydaers in the Palace had already been inside, as if hiding there. Or living there—

"I know what to do." Nico struggled to climb to his feet. He picked up the launcher and removed the grenade.

"What're you doing?" Neil reached for the discarded launcher.

Nico held the light grenade upraised in both hands. "We're visitors to a foreign land." He stepped out into the middle of the street, activating his contacts and the blue world.

The Pandirus pounded their arms together once, twice, three times. Echoes reverberated down the street, causing Nico's skin to crawl. His ears burned. They were exposed now. He hoped this wasn't a suicide run.

The red and yellow outline of Neil's body moved beside him, offering no support or criticism. The Pandirus moved to block their path. The Mydaers surged forward, climbing sideways on vast blue walls until Nico and Neil were completely surrounded. The fliers swarmed overhead until the red and orange of their bodies swallowed up the blue.

Nico felt a desperate desire to press his back against something solid. Marching forward, he held the grenade aloft. He felt blind despite the red outlines of every creature in the area.

As they reached the first Pandirus, Nico clutched the grenade hard, fighting his instincts to run. The Pandirus silently shifted aside, clearing a path. Each subsequent Pandirus followed suit. Every creature was trained on them, but all held their ground. Nico bit his lip.

They walked between the Pandirus guarding the empty courtyard outside Juliet's home. Nico's desire to see forced him to deactivate the contacts. An open doorway on the right led into the two-story stone house; above it loomed Juliet's balcony, which had actually not been added until the 1930s. At the back of the courtyard stood a bronze bust of Juliet in front of a door.

Before Nico could hazard a guess as to how to complete their final task, the stones behind them shook. He spun, reactivating his contacts. A winged Pandirus had landed behind them, cutting off the entrance to the alley. It was larger and fatter than any of the previous Pandirus they'd seen, and possessed a third orb on its head, creating a triangle. Without knowing why, Nico guessed a queen.

Her body flexed with contained violence.

Nico's knees weakened. It took every ounce of remaining strength not to crumple to the ground. Instead he stepped forward, raising the grenade. The queen remained taut, but lowered her head to examine the grenade. After a few seconds, she lowered her arms and pressed lightly against the grenade, somehow avoiding crushing his hands in the process. She raised it up in the air. Holding it close to her mouth, she leapt back to the roof.

Nico took an involuntary step back and bumped into something cold and hard. He deactivated his contacts. Juliet's bust. He grabbed one of its arms for support.

Neil turned to him, a triumphant grin on his face, then toppled backward, arms flailing. Nico fell as well, Verona gone. He clung to the statue like a life line, reaching with his free hand to latch on firmly to the statue and pull himself close.

Am I Romeo, destined to die in Juliet's arms?

The wind tore at him, threatening to dislodge him. It battered his face, making it difficult to open his eyes. He clung to the statue. But that wouldn't help him end the sim.

Finally opening his eyes, he noticed four glowing zeroes on the statue's right arm. It took him a moment to recognize they were digital numbers with four small buttons beneath them. Fighting his need to cling to the statue with both hands, Nico loosened his grip and slid a hand toward the left button. He pressed it and the zero above it changed to a one.

His whole body surged with hope. A four-digit code had come with the riddle. He closed his eyes, trying to visualize it in his mind.

The riddle came easily enough. The four numbers beneath it—Eight—Two—

The last two numbers were fuzzy.

Wind pounded his ears, buffeting him, disrupting his focus. His muscles ached from the strain of holding on. Nico pressed the first button seven more times, then the next one twice. Reaching for the third button, Nico pressed it slowly, stopping at each number to see if the combination shook his memory. When he reached eight, he remembered!

Eight—Two—Eight—Four.

Sliding his thumb to the last button, he pressed it four times and fell hard to the floor of the large circular cage in the enormous white sims warehouse. He gasped, pain shooting through his body. He shivered so hard he thought he was seizing.

Neil shouted ecstatically from his own cage. "That's how you do it!"

Once Nico caught his breath, he controlled his muscles enough to push himself to a sitting position. They needed to get to medical for treatment, but they'd made it.

Neil climbed to his feet and hobbled from his cage. "Brilliant. That's what the academy expects from us."

Nico forced himself to his feet, though he wanted to lie in the cage and wait for help.

They'd completed a fourth-year sim trial. He wished he could share this with his mother. Maybe a real visit to his aunts would do. He could tell them the story, though they'd never believe a word of it.

Doctors Without Planets

Chapter 1

Summer was free time. Chisel it in stone.

The moment Trini completed her final exam on Mars, she'd started to catch up on movies, shopping, and most importantly, extensive Academy Games training.

Aunt Teresa had no respect for the sacredness of summer.

The Ukka on Letos had suffered another breakout of maleze. As Space City's leading field doctor, Aunt Teresa had told Trini to pack her bags. They were headed for a summer with no electricity, running water, or conveniently 3D printed meals.

Basically the Middle Ages.

"I could've spent the summer in the academy dorms," Trini grumbled, shuffling through Space City Games videos on her wrist-comp. She loved watching replays, especially of Gabriella Munoz. Gabriella's decision-making and fearlessness during a match was incredible, and Trini hoped to one day be as talented a Games player.

Aunt Teresa piloted the ship toward Letos, but took a second to cast Trini a disapproving glare. "I need your help. Plus the experience will do you good."

Her aunt planned for her to become a doctor after graduation, no matter how many times Trini insisted she had no desire for it.

"I need to spend the summer training." Trini had never considered herself a genius; neither had her instructors. And Aunt Teresa had once lamented—after too much Christmas brandy—that Trini's mother hadn't exactly passed on her stunning good looks.

But Trini was a great Academy Games player. In her first game, she'd charged through the stadium forest when a much larger boy from the opposing team surprised her. Instinctively, she had screamed at him. Startled, his shot went wide, allowing her to light up his chest target to disarm him. And thereafter, screaming like a banshee as she bore down on opponents became her thing. It had also earned her the nickname wolf spider. Female wolf spiders ate the males, and her dominance of many of her male counterparts in the Games made it stick.

Aunt Teresa pressed her lips together in a thin line. After a short pause, she responded. "Doctors make a real impact in the universe. Too many humans and aliens in this universe suffer from a lack of quality medical attention. They need our help."

"They need your help," Trini said, falling into her usual argument. "Your help and others like you who are driven to heal. Not everyone can do that."

"You've never tried," Aunt Teresa snapped. It didn't take much these days for this discussion to unravel.

"And what if I get sick?" Trini asked. "You're endangering me. What if I miss the school year because of it?"

Aunt Teresa sighed heavily, clearly exasperated. "That's why I gave you our standard field medications, and you'll continue to take them while we are on Letos. They'll reduce your chances. You'll be fine."

Trini stared out at the stars, weary of their circular argument.

Silence stretched uncomfortably between them for several minutes, before Aunt Teresa continued with a hint of pleading, "I just want you to see the Ukka. What they're going through. The difference we can make in their lives."

"It's your passion," Trini replied. Why wouldn't her aunt recognize that medicine wasn't for her?

Aunt Teresa nodded. "It is. It can be yours—"

Trini cut her off, "The Games are my passion. I love to compete—to challenge myself. I'm happiest on the field."

"If all you want from life is fun and games, I should've left you on Earth with your parents," Aunt Teresa said, voice dripping with disgust.

Trini gasped.

Aunt Teresa tensed. "Trini, I'm sorry. I didn't mean that."

Trini unbuckled herself and rose, retreating to the main cabin, which held two racks built into the walls for sleeping, a small kitchen with a 3D food printer and recycling shoot, a large number of wall cabinets, most of which held medical supplies for the sick on Letos, and a small bathroom at the back. Her aunt didn't call after her, and when Trini reached her rack, she sunk into it. Her eyes burned, but she refused to cry.

In the five years since Aunt Teresa had rescued Trini, they had rarely discussed her life with her parents. Aunt Teresa had certainly never threatened the possibility of Trini returning to Earth.

She'd never go back.

Trini lay on her rack a while, cycling through more Games videos, but mostly stewing over Aunt Teresa's jab. Her aunt had no right. It was too cruel. If she could just make her aunt see how different they were. Not everyone could be a doctor. Teaching her would only slow Aunt Teresa down. The Ukka couldn't afford that. And back on Space City, she could train like she needed for the upcoming year.

Striding back into the cockpit, intent on appealing to her aunt one last time, Trini spotted Letos through the ship's front screens. From up here, Letos looked a lot like Earth, which unnerved her. For a fleeting breath she panicked. Irrational fear whispered that her aunt had decided to return her to Earth after all.

"We're landing on Letos in five minutes," Aunt Teresa called over her shoulder.

Trini exhaled softly.

Her momentary anxiety gone, curiosity took over. What did the Ukka look like? Maybe she could wait until after they landed on Letos to speak with her aunt about returning to Space City. A few hours delay wouldn't make much difference in her training. A day at most.

*****

Aunt Teresa landed a short distance from the village; the Ukka weren't accustomed to spacecraft dropping out of the skies. Before debarking, Trini and her aunt had slipped on large backpacks filled with medical supplies. They weighed a ton!

Would be good to train with one of these, though, Trini thought. *How far could she run while carrying one?*

Her first sight of the Ukka caused her to miss a step. The Ukka adults stood ten or eleven feet tall, like human giants. Even a majority of the children scampering through the village had a head or more over her. Their skin possessed an orange hue. And they were all bald. Men, women, children. All with hairless noggins. No facial hair either. Not even eyebrows. They all wore simple gray garments and moved around barefoot.

Long, thick branches, lashed together, formed the frames of the modest homes the Ukka lived in. Flowering vines grew from the roofs down the sides, providing limited privacy. All the homes were huddled close together in fairly straight lines, despite plenty of space on the plains around them.

"Good dayspring to you, Teresa Flores," an Ukka greeted when they reached the edge of the village. He carried a staff decorated with purple symbols.

Trini's tradutor, a tiny earbud, translated the Ukka tongue into English for her, while also translating anything she said in response into the Ukka tongue. It allowed for smooth communications, especially with alien races the citizens of Space City didn't encounter much.

"Good dayspring to you as well, Jarin." Aunt Teresa clasped her hands, one over the other, and nodded slightly. "This is my niece, Trini Flores."

"Good dayspring to you, Trini Flores," Jarin said. His voice was gentle.

Trini returned the greeting.

"How are your people?" Aunt Teresa asked.

Jarin's broad shoulders sagged. "The illness afflicts many. I've spoken with our closest neighbors. It is widespread." He hesitated, as if debating how to proceed, before adding simply, "It's good you've come."

"We're ready to help." Aunt Teresa gestured for Jarin to lead. "Trini will support me."

"Yes," Trini agreed, not wanting to argue in front of him.

She had known that the Ukka possessed limited technology, and therefore lacked all but very basic medicine. She didn't really understand what that meant until she followed her aunt through the village. Sick people lay on mats inside their huts. They lacked a hospital with beds, with doctors or nurses caring for them. Since Aunt Teresa had visited once before, this marked the second time most of them had ever seen a real doctor. For diseases like maleze, the Ukka simply made the ill as comfortable as possible and hoped for the best.

"I'd like to set up one location and bring as many of the ill there as possible," Aunt Teresa said. "I have a great tent in my ship. Do you have some men able to set it up?"

"Will six be enough?" Jarin asked.

"Plenty."

Jarin rounded up the men. Aunt Teresa led them back to the ship and directed them to the tent, while Trini retrieved the quad doc, a drone equipped with a container for carrying blood sample vials.

Once the Ukka had carried the tent back to a site to begin erecting it, Aunt Teresa insisted on immediately seeing to the sick. Drive was one thing she and Trini shared.

Their first patient was a girl, not more than a toddler, and the only Ukka Trini had seen who was actually shorter than her. The girl lay on a mat in her home, covered with an animal skin blanket, head slick with sweat. Her mother hovered over her, a bowl of water and a wet cloth in her hands, the latter of which she used to wipe the girls head.

"What's your name?" Aunt Teresa asked the little girl—little being relative since she was not all that much shorter than Trini.

"Sepi," the girl croaked.

"Good dayspring to you, Sepi. My name is Dr. Teresa, and I'm going to check your temperature. Would that be okay?"

The girl nodded weakly.

As Aunt Teresa worked, she spoke to the mother. "What symptoms has she shown?"

"She's been hot the last two days, complaining her head hurts, and vomited a couple times. Once this morning. First time during the night."

"Her temperature is running a little high." Aunt Teresa returned her thermometer to her pack and withdrew a syringe. "Trini, I'm going to show you how to take blood samples."

"Um, ok." The thought of doing so made Trini's stomach twinge, but she didn't argue.

After giving her a quick phlebotomy lesson, Aunt Teresa deposited the marked blood sample in the quad doc container. She then withdrew a vial from her pack and handed it to Sepi's mother, along with a syringe.

"Give her five milliliters of this medicine every four hours." Aunt Teresa demonstrated filling the syringe from the vial and gave it to Sepi orally.

"I understand," Sepi's mother answered.

Aunt Teresa stood. "I've got some of your neighbors constructing a makeshift hospital. I'd like you to bring Sepi there later today, so that I can monitor her more closely."

Trini felt for Sepi, knowing the girl was suffering. She would continue to suffer until Aunt Teresa was able to devise a solution, or the illness ran its course. Assuming it didn't get worse. Trini tried not to think about what worse meant.

For everyone else they visited, Trini drew the blood samples, while Aunt Teresa focused on distributing basic medicines to treat symptoms. Unfortunately, all those would do was give the Ukka a little relief for the time being, until they could pinpoint the source of the outbreak and develop some sort of a treatment.

Trini worked quickly, terrified of hurting the first few patients she drew blood from. But after several successful draws, she grew more confident, promising nervous children that a pinch on the cheek or ear from their mother hurt worse than a needle stick. Each time the child had glanced uneasily at their mother as if fearing a pinch to prove Trini's claim. She made sure to hide her smile at their concern.

Not one of the children cried, and afterward, Trini gave each of them the traditional lollipop to make up for any suffering.

If only a dose of sugar could *cure.*

It took her a few hours to draw blood samples from all the ill Ukka in the village. In that time, more had come in from the surrounding villages, drawn by the news that a doctor had arrived. When she noticed how many new patients had filtered in, she knew she'd be busy for the next several days taking samples for Aunt Teresa to analyze. There was no going back to Earth. But seeing their suffering up close, she no longer wanted to return home. What did training matter right now in comparison to this? She'd have plenty of time to practice when she got back without losing a step in her game.

Jarin's men had just finished with the medical tent when Trini and Aunt Teresa returned, loaded with blood samples. Easily the size of four Ukka huts, the white tent had one flap to cordon off a small area for Aunt Teresa to analyze the samples and conduct basic research on the maleze strain. The rest would be filled with mats for the sick. Trini wished they could've offered beds, but they had no way to easily transport any from Space City or anywhere else.

As Trini organized the blood samples, her aunt approached her, Jarin at her side. Aunt Teresa handed Trini a bottle of water. "Have you eaten since we arrived?"

Trini shook her head. She'd been ignoring her rumbling stomach for the last couple of hours.

Aunt Teresa placed her hands on her hips. "You need to keep yourself hydrated and fed. You'll need your strength if you're to help anyone."

Trini drank, not bothering to point out that her aunt hadn't eaten anything either.

"I can have food brought to you," Jarin offered.

Aunt Teresa waved her hands dismissively. "Save what you have for your own. We've got plenty on our ship."

"Jarin. Jarin," a boy yelled, running toward them. He was only the third Ukka that Trini had seen who was shorter than her, though he reached her eyebrows. The boy looked to be no older than five or six. In one hand he clutched a wooden carving of a long-necked dinosaur. "You must come. Grandpa is sick."

"Otso, when did this happen?" Jarin asked, face paling.

Otso stopped before them, eyes welling with tears. "He just fell. Please come."

*****

Otso was inconsolable the whole way to his hut on the outskirts of the village. He pulled urgently at Trini's hand until she wanted to run with him to his grandfather. In his other hand, he clutched the wooden dinosaur.

"Tell me what happened, Otso," Jarin asked.

Otso sniffled. "Grandfather went fishing early as usual. He returned with no fish, and he was pale. He told me, 'Otso, fetch Jarin'." The boy imitated his grandfather's voice. "Then he fell. I couldn't wake him, so I came as fast as I could."

He started sniffling again. Trini wanted to scoop him up and hug him tight.

"No fish?" Jarin asked skeptically. "Ahti always catches something."

Trini frowned, wondering why Jarin was worrying about fish when Ahti had just collapsed.

Otso shook his head fervently. "He had his gear, but no fish."

Jarin's brow darkened, the news clearly bothering him, but he said nothing.

They found Ahti lying on a mat inside the hut, partly covered by a blanket. Trini guessed Otso had dragged him to it, no small feat for the boy. Ahti had fallen into a feverish sleep. Otso started for his grandfather, but Trini clutched his hand and pulled him back against her, both as a measure of comfort and to keep him out of the way so her aunt could examine Ahti unhindered.

"Let Doctor Teresa look at him," Trini said. "She's very good. She'll take care of him." She hoped fervently that this wasn't one of those times when it was already too late.

Aunt Teresa checked Ahti's temperature while they watched in silence. She clucked her tongue and shook her head, before soaking a rag with water and placing it on his forehead. The instant the cold compress touched Ahti, his eyes fluttered open.

"Jarin, what you doing here?" Ahti gasped.

Aunt Teresa prepared to take a blood sample, as she answered him. "You're sick. You collapsed."

"Otso?" Ahti called.

The boy scrambled out of Trini's grasp and over to his grandfather's side, still clenching the wooden dinosaur. "I'm here. Are you okay?"

"I'm fine." Ahti patted his grandson's hand to reassure him. "Probably just too much sun."

Trini knew that wasn't true, but kept silent. Otso needed comforting, not the truth.

Aunt Teresa capped the vial of blood. "How long have you felt tired?"

Trini took the sample from her aunt and added it to the quad doc, thankful that it was programmed to follow her automatically until she gave it direction otherwise.

"Yesterday," Ahti answered. "I pushed myself a little hard is all. People need food."

"Ahti is our best fisherman," Jarin explained. "With so many sick, there's few hands to keep everyone fed. I'm not sure what we'll do now."

"I can fish," Otso piped up. "I'll go with Grandpa."

Jarin squatted in front of Otso. "Your grandfather needs to rest awhile."

"Then I'll go myself. I can go now." Otso rose and made for his grandfather's gear.

Jarin grabbed Otso's wrist, stopping him short. He shook his head. "We'll find another way to feed the village."

Otso yanked his hand away and frowned. "I can do it. I've fished alone before. Maybe Satu will help me."

"Maybe later." Jarin smiled and rubbed Otso's head. "For now, you need to stay with your grandfather. Keep an eye on him."

"I can fish by myself," Otso shouted, eyes flashing.

"Otso," his grandfather said.

Knowing an upset grandson wouldn't be good for Ahti right now, Trini decided to distract the boy. "Who is this Satu?" she asked. "Is he a friend?"

"It's a superstition," Aunt Teresa called over her shoulder.

"He's real!" Otso stomped his feet and glared at them, before holding up his toy dinosaur, which possessed two large, webbed rear feet and two flippers up front. "He looks like Isu."

"Otso, now isn't the time for your imaginary beast," Jarin said disapprovingly.

"Jarin, the world is filled with more than most believe." Ahti's words came out as a wheeze.

Jarin shook his head and chuckled. "Your fever must be making you senile, old man."

Real or imaginary, Satu would distract Otso right now, so Trini held out her hand to him. "He looks pretty cool. Where does he live? Can you take me?"

Getting the boy out of the hut would allow Aunt Teresa to tend to Ahti without hindrance. If Trini had to guess, Ahti had probably been displaying symptoms for a couple of days now, maybe even a week, but had hidden them, either because he had to keep fishing for the village, or more likely, he didn't want to scare his grandson.

Trini and Otso walked down the hut front steps. The boy led her north out of the village and toward foothills. The exercise was nice.

"Is Satu little like your toy?" Trini pointed at the dinosaur carving.

"He's big." Otso raised a hand high over his head to accentuate his words. "Way bigger than my home. He's got gray, oily skin and he's kind of fat."

"Where does he live?"

"He lives in the lake where we fish."

"But he comes ashore?" she asked. Perhaps Ahti has been humoring the boy.

"Oh yes," Otso promised. "I'll show you. He's my friend. He visits grandfather and me sometimes when we fish."

"Your own guardian angel."

He looked puzzled. "What's a guardian angel?"

"You don't know about guardian angels?" She opened her mouth wide in mock disbelief. He was cute, and she wished she had a younger brother like him.

He pursed his lips, considering for a moment. Finally, he shook his head. "No. Are they strong?"

She grinned. "Very strong. A guardian angel is someone who looks out for you. Protects you from harm."

"Like grandfather?"

"Yes, like your grandfather. He makes sure you're safe."

"So I have two guardian angels?" He beamed.

"Looks like it. You must be a very lucky boy. It's rare to get more than one guardian angel."

His chest puffed up, and he picked up his pace. With the late afternoon sun shining on them, she was glad for the short break. It had been difficult seeing all of the suffering in the village. Men, women, and children alike, stricken by a disease they were powerless to fight. If her aunt hadn't come, the Ukka would've been forced to brave it and hope to survive. Even with her here, many might still perish.

Trini hated to think what Otso had seen already, or what else he'd see in the days to come.

"There it is," he said excitedly, pointing ahead. He charged forward.

She ran after him, anxious not to lose him. He stopped fifty yards ahead and stared down at large indentations in the dirt. As she caught up, she realized the tracks were larger than she'd expected. The indentations were long enough for a full grown Ukka to lay down inside without touching the ends. Based on the shape of the tracks, they certainly could've come from something that resembled Otso's toy dinosaur. Could it be real?

"I told you," he said, smiling broadly. "It looks like Isu." He held up the wooden dinosaur, pointing at its flipper like feet, then at the tracks in the ground.

On Earth she would've suspected someone of faking the tracks for a prank. That was certainly possible here, too, but with so many ill, who would waste the time?

"This Satu lives in the lake?" She was certainly intrigued.

Would Space City have any record of the creature? She guessed based upon Aunt Teresa's comment that they did not. She took a picture of the tracks with her wrist-comp. If she got a sighting of whatever had made those tracks, she might be able to use the discovery for a class project next year.

"Yes. Come. I'll show you." He reached for her hand as he pointed ahead.

She pulled back, suddenly uneasy about continuing onward. She wanted to see the creature, but if it was as large as its tracks suggested, it might pose a danger. She didn't know anything about it. His belief that it was friendly could just be in his head. She needed to be careful. "We should go back. It's getting late and I haven't eaten all day. Can we go later?"

He looked disappointed, but nodded, then brightened once more. "I can get you food. Let's go."

She let him lead her back to the village. But she was curious about those tracks. Was it possible most of the Ukka didn't know about the creature? Was there a creature?

She'd seek it out later tonight. Alone.

Chapter 2

Sneaking out of the village late that night, Trini retraced her steps north into the steadily rising foothills. Her stomach was stuffed with lemonfish, so the exercise was welcome. The spices the Ukka had cooked the lemonfish with had given it a fiery flavor. It had come with a side of baked white roots mixed with some sort of greens, as well as pacush, which reminded her of yams. She had put away two helpings.

Once she had safely escaped the village unseen—she didn't want word of her late night excursion getting back to her aunt—she used the flashlight app on her wrist-comp to light her path. The villagers had assured her the lake was huge. She couldn't miss it.

Before leaving, she'd changed into her silver Space City suit with active lasers. Seemed like a smart precaution. Despite Otso's assurances, she had to assume the creature would be wild and hostile. If it was real. Plus, there were other predators to be wary of, though with the limited ground cover and ample moonlight she should see anything coming well before it reached her.

She topped a hill and an enormous body of water awaited her about a quarter mile ahead. In the darkness, she couldn't see its far side. Could the tradutor have confused the Ukka word for ocean with lake? Or perhaps the Ukka didn't have such distinctions. The land on her left continued to rise steeply, creating a cliff overlooking the water. She picked up her pace, adrenaline causing her to shiver. Would she find Otso's fabled creature?

Yellow light illuminated the water around one particular rock ledge that jutted out a little into the lake. Trini headed for it, curious what caused the water to glow like that, as if a fallen star had landed in the lake.

When she reached the end of the rock shelf, she found numerous large fish milling about, skins glowing like yellow neon lights.

Or mini stars.

Lemonfish.

Why were the fish congregating here? It was almost like a fish farm, except she knew the Ukka weren't sophisticated enough for such a thing. Nor was their population large enough to require it.

Dropping to her hands and knees, she leaned out over the water, entranced. The fish chased each other, darting this way and that. Some nipped playfully at each other, their tiny mouths seemingly useless next to their large, round bodies.

Without warning the fish scattered in all directions. She squinted, trying to identify what had spooked them. One lemonfish darted straight upward for the surface. Would it leap straight out of the water?

Too late, she noticed the mouth surging up from below the fish, a great dark mass like that of a whale. The mass breached the lake's surface around the lemonfish, spraying water in all directions. She flinched back, but not fast enough to avoid a blow to the head that sent her reeling.

Gravity swung out of control.

Helplessly she flung out her arms for something to steady herself. She plunged into the icy water, which sent a shock through her system. Water poured down her throat. She coughed, trying to clear it. She fought to get her head above water. As she gasped for air, unconsciousness threatened to overtake her. Instinctively, she tried to swim, frantic to get out of the water and away from whatever was there with her. But her body slammed straight into a wall and she blacked out.

Chapter 3

Trini's spasming jaw woke her. She lay on rocks, one cutting into her thigh. Her head pulsed like a bass speaker.

Where was she?

The last thing she could remember was two enormous rows of teeth. And neon lights underwater. No, glowing fish. The lemonfish all huddled together. The pieces came together, sending a surge of panic through her. She lurched upright, which made her head do loops. Her vision blurred and everything went dark again.

*****

The second time she woke, her stomach was an acidic mess. Her jaw ached as if she'd ground her teeth during sleep. A wet, jagged rock dug into her cheek. She shivered. Every bit of her was soaking wet, as if someone had dumped water on her bed. She struggled to open heavy eyelids, but could barely see other than to discern it was still night.

In a rush, memories flooded in of a large creature leaping up from the lake's depth. Her whole body clenched as she recalled it striking her.

Was it still here?

She started to push herself upright, but the nails shooting through her brain stopped her. It took her several deep breaths to adjust to the pain. Her eyes acclimated first, showing her the lake mere inches away. Water from the surf sprayed her.

Had that creature been Satu?

If so, it wasn't a superstition. It had hit her like a wrecking ball. She was lucky the impact hadn't killed her. And that she hadn't drowned.

Slowly, she pushed herself to a sitting position, gasping to soothe her aching head. Her arms and legs throbbed.

Though she desperately wanted to lie back and sleep, she forced herself to her feet, groaning all the while. The glowing yellow lights had returned near the ledge a short distance from her. This time, she had no desire to check it out. One encounter with the strange creature in the lake was enough.

She didn't think it had been lunging for her, though. If it had, she would be dead. No, she'd just had the misfortune of being in its path as it went for the fish. Thankfully, she must've washed up on shore before drowning.

Every step back to the village jarred her head, so that she constantly fought the urge to lie down and quit, as well as to empty her stomach all over the ground. She pushed on only by telling herself that she'd find no relief on the freezing ground.

It took a hundred thousand steps to return to the village, she was pretty sure. There was no one out and about, the only noises were moans coming from some of the huts. In the darkness, she had difficulty locating the hut the Ukka had set aside for her and Aunt Teresa, but once she reached it she wanted nothing more than to lie down and sleep.

"Trini?" Aunt Teresa called from her side of the hut—she had hung a sheet in the middle to give themselves some privacy. "Where have you been?"

Squeezing her eyes shut to control her voice, Trini replied, "Couldn't sleep. I went for a walk." She bit her lip to prevent herself from asking for help. Part of her wanted to beg her aunt for medicine for her head, but the last thing she wanted was to be questioned or receive a lecture. Besides, sleep would solve everything. "I'm half dead now. I'll see you in the morning."

"Good. You need your sleep," Aunt Teresa replied through a yawn. "We've got some long days ahead of us."

Trini stifled a groan. She stripped out of her clothes, fighting the desire to crash with them still on. She forced herself to dress in fresh clothes, hanging her wet ones over a wall post.

She grabbed a water bottle from her pack and drank greedily. The water settled her stomach a little. She took a couple more gulps before crawling under the blanket on her mat, wishing she had three more to bury herself under. Even with the fresh clothes, she shivered uncontrollably. Despite that, she quickly lost consciousness for the third time that night.

Chapter 4

Sunshine bullied Trini awake. It needed a dimmer switch. Or tinting. Her headache hadn't subsided and chills spiraled through her. She curled up in a ball and groaned as she pulled the thin blanket over her head. The sun had no right to be so happy.

"You might be better rested if not for your late night stroll," Aunt Teresa chided from her side of the hut. "I could use your help as soon as you can drag yourself from bed."

Trini wished sleepiness was all that ailed her. Instead, she felt exactly how she imagined someone would feel after getting smacked around by a whale-sized creature.

"And don't forget your medication regimen."

She poked an arm out from under the blanket, feeling around for the water bottle. She wasn't ready to brave the sun just yet. But if she stayed in bed too long, she'd never hear the end of it. Her fingers found a corner of the bottle, and she yanked it under the blanket.

She gulped down half the bottle before she could make herself face the day. She dragged herself from under the covers, wincing and blinking against the sunlight pouring in. By that point, her aunt had already gone.

A bowl of warm water waited on the hut porch, left by the Ukka for washing. Trini reached for the bowl and spotted a couple of long, narrow cuts on her left arm. She touched one gingerly. It stung a little, but wasn't bad. There were two more like it under her arm, and as she studied them, she thought they looked like giant teeth marks. As if the creature last night had bitten her. Seemed she was lucky it hadn't eaten her.

She retrieved the water bowl and a fresh cloth from her pack and cleaned the cuts, and then the rest of herself a little. She put disinfectant on the cuts. With that done, she donned an old, long-sleeved gray shirt and jeans, something simple to work in for the day.

Her stomach bubbled like a cauldron of witches' brew. She couldn't possibly keep any food down. As she glanced at her pills Aunt Teresa had prescribed, she wasn't sure she could stomach them either. Best hold onto those for a few hours until she felt well enough to eat something. So she slipped the pill container into a pocket and departed for the medical tent. She did continue to down water. Had the collision with the lake creature caused internal injuries that made her feel so sick? Or something in the water she'd ingested when she fell in?

She ducked into the medical tent, now filled with Ukka. The mats held the sickest patients. Healthy Ukka, or at least those not too sick to stand, tended to their loved ones on the mats. Trini waded through the aisles to the research room where Aunt Teresa studied the blood samples.

Aunt Teresa looked up from her microscope only long enough to take measure of Trini. "You look terrible." Another jab at Trini's late night.

But Trini was relieved her aunt was too focused on work to pay closer attention. "I'll be fine. How can I help?"

Without looking up, Aunt Teresa pointed to a gray medical bag in the corner. "Check on Ahti for me? Until I get a better handle on this maleze strain, I can't treat anyone. I can only make them comfortable and hope for the best."

"I've got it." Trini crossed the room and retrieved the medical bag. She fished around in it for some nausea medicine.

"Once you finish there, make a round through the village. I want to know if there are any seriously ill still in their homes. I also need to know about any new cases."

"Yes, captain. Anything else?" She took two nausea pills and washed them down with water.

Aunt Teresa cast her an annoyed look. "Oh, get out of here."

Trini smiled, then departed.

Walking to Ahti and Otso's home exhausted Trini. She stumbled up the wood log steps. At the top she leaned against a frame post, breathing heavily. Hardin would mock her if he saw her like this. Some professional Space City Games player she'd make if she weakened so easily. She felt like an android on low battery power and still ached all over. Last night must have taken a bigger toll on her than she thought.

"Trini?" Otso called from inside the hut.

She straightened, trying to hide her fatigue. She grabbed the bowl of cleaning water from the steps before entering. "Morning Otso, I'm here to check on your grandfather."

The boy sat in a wooden chair fingering a simple fishing pole. The little wooden dinosaur, Isu, rested beside him on the chair. Ahti lay unconscious on his mat, head drenched with sweat. The smell of vomit lingered, though the floor and mat were spotless.

"Grandfather is sleeping late," Otso said, frowning at Ahti. "He promised we fish when he woke."

She sat beside Ahti. "Your grandfather needs to rest." She soaked a rag in the cleaning water and wiped the sweat from Ahti's brow.

Otso jumped to his feet. "Since you're here, you can stay with grandfather. I'll go fish."

"Actually, I'd like to ask you some questions," she said.

"Someone needs to fish." He glanced at the door as if debating running off anyway.

"I believe I saw Satu."

He dropped the fishing pole against the chair. The pole bounced off the chair and clacked to the floor. He ignored it as he plopped down beside her. "Here in the village?"

She shook her head. She wanted to be careful in how she responded. "Late last night I couldn't sleep, so I went for a walk. I came across the lake."

"He's big!" Otso's eyes were bright. He absentmindedly grabbed up Isu and held it in his lap.

"Huge," she agreed.

"I see him the most." He rocked back and forth. "We're friends."

She bit her lip. She didn't want to upset him, but Satu seemed anything but friendly. *She'd* been lucky to walk away from the encounter. He might not be so fortunate. But if he considered the creature his friend, it would be difficult for her to persuade him otherwise. He might not even believe what had happened to her. Children always saw the best in the people and things they loved.

"Is your grandfather friends with Satu, as well?" She rinsed the rag in the water and proceeded to wash Ahti's cheeks and neck. His skin had paled, which worried her.

Otso nodded eagerly. "Yes, he told me about Satu. He knows all the stories."

"Do you two play with Satu?" she asked, thinking of the cuts on her arm.

"I love to play with Satu," he replied.

"And your grandfather?" She fished out a couple of pills that her aunt had marked for Ahti. She forced them between his lips. He swallowed without opening his eyes, and when she placed a water bottle to his lips, he sipped, choking a little in the process. Inexperienced as she was, she still recognized his rapidly declining health.

Otso frowned, staring at his grandfather. "I think so. I've only seen Satu by myself."

"I see."

Had he just been lucky to this point?

She didn't like it. Reluctant to leave him alone and risk him deciding to fish on his own, but with a full day ahead of her, she convinced him to help her check on the other villagers. Ahti would be fine for a few hours; Otso placed Isu beside his grandfather's head to keep him company. And if the boy felt he was helping out, he'd be satisfied.

As they made their way around the village, Otso diligently helped her out, carefully listening when she assigned him tasks. He showed a child's enthusiasm for doing something new and feeling helpful.

Unfortunately, many of the Ukka they encountered didn't display similar enthusiasm. They found a number of Ukka complaining of headaches or shivering under extra layers. But none of them wanted to go to the hospital tent, or even admit they were sick. Trini advised—and in a few cases used her position as a representative from Space City to order—them to visit the hospital tent to get checked out. Maleze wasn't something to take lightly, even for the toughest of them.

Late in the afternoon, as she and Otso departed a hut, four Ukka passed carrying someone on a stretcher covered by a blanket, headed out of the village.

Their first death.

Mood dampened, Trini headed to check on Aunt Teresa; see how her research was progressing. Besides, she needed to eat and rest a bit. It took all her energy to place one foot in front of the other. Otso bounced around her on their way, full of energy. Trini envied him.

The medical tent was crowded to overflowing when she returned. There was no more room for anyone inside, so the ill rested on the ground outside the medical tent or up against nearby homes. The healthy or healthier tended to them with water, food, or simple company.

Entering the medical tent, she spotted Aunt Teresa bent over an Ukka woman, checking her vitals. Every cot and chair were taken, and with so many people in the tent, it felt a good bit hotter than outside. Trini felt a little bit claustrophobic and wondered if this was a mistake. Perhaps she should head back to their hut to rest a bit.

But when Aunt Teresa stood and noticed Trini, her mouth dropped open.

"Trini, what happened to you?" Aunt Teresa hurried over, her patient forgotten.

"I'm just tired." Trini forced herself to straighten.

Aunt Teresa shook her head and grabbed Trini's arm. She motioned for a male Ukka to vacate his seat and forced Trini to sit. "You're not fine. You're sick."

"I'm just a little worn out." Trini waved dismissively.

"No, you've got maleze." Aunt Teresa began an examination of her.

"No, I don't," Trini protested. She tried to rise and wave her aunt off, but hadn't the strength.

*****

Aunt Teresa took a blood sample from Trini, handed her a fresh bottle of water, then disappeared back to her office. Trini sipped nervously. Despite the efforts of the recruited Ukka nurses, the tent smelled heavily of sweat and vomit, which didn't help matters. She doubted her ability to stand, but dismissed it partially as recovering from last night and also from traipsing through the village for hours. Her aunt was wrong.

"Trini, are you sick?" Otso's eyes glistened.

She reached for his hand. "No, Otso. I'm just tired is all. We've worked hard. Just need to eat."

A nearby nurse gave her a sympathetic glance. Trini wanted to tell her she didn't need her concern, but bit her tongue. Snapping at the nurse wouldn't help matters.

"I could get you food," Otso offered.

"That would be great." She did her best to sound excited, though her stomach remained an acidic mess. She wanted to eat because she knew she needed to, not because she desired it. Plus it would give him something to do.

"I'll be back quick." He scrambled from the tent.

He returned shortly with fish, but she only nibbled at it. She was fine. She just needed to get back to work. She tried to rise, but her legs refused to cooperate.

Maybe ten more minutes.

Twenty minutes passed before Aunt Teresa rushed back, medicine bag in hand. "I'm sorry, Trini. I've double-checked. It's positive."

Trini's hand started to shake. She tried to stop it, but failed. "I'm sick?" The words sounded strange, without real meaning.

Aunt Teresa handed her some pills, the ones she had dispensed for fever and nausea. Trini stared at the pills blankly.

"I'm sorry, honey." Aunt Teresa's shoulders slumped. "This wasn't supposed to happen."

"What do I do?" Trini asked, unable to think of anything more.

"Can you get back to the hut?" Aunt Teresa asked. "You need to lie down and there's nowhere left here."

"I can help her," Otso offered.

With Otso's help, Trini stood, though she had to lean heavily on him. She colored with embarrassment, but it *was* a relief.

"I'll come by a little later to check on you," Aunt Teresa said, before bending down over an unconscious patient.

Otso walked slowly, not rushing her as they navigated out of the tent and past all the Ukka huddled outside. The cool air brought immediately relief. They had to stop a couple of times along the way to rest, but finally reached the hut.

As soon as she made it inside, she collapsed on her mat.

"Do you want me to get you anything?" Otso asked, pulling the blanket back over her.

"No," she murmured, eyelids growing heavy fast. "I just need—"

*****

Trini awoke worse than ever. Her headache had expanded to a throbbing pulse. Her stomach clenched repeatedly, threatening to empty its contents everywhere. She moaned. There was no mistake about it. She had Maleze.

Beside her was a bottle of water and a bowl of cold broth. The thought of consuming either made her stomach clench harder. She wanted nothing but to sleep. And medicine from her aunt. But she also knew her aunt lacked a real cure. Until Aunt Teresa had a breakthrough, her only hope was for her immune system to fight off the infection. And to do that, she needed to nourish her body.

Forcing herself to sit up, she took the bowl of broth in both hands and drank. As she did so, she tried to figure out how she'd gotten sick. The disease wasn't passed from one person to the next. On Earth, people got malaria when infected insects bit them. But despite the similarities between malaria and maleze, Aunt Teresa had ruled out insects here. Had Satu somehow infected her? She pulled back the sleeve of her shirt, revealing the cuts. They had scabbed over.

But most of the other villagers thought the creature was a myth. They hadn't come in contact with it. Had they? She hadn't seen anyone else with cuts like hers. Was there a way for them to come in contact with the beast without their knowing it?

She decided she couldn't just lie here and wait to see if she survived. She needed to fight this. Needed to help her aunt find a cure for them all.

Climbing to her feet to prove she could, she debated heading to the medical tent. No, she couldn't help her aunt there. She lacked the medical training to help with the research. Nor would her aunt allow her to tend to the other patients now. Aunt Teresa would insist she rest.

She needed to think outside the box. Come up with something that all of the Ukka had in common. Despite the absurdity of the idea, her

75

mind kept drifting back to Satu. She didn't know why, but something told her she needed to at least rule out the creature.

Groaning inwardly at the prospect of heading back out to the lake in her present condition, she refilled her water bottle anyway. She had no choice. There was already one fatality from the outbreak, and likely would be many more soon if they didn't discover the source of the outbreak.

Otso would go with her, but she resisted that idea. It would be nice to have his support, but she couldn't risk him if she encountered Satu again. No matter what the boy believed, she couldn't trust that the creature was friendly.

Instead, she grabbed a couple of health bars from her aunt's stuff, then headed out alone. Every dozen paces or so she had to take a mini break, gulp down a few mouthfuls of water, and reassure herself that she could do this.

The Ukka depended on her.

Otso and Ahti depended on her.

It felt a little like the Games, on the attack for her teammates. She wouldn't let them down.

Not far from the edge of the village she came back across the enormous prints from the first day, which Otso had told her belonged to Satu. Near the prints lay the partially eaten remains of a yellowfish, which she hadn't noticed the first time.

Saliva! It stood to reason that Satu was the one who'd eaten that fish, though why it had dragged the fish so far from the lake was beyond her. Thankfully it had, because it would've left behind saliva on the carcass, and while dried by now, she should be able to test some of it.

Dropping to her knees, Trini removed her wrist-comp and a test tube. Using a knife, she cut off a portion of the fish around where it had been eaten. She placed the sample in the test tube which analyzed the tissue.

Five minutes later, her wrist-comp beeped. Scanning the results, she wanted to leap like a dolphin.

Test positive.

The creature had eaten the fish and left the disease on the carcass. She had the source! Aunt Teresa could develop a cure!

Chapter 5

"I've got your source!" Trini held the test tube up as if about to propose a toast.

That little gesture sapped her strength, forcing her to lean on Otso, who'd helped her back to her aunt's private research room in the back of the medical tent after she nearly collapsed on her way through the village.

Aunt Teresa's eyes narrowed, lips pursed.

Trini recognized the signs of a scolding coming from her aunt and overrode her. "Satu's the source of the sickness. I've got proof."

"Satu?" Otso squealed, jostling Trini so that she nearly lost her balance and fell to the ground. "Satu hurt grandpa?"

Aunt Teresa exited the hologram she was studying and crossed the room, taking the test tube. "How? What did you do?"

"I need to sit." Trini sunk onto a knee-high crate, taking a couple deep breaths to compose herself. "I got a sample of his saliva."

Horror marred Otso's face. He clutched Isu to his chest.

"Otso, I—" Trini reached for his hand, realizing too late that she should've taken more care in how she revealed her discovery.

He backed out of her reach, tears brimming in his eyes. "How could Satu do this?" He bolted.

Trini wanted to go after him, but couldn't muster the strength. She'd pushed herself to the limit getting the sample.

"Satu's a myth," Aunt Teresa said. "You're sick. You must be imagining things."

Trini shook her head and pulled back the sleeve of her left shirt, revealing the pair of long scabs on her forearm. She turned her arm over to show the matching set on the underside of her arm.

"Where did you get those?" Aunt Teresa took Trini's arm in her hands and studied the scabs.

"The other night. When I went for a stroll," Trini said as Aunt Teresa retrieved a salve and started dabbing some on the scabs. Trini debated telling her aunt she'd already cleaned the cuts, but decided to just roll with it. "Once you diagnosed me, I tried to figure out how I got it. You said maleze doesn't pass through simple contact. My encounter with Satu is the only thing I've done, besides helping you. I found the remains of a fish it had eaten, took a sample, and tested it. Came back positive."

Aunt Teresa started laughing, shaking her head. "Silly girl."

"What? I found what you needed." Trini felt her anger rising at this dismissal.

"You did, but Satu's not the source."

Trini bit her lip. "But—"

Aunt Teresa retrieved the sample, which she'd deposited on the table. She carried it to a gray analysis machine and slipped the tube inside. "It's not Satu. It's the yellowfish. The main *staple* in the Ukka diet."

Trini's mouth widened in an "O" of understanding, but was short lived. "If it's the fish, why haven't the Ukka always had problems?"

"They've become contaminated somehow. Maybe a mutation." Aunt Teresa moved to the tent flap and looked out into the main area. "Jarin, will you have someone bring me a sample of the yellowfish? Uncooked." Without waiting for a response, she returned to her wrist-comp and re-activated her hologram she'd been studying earlier.

Trini couldn't wait to deliver the news to Otso. He'd be thrilled to learn that his friend wasn't responsible for his grandfather's illness.

Ilta, a wrinkled old Ukka whom Aunt Teresa had recruited as a nurse, entered with a tray of broth and crackers, which she delivered to Trini. The broth was warm, and while she still lacked any desire for food, she knew she needed it.

"Otso! Otso!" a voice yelled from outside. "Put me down and get Otso." It was Ahti.

Trini tried to rise, but her legs wobbled, unable to hold her. Leaning against storage containers within arm's reach was a pair of crutches. She grabbed one and used it to climb to her feet.

"Be careful," her aunt said. "Don't push it."

"I just need to check on Ahti. Something's wrong." Trini pushed through the tent flap out into the main area of the tent. Ahti tried ineffectually to lift himself off a cot. When had he been brought in?

"Ahti, what's wrong?" She struggled to maneuver with the crutch around Ukka and cots.

"Otso. He's gone," Ahti cried. "Went after Satu. Said he had to punish it for making me sick."

Trini inhaled sharply. Someone had to locate him before he found Satu.

Ahti struggled to rise and continued hollering for his grandson.

"I'll go," Trini placed a hand on the old man's shoulder. "I'll get him."

The old man ceased shouting and turned to her, eyes imploring. "Please. Otso is all I have." Tears streamed down his face.

Trini had to fight back her own. "I'll find him."

He slumped to the cot. "Thank you! Thank you!"

She closed her eyes, taking deep breaths, trying to muster the strength to go after Otso. Even with the crutch for support, she was daunted by the prospect of heading back out to the lake.

Get it together, Trini. This was about mind over matter. She could do this. Had to for Otso's sake.

Grunting from the effort, she moved the crutch forward. Her legs trembled. She took several steps toward the tent entrance, clutching the crutch like a lifeline. She focused all her energy on putting one foot in front of the other, afraid that if she stopped for even a moment she'd never get started again.

The cots were not well aligned, and many without cots had simply taken up spots on the ground in random places. Trini had to navigate through. One step forward, two diagonally left, three forward, one right, and so on until she reached the exit.

On the ground outside, she spotted Isu, the little wooden dinosaur, lying discarded in the dirt. She bent, one hand on a lower point of the crutch, in order to retrieve the toy. As she rose, she spotted the ship on the outskirts of town. She didn't have to hike all the way out to the lake. Just to the ship. Then she could fly to find Otso.

The flowering vines on the homes she passed were all wilting. Animals milled about in pens, some bleating in hunger or thirst. And for the number of people filling the village, it was fairly quiet. All conversations were hushed, few Ukka still standing. It had only been a couple of days, but the look of defeat was evident everywhere. She wanted to tell them all there would be a cure soon, to reassure them that things would be all right. But for some of them it might not be. It would still take her aunt some time to develop a treatment.

And right now she had to get to Otso.

She wasn't sure how long it took her to reach the ship, but she made it, every muscle in her body screaming to lie down, threatening to mutiny if she ignored them. Entering the side door, her eyes fell on her bunk, which called invitingly to her. She had to force herself to look away and push on, using the ship's walls for support in addition to the crutch, up to the cabin.

Good afternoon, Trini, popped up on the pilot's screen. She ignored the greeting as she leaned the crutch against the passenger seat. She sat in the pilot's seat, sighing deeply, and activated the ship's controls. Firing up the engine, she lifted off.

Otso had likely reached the lake by now, but with any luck, he wouldn't have found Satu waiting for him. If he was harmed, it would be her fault.

Please don't let him find Satu.

*****

The placidity of the lake offered little comfort as Trini flew over. No sign of Satu or the boy. The ship's bio scanner registered only birds and other small creatures. No sign of Otso. Her mind flashed back to waking up along the shoreline after her encounter with Satu, except now she saw Otso in her place, floating face down in the water. No!

That wouldn't happen. She'd stop it.

Flying slowly along the shoreline, she covered a distance much further than Otso could've hiked in the time he'd been gone. She circled around and flew back, panic on the rise.

Otso, where are you?

This wasn't working, so she landed near the rock ledge where she'd encountered Satu. For a moment, she simply sat there. Just thinking about rising and going out to search for him exhausted her. She was weak. Aunt Teresa would've wanted her on a cot resting in the medical tent. But there was no one else to help Otso out. She was all he had.

Taking several deep breaths, she grabbed Isu and the crutch and struggled to her feet. It took a couple of more seconds to get going to the ship's exit. She hobbled across the rock ledge to the water. A few of the yellowfish swam nearby, but no Satu or Otso.

A scream up in the hills froze her. She looked up the steep incline, sure the scream had come from Otso. If it was him he was out of sight. She pressed forward up the hill, focusing on staying upright over the rocks and roots that threatened to topple her.

"Otso! Otso, are you okay?"

No answer.

The hair on the back of her neck stood up. "Otso! Otso!" Her breathing came in gasps as she trudged upward. She gripped Isu tightly, seeking emotional support from the wooden dinosaur, as she scoured the trees for any sign of the boy.

"Trini?" A hoarse voice called from her right.

She rerouted toward the voice and almost lost her feet as little rocks slid out from underfoot, threatening to throw her off a cliff overlooking the lake. She clutched the crutch with both arms to steady herself. She hadn't realized she'd been that close.

"Otso?"

"Down here," Otso called from below.

Bracing herself with the crutch, she leaned over the edge. He stood on a narrow ledge about twenty feet below, waving his arms up at her.

Otso cupped his mouth with his hands. "Can you help me up?"

"I don't have a rope," Trini replied, angry at herself for not bringing any rescue supplies from the ship.

A few rock shelves poked up from the lake directly below.

"How did you get down there?" she asked.

His shoulders slumped. "I fell searching for Satu. The edge crumbled beneath me, and I fell." His chin dropped to his chest.

She took a step backward, checking the ground nervously. It seemed steady enough.

"Don't leave me," he yelled, voice tinged with fear.

She took careful steps to the ledge, cringing, and leaned over so he could see her. "Are you hurt?"

"No." He looked himself over as if searching for injuries.

Thank goodness for that at least. She regarded her crutch, but even if she lay down on the ground and lowered it over the edge, she wouldn't be able to reach him.

"Otso. I've got rope in the ship. I need it to help you. I won't be gone long."

"No!"

She clenched Isu so tightly it hurt her palm. Hearing the anxiety in his voice made her feel guilty for having to leave him, even though she had to in order to rescue him. Then she had an idea.

"Otso, I have Isu." She knelt and held the wooden dinosaur out where he could see it. "I'm going to drop it to you. It'll stay with you until I can return."

"No. I don't want it," Otso cried back. "I want you."

"I'll be back as fast as I can. I promise. In the meantime, Isu will stay with you. Okay?" She dropped the wooden carving, hoping it wouldn't break when it hit or bounce off the ledge into the water. It landed in a patch of weeds and Otso retrieved it, once more clutching it tightly to his chest as he looked up at her.

"You'll be fine," she said. "Will you do something for me? Will you sit with your back against the cliff and stay there until I return?"

For a few seconds, he didn't respond. Tears welled up in his eyes. All bravado was gone. This was too big for him to handle.

Nevertheless, he replied, voice so quiet she barely heard him, "Okay." He promptly sat, pressing his back against the cliff. His knees hugged his chest, Isu cradled in between.

She opened her mouth to offer him a final bit of encouragement, but was interrupted by a head poking up out of the lake. A long gray neck like that of a brontosaurus followed the head. Next came a massive body. The creature floated on the surface like a waterfowl, though it also had a couple of front flippers, like a seal.

Satu. It must be, though it looked a lot different than she remembered from her encounter, limited though it was. It crawled up onto the rock shelf far below. Then the beast stretched up its long neck toward the ledge on which Otso sat, but it only covered half the distance. It cried up at the boy.

Trini stood frozen, awed by the size of the creature, which was easily thirty feet tall. The awe was quickly replaced by worry for the boy. She had to get Otso up before Satu figured out a way to reach him. If only she'd thought to bring a weapon to scare it off. The ship had several, but did she risk leaving him now that Satu had appeared? For a split second she debated throwing the crutch at the creature to try to scare it off, but that wouldn't bother it much. And then she'd be stuck here with no way to get back to the ship.

To her consternation, Otso scrambled to his feet, approached the edge, and shook his fist clutching Isu at the beast. "Bad Satu. You made grandfather sick. I hate you."

Satu lowered its neck, then leapt. As it jumped, it kicked out its hind legs, flattening itself as much as possible. The beast had great strength in its limbs, allowing it to spring up a good distance above the rocks, but not enough to reach the ledge where Otso stood.

"No! Otso, get back!" She didn't have time to return to the ship. She had to find another way to help Otso up.

Satu landed, gathered itself, and sprang again. Once more it kicked its legs out, creating a relatively flat surface with its back. It was the most bizarre thing Trini thought she'd ever seen. Kicking outward and flattening itself was taking a lot out of the creature's jump. Surely it would realize it couldn't reach Otso this way and try something else.

Otso, for his part, kept admonishing the beast.

After the second jump, Satu stretched up its neck toward Otso and cried. The cry was neither angry nor threatening. If anything, Trini thought it looked frustrated with Otso. It lowered its head and leapt for the third time.

This time, a strange thought crossed her mind. What if Otso was right? What if Satu *was* friendly toward the boy? Taken in that light, the creature looked to be creating a cushion of sorts that Otso could safely land on if he jumped. Like a fireman's life net outside a burning building.

But that would mean trusting the creature. Despite Otso's previous assertions, it was hard to believe Satu would really view him as a friend.

Before springing a fourth time, Satu looked up at Otso, before deliberately glancing down at its back. There was no mistaking the gesture. Or was that her sickness talking, making her delirious in her exhausted state?

As if to underscore that thought, her legs gave out, dropping her into a heap, inches away from tumbling over the edge. The crutch slipped from her grasp, toppling over the side. It fell past the ledge Otso stood on, clanked against the cliff a couple of times, then hit the water and sank.

Gasping in frustration, Trini tried to pick herself up, but all her remaining strength had deserted her. There was no going back to the ship to get anything to help Otso up. There was nothing she could do.

They could wait around until someone from the village realized they'd been gone too long and come looking for them. Which might take hours. Or days.

Or she could trust Satu.

Hoping she wasn't making a serious mistake, she leaned over the ledge. "Otso, I think Satu wants you to jump down onto it's back."

"No!" Otso backed away from the ledge. "I hate him. He betrayed us."

"Otso, Satu didn't make your grandfather sick. It was the fish."

"The fish?" Otso turned to look up at her, mouth ajar, eyes emitting hope. "Not Satu?"

She shook her head. "No. I made a mistake. Satu didn't hurt Ahti."

A smile broke across the boy's face, underscoring his young age. He turned and looked down at Satu. The beast had raised its neck up toward him once more.

"I'm sorry I said I hated you," Otso apologized. "I didn't mean it."

Satu cried up at him once more. Acceptance? Impatience?

"Otso, have you gotten close to Satu before?" Trini asked.

"Oh, yes," he replied. "We've swam together several times."

"You promise?" she asked. His fate rested on her.

"Yes!"

She chuckled at the insanity of this, but it was their best choice. Perhaps their only choice.

"Otso, when Satu jumps, I want you to leap down to his back. Aim for the middle."

"Really?" His eyes lit up.

She didn't like his eagerness, making her reconsider if this was the right course. But she couldn't see any other way to help him. "Yes."

Otso shuffled to the lip of the ledge, legs bent and ready to leap. Trini held her breath, wishing she could trade places so he'd be safe.

Satu sprang again, stretching flat as possible, and Otso dropped. Every muscle in her body tensed as he fell, landing in the middle of the creature's back just as it reached the highpoint of its jump. When it landed, it maintained its flat back. Otso bounced, but didn't fall off. A moment later, Satu slipped into the lake, keeping his back above the water as he carried Otso along the shoreline.

Trini rolled onto her back and sighed. Her body ached all over, and she needed sleep. Fifteen minutes later, Otso started calling for her. She shouted for him to come up. It was the most she could manage.

He soon hurried up to her, face beaming. "Did you see me? Did you see Satu catch me?"

She smiled. "I did. You did great."

When she didn't rise, his brow furrowed. "What's wrong?"

"I pushed myself too hard. I need to rest awhile."

"I can carry you back." He knelt beside her.

The offer was both humiliating and amusing. She hadn't been carried since she was a little girl on Earth. And Otso was but a child. A large one, but still a child. She also knew it would be a while before she had enough strength to get up.

"I'm not sure you can," she answered.

"I can." He gave her Isu, which she accepted gratefully. Then he slid his arms beneath her and lifted her straight up without even a grunt from strain. He turned and headed downhill as if she were nothing to carry. She was unsure if she should be happy or embarrassed by this.

"You don't have to carry me all the way back. Just down to my ship. We'll fly back."

"I get to fly with you?" Otso asked, eyes widening.

"I'm not letting you out of my sight until I've got you back to your grandfather." It was a strange sensation to be cradled and carried, but she accepted it. Better than lying at the top of the cliff for the next several hours. Fortunately, she could set the ship on autopilot.

Chapter 6

For the next two days, Trini lay on her bunk in the ship, too weak to rise. She shivered, her jaw rattling whenever awake despite the warm temperatures and three blankets covering her. Plus, she'd swear a lumberjack was splitting her head open with an axe repeatedly.

Aunt Teresa and Otso checked on her periodically, bringing her broth and crackers, and replenishing her water. During Aunt Teresa's visits, she'd update Trini on the progress toward a cure, though Trini understood little of it. Her aunt had black rings under her eyes, and Trini wished she could be up helping her.

Otso gave her updates on his grandfather, who had fallen into a coma the night before, his strength ebbing. Otso's shoulders were slumped and his eyes dull every time he visited, and he never let Isu go. She tried to reassure him, missing his incessant energy and enthusiasm, but anything she said paled in comparison to the state he was seeing his grandfather in. It broke her heart that she couldn't get up from her bunk and do more to help Otso, Ahti, her aunt, and the rest of the Ukka.

On the third morning, she awoke thirsty, but stronger than she'd felt in days. She downed an entire bottle of water. She tested herself, finding she could rise to a sitting position. She stretched, her muscles tight and cramped after the extended inactivity. On a table at the base of her bed were a couple of energy bars. The first pangs of hunger in days stirred in her belly. She opened one of the bars and ate. She finished off two.

Hunger alleviated, it was time for a fresh change of clothes. She removed a plain gray shirt and jeans from a drawer beneath her bunk and changed, taking a few minutes to wash herself off with water from the ship's sink. Feeling reasonably refreshed, it was time to head back into the village and see what she could do to help.

In the time she'd been recovering, five new medical tents had been erected; no more sick Ukka lying on the ground. Only a contingent of healthy Ukka, and a small army of Space City medical personnel, moved around the village, tending to the sick and handling supplies. In the original medical tent, there were fewer patients, some having been transferred to other tents. And the cots had been re-arranged into orderly rows along which nurses moved, checking on the status of each patient.

Trini navigated through it back to her aunt's research area, which had been expanded to triple its original size. Two doctors, Devonte Smith and Shi Kuang, were now here, each carefully studying hologram projections from their wrist-comps.

"We've done it!" Aunt Teresa exclaimed upon seeing her. "Developed a basic treatment."

"That's wonderful! How quickly can we use it?"

"Later today we'll have the first batch ready." Aunt Teresa strode over and studied her. "How are you feeling?"

"Good. Still drained. But I'll be fine?"

Aunt Teresa nodded. "You will. Your immune system fought it off. You'll only need a small dosage of the medicine to make sure you're over it."

"Ahti?" Trini asked, anxious for good news for Otso.

Aunt Teresa pursed her lips, sobering, and shrugged. "Hasn't woken back up."

"You'll give him the medicine as soon as its ready?" Trini knew it was wrong for her to ask for preferential treatment for Ahti and Otso, but she couldn't help herself. She didn't want Otso to lose his grandfather.

Aunt Teresa simply nodded.

"Thank you." Trini looked around the room at all the new equipment, including four 3D printers; a technician moved between them, monitoring their output.

"Anything I can do to help?"

"Only rest." Aunt Teresa rotated her around. "Dr. Smith and Dr. Kuang are here helping with the medicine development. Other volunteers have arrived with 3D food printers containing enough supplies to feed the Ukka for a couple of months. Also restocked on other medicines. So I have all the help I need. You need to focus on recovery."

Aunt Teresa pushed her out of the research room. "Go find some food."

Trini maneuvered back through the tent, seeing all the severely weakened Ukka who wouldn't recover without the medicine Aunt Teresa was making. Just hold on, she wanted to say to them. A little bit longer now. If only there was something she could do to speed things up.

Ilta appeared at her side, offering her a plate of strawberries, cheese, and a couple of slices of bread. Trini accepted gratefully and began to nibble on a strawberry as she stepped outside the tent.

A short distance away, Instructor Tereshkova tended to some of the Ukka's domesticated animals in a pen. And there were others, feeding and watering the various neglected animals throughout the village, so that once the outbreak had been beaten, the Ukka wouldn't have lost too much of their livestock upon which they depended. But the shortage of healthy Ukka moving about the village underscored the severity of the outbreak.

Out of a nearby medical tent, Jarin exited slowly, shoulders slumped, clearly as exhausted as anyone. Red-rimmed eyes punctuated an anguished face. Behind Jarin, four Ukka emerged from the hut, carrying a stretcher with a shroud-wrapped body. Something about the procession gave Trini pause

"Jarin!" Otso ran around a corner and headed for the village elder. "How is grandpa?"

Jarin stepped into Otso's path and knelt, holding out his arms to the boy. "Otso, I'm sorry."

Otso slowed to a halt, face turning wary. "What is it?"

Trini's stomach turned and she looked at the stretcher, searching for signs of who lay on it, hoping she was wrong about what was happening.

"It's your grandfather." Jarin wrapped the boy up in his arms, holding him close. "I'm sorry. He's gone."

Otso struggled to get free, yelling for his grandfather, but Jarin held him tightly. The boy burst into sobs.

Trini suddenly wished she hadn't gotten up out of her bunk. Ahti couldn't be gone. They were so close to having a treatment ready that would've healed him. He had held on so long, and now when they finally had hope… it wasn't fair.

She made herself walk over, trying to come up with comforting words for Otso, but her tongue abandoned her as the four Ukka carried the stretcher from the village.

Otso slumped to the ground, out of Jarin's grasp, Isu in his lap. Trini numbly approached. The boy looked up at her with tear-streaked cheeks. "Can't you bring him back? Dr. Flores says she has medicine. Can you give him some?"

"I wish I could." She hugged him, but it wasn't enough. Nothing was enough.

He pulled away. "What will I do? I have no home now."

"You can live with me," Jarin assured him. "Or Lida. You'll be taken care of. You are important."

Otso shook his head. "I don't want to."

Trini could only guess how alone Otso must feel, his only family gone.

"You could come with us," Trini blurted out without thinking. She wasn't sure why she said it.

"Really?" Otso asked.

"Yes, of course. We'd love to have you. If it's okay with Jarin?" Why had she made this offer? It was hasty and illogical. The Ukka would probably not except anyone taking away one of their own children. She'd misspoke.

But when Otso gave the village elder and inquiring glance, Jarin said simply, "If that's what you wish, Otso. We would miss you."

There was no recrimination or discomfort in Jarin's expression for her. Perhaps, with all the work that would be involved in getting the Ukka healthy and back to their normal lives, Jarin recognized this might be better for the boy.

Otso smiled, hugging her again. She'd have to talk with Aunt Trini, but she knew she wanted this to work out. She'd always wanted a brother. She could teach him all about the Academy and Space City Games. He'd be a great player once he was big enough.

*****

Otso's eyes were wide as saucers as they departed Letos a couple of days later. Isu momentarily forgotten beside him on the seat, he silently stared as the ship took off and departed the planet's atmosphere.

"Guess you're not going to get much of a break before class starts," Aunt Teresa said apologetically.

Trini smiled as she leaned back in her seat. "That's okay. When I get back I plan to let the instructors know I intend to change my major anyway."

"Oh?"

"I'm going to switch into the medical field,' Trini confirmed. Her life had changed more than she ever thought possible. She felt motivated to accomplish new goals she had never really considered before.

"What about the Space City Games?" Aunt Teresa asked. "You love it, and I don't want you to lose out on the things you love. Life is too precious to waste it unhappy."

"I still want to play," Trini admitted. "I feel at home in the arena and that will never change. But I can't play forever. I need to think about a career for when I'm through. Plus, I'll have the offseason. I can make a great difference and still do what I love. I've got room for more than one passion."

Aunt Teresa reached out and gripped her hand. "I know you can do both."

"Will we hit the fireflies?" Otso suddenly asked.

"Huh?" Trini asked.

"The fireflies." Otso pointed out the front windshield at the stars. "They're everywhere. We won't hit them, will we?"

Hunted

Chapter 1

Jiro Takeda cycled through the hunting details for rhino boars for the fifth time on his wrist-comp. He found it difficult to focus for more than a line or two. Most of the information on the beasts he could recite from memory, but kept pouring through it for any new detail that might ensure a successful first hunt.

"Rotate engines for landing," his father said.

Jiro dropped his wrist-comp into his lap. They approached the exomoon, Herne, orbiting the super-giant, Wodan. Leaning forward in the co-pilot seat, Jiro ran his hand over the ship's computer screen, flipping to engines control display. He tapped the controls for all four quantum engines and rotated them ninety degrees. The ship jolted upward, throwing him hard against his seat.

"Not yet!" His father's face darkened. "We haven't entered Herne's atmosphere."

Jiro lunged forward and reversed the engines back to normal. "You just said rotate the engines."

"I said check the monitor and be ready to rotate the engines," his father corrected. "You weren't paying attention." Daichi was a lean man with a short stature, but when his brow furrowed, grown men paused. He possessed a will that demanded respect.

Half a head shorter than his father, even at sixteen, Jiro felt like he had shrunk back to a ten-year-old version of himself. This was not how he wanted to start his first hunt with his father.

"I was studying," Jiro said defensively. "Wanted to be ready."

His father didn't respond. His body went rigid as the two-man ship encountered turbulence entering Herne's atmosphere.

Itching to review the data on the saber-toothed cheetah one last time, Jiro forced himself to slip the wrist-comp to the floor beside his chair. Father wouldn't let him take the device once they landed anyway. Instead, Jiro focused on the ship's computer, waiting.

The ship calmed as it descended toward the exomoon's surface, sending a buzz through Jiro. He'd anticipated this day for months, ever since his father announced they were going. Truth be told, his brother's stories about hunting with their father had triggered Jiro's longing years ago.

"Decelerating," Daichi said. "Rotate the engines in five… four… three… two… one."

Jiro reactivated the engine rotation and the ship slowed to a glide, nose rising slightly before landing. His father powered down.

Unbuckling, Jiro scrambled back to the small cabin in the aft of the ship. The cabin had one bench for passengers, a single gray equipment locker, and an exit door. He seized his pack from the equipment locker. Out of the pack's side pocket he pulled a black-handled hunting knife with a four-inch steel blade in a camouflage sheath, which he clipped to his belt.

"Don't work yourself up." Daichi retrieved his own pack. "A calm hunter is a safe hunter."

"Yes, sir." Jiro took a deep breath to show he was listening, though it took some effort to keep it from becoming a huff.

He knew his father's hunting maxims by heart.

A calm hunter is a safe hunter.

A patient hunter is a successful hunter.

A smart hunter chooses his game rather than be chosen by it.

He didn't need the reminder. He ran his hands through his black hair, cropped short like his father's. Same as it'd been for as long as he could remember, unlike his brother, Noboru, whose hair nearly reached his lower jaw. Noboru had always been the braver of the two.

Checking his pack, he found two spare light charges for his rifle, a water canteen, compass, flashlight, a turkey and Swiss sandwich, two purple melons, nutrient bars…and a first aid kit his mother insisted he bring. He'd argued his pack was full and the ship held far more medical supplies than they needed, but she wouldn't hear of it. You'd think he was still five years old.

Lastly, he grabbed his lucky tooth, a sharp, two-inch canine which he tied to his rifle sling. Noboru had given Jiro the tooth for his eighth birthday, a few weeks after his brother had killed a saber-toothed cheetah. That tooth had gotten Jiro out of a makeup test in third grade. In fifth grade it had helped him escape Patrick Duffy and Caleb Thornton, who had wanted his lunch money. And Noboru had won the Sun trophy two years ago while Jiro cheered in the stands, the tooth clutched in his hand throughout the entire Academy Games championship.

"Ready?" Daichi asked.

Over Jiro's shoulders went the pack and he grabbed his rifle. "Yes, sir."

They'd landed on rocky ground, with limited plant life. A light fog, common during the late fall and winter months, gave the exomoon a ghost-like quality from which it received its name.

To the east, the early morning sun peeked over the treetops of a deciduous forest devoid of leaves. Numerous game options awaited within. But it was Wodan, which dominated the morning sky, that drew his attention. It was like a god's swirled bowling ball, underscoring how small Herne, and by extension himself, really were. He had a concept of how large the universe was based upon the number of different planets he'd visited and the knowledge of how many galaxies existed. This was a more visceral experience. He felt like an ant in his bones.

A shiver from the cold and damp fog drew him back to his surroundings. Thankfully, he'd worn a long-sleeved camouflage shirt and pants, although it made him easier to spot here in the open.

"I studied up on rhino boars, saber-toothed cheetah, and long-antlered deer," Jiro said.

Noboru had told him repeatedly to pick one animal he planned to hunt before he ever left. Jiro had tried to choose, but his mind had changed from moment to moment for the last three weeks.

"A giant sloth is a good first target." His father studied the landscape.

"Giant sloth? Noboru killed a long-antlered stag his first hunting trip." Jiro let the rifle fall to his side.

"Keep your voice down," his father said. "We stumbled onto that one."

Jiro felt like a hot air balloon that someone had shot a hole through. Playing on the Ursa team in the Academy Games during his first year, he had faced serpent hawks, club tails, and in the championship match, Terocrocuses. Now his father wanted him to hunt a sloth? Granted they were bear-sized, but a sloth was still a sloth.

"It's a great time for long-antlered stags," Jiro said, hoping to salvage some dignity for his return to Space City.

"Jiro."

His shoulders slumped. He recognized that stern tone of voice. His father had heard enough discussion and expected him to comply with orders. No further comment. But if his father wanted him to hunt giant sloths, they might as well have gone to Herne's Southern Hemisphere as his mother had requested the previous night.

"What if something happens?" Aimi fidgeted with the mixed vegetables and chicken in the skillet. "The southern lodges all have good medical doctors, and the hunting grounds there are renowned."

Pretending to read his wrist-comp at the kitchen table, Jiro bit his tongue.

"The lodges already staff butchers and taxidermists, and gourmet chefs will prepare dinner using a portion of your game," Aimi continued, seasoning the meal. Thanks to 3D printing, they could just print their meals, but Aimi insisted on cooking as often as possible.

"No son of mine will settle for a tourist hunt." Daichi crossed his arms. "The whole point of hunting is to get away."

Jiro stifled a smile. For years, Noboru had regaled Jiro with tales of his hunting trips with their father in the unpopulated north; the warmer climes of the south drew most hunters. But by the time their parents had allowed Jiro to learn to shoot, Daichi had joined the Space City council, leaving him far too busy to hunt.

"Fine," Aimi replied.

Why had she lobbied for them to hunt the southern continent? She had never done that to Noboru.

Tiny lizards skittered across the gray stone covering the landscape, diving down holes when he got too close.

It's a wonder Father doesn't decide there are ample lizards to shoot and call it a day, Jiro thought. Why had his father insisted on coming to Herne just to hunt giant sloths?

"Let's spread out a little," his father said.

That was a suggestion Jiro was more than happy to comply with, and he quickly put about fifty yards between them. A part of him hoped they failed to even find a sloth today. Neil and Riagan would laugh if he returned with a hologram of a sloth after bragging for the last few weeks that he intended to take down a saber-toothed cheetah.

Movement to the south caught his attention.

Stepping out from the leading edge of trees a couple hundred yards away was a rhino boar! It dug around for roots and tubers, though it would eat a dead carcass if it found one. It had rough gray skin, a large-humped back, and two tusks rising up from its lower jaw that were about half the size of Jiro's forearms. Reddish skin capped the boar's head and circled its eyes.

Should he get closer? His father would tell him to let it go, reiterate they were here for a sloth. But Noboru had stumbled on his first kill, too. This had to be fate.

At the moment, Jiro was downwind of the rhino boar. Boars had poor eyesight. He could sneak closer before taking a shot, as long as he kept quiet.

He had to try.

He stepped cautiously, restricting the movement of the upper half of his body, until he had closed to within a hundred yards of the boar. It dug around for more food, nose sniffing the ground, broad side toward Jiro. The details on where to shoot a rhino boar flashed through his mind. Looking through his rifle scope, he aimed slightly below the ear at the neck. He took one more calming breath. He fired.

The boar's head twisted sharply right. It squealed, but rather than go down, it bolted. Refusing to lose the boar, he charged after it. Noboru hadn't failed his first hunt and neither would he.

"Jiro!" his father shouted.

Jiro ran hard in pursuit. He wanted to shoot the boar again from behind, but he'd never make the shot on the run. As he gave chase, he realized what had happened. He had scoped the rifle for a hundred yards. He hadn't accounted for that when he took the shot from no more than fifty. The shot had struck high, grazing the boar at best.

The fog swallowed the boar. Jiro squinted, trying to pierce the smoky curtain. The boar wasn't getting away. He reached for all of the strength he could muster and pushed himself harder. This boar was his. He checked right and left in case it had changed directions, and the rocks ahead disappeared.

The drop-off barely registered before he plunged down a steep hill. He threw out his arms, trying to catch anything with his free hand. As he tumbled, rocks struck his arms, back, legs, and side. The rifle ripped free from his grasp. He spun too fast to stop until he crashed into a hard surface and searing pain shot through his right arm.

Scolding himself for such recklessness—a calm hunter is a safe hunter—he lost consciousness.

Chapter 2

A pounding headache woke Jiro. As he reached to cradle his head, his right arm convulsed, forcing a gasp from his lips. A large rock dug into his side. What happened?

"Jiro. Jiro, are you okay?" his father's words, laced with pain, brought Jiro wide awake.

Confused by his injured right arm, but not wanting to make it any worse, he pushed himself up with his left. This caused his head to throb even more, his stomach churning. He closed his eyes—fighting down panic—before looking for his father.

His father lay at the bottom of a steep slope half covered with loose stones and pebbles. Several feet away lay a rhino boar. Jiro scrambled backward a couple feet before realizing its head was angled awkwardly in a way that made Jiro shiver. A wave of rocks partially surrounded the boar.

"Jiro, thank God," Daichi said. "I feared you were…" He didn't finish the sentence. Back against a boulder, his already red face contorted in pain.

"How did we get here?" Jiro had a vague memory of falling.

"You fell… down… hill," Daichi replied through clenched teeth. "Knocked you… out."

Everything came rushing back. Jiro groaned, this time not from the pain. Why was he so stupid?

"How… do you feel?" Daichi asked.

Jiro breathed through the pain in his head and arm. He tested his right arm again, but the slightest movement sent daggers shooting through it. While trying to avoid jostling it too much, he examined it. His shirt was intact. No blood stained it, but it felt like it might be broken.

"I'll be fine," Jiro lied. "What happened to you?"

"Lost… my balance."

Gashes marred his father's pants. He made no effort to move or stand.

"How bad are you hurt?"

"My leg, it's broken," Daichi said. "At least two places."

Fresh guilt flooded through Jiro. His recklessness had not only hurt himself but his father as well.

Will he ever bring me hunting again?

Determined to fix this mess, Jiro used his left arm to support himself. Little rocks cut into his palm as he climbed to his knees. He ignored the little pains and hauled himself to his feet. Everything ached.

His childhood instinct had been never to approach his father when he screwed up, and this was a monumental blunder, but he forced the feeling down and limped toward his father. "Let me help you up."

"No." Daichi shook his head. His rifle rested in his lap. "Can't… climb… with broken leg. You'll… have to go back… to the ship. There's… a transporter… in back. You need… to get it and come back."

"I won't leave you." Jiro reached to tap the tradutor in his left ear to turn on the emergency frequency, but the small earbud was gone. He silently cursed himself. "I lost my tradutor. Do you have yours?"

Daichi shook his head.

It took all Jiro had not to bury his head in his hands. Neither of them had communication devices, all because he'd wanted a boar. He'd gotten it, but it wasn't a story he wanted to share with anyone.

"You have to go back to the ship alone," his father continued. "You can… make it."

Jiro didn't want to leave his father here with his broken leg, but with only one good arm, Jiro couldn't help him up the hill. He might not make it up himself. He had to try, though. He had to fix this.

His light rifle lay next to his pack, partly buried, but his knife remained hooked to his belt. He grabbed the rifle and examined it carefully. Appeared unbroken. But his lucky saber tooth! It had come off!

He dropped to his knees, ignoring bodily protests, and shoved around the little piles of rock, stomach bubbling nauseously.

"What are you doing?" his father called.

"My saber tooth."

He lifted his pack, one strap broken and a hole in the side, hoping to find the tooth underneath it. There was only his first aid kit, a nice *see-I-told-you-so* from his mother.

"It's just a tooth, Jiro. You need to focus on getting back to the ship."

For a few more seconds Jiro scrounged around for the tooth. When it was clear it wasn't buried close by, he scanned the immediate area.

"Jiro!"

Fighting back sudden tears, Jiro made himself rise. His father was right. It was foolish to waste time looking for the tooth. Maybe it was somewhere on the hill and he'd come across it on the way up. Or perhaps he'd find it after he got the transporter and returned for his father. Either way, getting medical supplies was his first priority.

Holding his right arm protectively to his chest, Jiro stepped on the pack's strap so he could unzip it with his left hand. All that remained was his water canteen and a single nutrient bar, along with several small rocks and a handful of dirt. He tossed it aside and retrieved the first aid kit, his face reddening as he did so. The kit held bandages, gauze, alcohol cleaning wipes, gloves, and pain medication.

"I've got disinfectant and bandages," he said. "Do you need some?"

"You never chase after a wounded animal," his father snapped. "In the fog, it could've gored you before you saw it."

Jiro recoiled.

After a moment, his father's tone softened. "You can fix this. You have to get to the ship."

Face burning, Jiro nodded. He grabbed his canteen and held it out. "Do you want my water?"

"No." His father patted the pack that lay on the ground beside him.

The canteen had a strap, which Jiro slipped over his shoulder. He dropped the nutrient bar in his pocket, before tossing aside the useless pack, hitting the dead rhino boar. His first kill had come from chasing it over a cliff. He imagined the jeers from classmates when they found out. There was no room for the whole medical kit in any of his several pants pockets, so he removed the contents and stored them before discarding the case.

"Back as quick as I can," he promised as he started back up the hill.

"Be careful."

Activating the safety on his rifle, Jiro used it like a cane as he climbed the hill. He knew it wasn't wise to use the rifle in such a fashion, but with the loose rock underfoot and the broken arm, he needed the extra support. Rocks slid with each step. One bounced down and struck Daichi on one arm. It was small enough that his father didn't seem to notice, but Jiro still shifted several feet over before resuming his climb. The last thing he wanted to do was bury his father under an avalanche.

At the summit, he rested on his heels, gasping. He wanted to rest longer, but he had to return quickly with a transport. Daichi had a rifle and charges, but what if the dead boar drew a pack of saber-toothed cheetahs? Unable to flee, could his father fight them off alone?

That gave Jiro pause. What more could he do to help his father? He had to get back to the ship. They both needed real medical attention. He had to send a distress call.

As Jiro trekked toward the ship, he searched for prowling animals. The swirling fog hid everything. He passed a pair of trees that, with their bare branches, looked like the hands of some buried giant trying to pull itself out of the ground. Maybe to hunt for someone to drag underground.

He shouldn't have tried to match Noboru. Hunting a giant sloth sounded great now.

Midmorning had arrived by the time the ship materialized through the fog. Relief washed through Jiro and he quickened his pace. He'd fly the ship to pick up his father and they'd return home. Injured and with an unsuccessful hunt, but all right.

Furtive movement near the door stopped him. A figure examined the ship. A couple of boulders nearby offered cover, and Jiro darted for them. Once he was safely hidden, he peeked out, the rifle gripped firmly in his left hand.

A Malsain. The green, lizard-like alien circled the ship, likely searching for a way to break in. Two fat brass rings stuck out from the sides of its ear holes, and another from its nostrils. The scales on its head were painted red, making it look like it had been scalped. What was a Malsain doing on Herne? Malsain rarely hunted for sport.

The fog between them cleared, revealing a black tattoo on the Malsain's greenish-yellow scales. No, not a tattoo. A brand. A skull branded onto the back of its hand.

A rogue Malsain, here on Herne.

Jiro's legs weakened. He fought the urge to run. Outcasts from their own kind, rogue Malsain were cruel scavengers, attacking any time they had the upper hand, usually against wounded men and women or even isolated children. In his present state, Jiro was the perfect target.

He debated running back to his father and warning him. But he may not have the time. The ship offered their sole means of escape or communication. How could he get rid of the Malsain? He couldn't aim properly with his left arm only. And he doubted a warning shot would scare it off. Maybe it would give up on breaking into the ship and leave.

The creature stalked behind the ship, still probing for a way inside. Jiro moved to the right side of the boulders, trying to catch sight of the Malsain again.

The Malsain suddenly fled as if spooked. Jiro frowned. The ship didn't have an automated defense system.

The aft end of the ship ruptured, sending shrapnel in all directions. Jiro thudded to the ground behind the boulders, his mind frozen.

A second detonation. He buried his face in his arms, waiting for another. When no additional blasts followed, Jiro stood to find their ship destroyed. The whole thing burned, filling the air with black smoke and the stench of molten metal. The heat from the blaze seared his skin, and any hope of salvaging anything from the wreckage vanished.

No way to call anyone in the south for help. No supplies. No shelter. They were alone.

Stranded.

The destruction proved too much for Jiro. He turned and fled, overwhelmed with a need to get back to his father. Almost immediately he realized he should have checked for the Malsain. Had it seen him?

He risked one glance over his shoulder. No sign of it, but he had no time or cover to make sure. Instead, he ran as though the Malsain was after him. The sooner he reached his father the better. Daichi would know what to do.

He had been an idiot. Ruined everything. Panic rose up his chest, stifling him. He couldn't catch his breath.

His father's maxims surged to the front of his mind. "A calm hunter is a safe hunter. A patient hunter is a successful hunter. A smart hunter chooses his game rather than being chosen by it." He repeated them over and over, especially the first one. Those words held his fear at bay. It didn't go away, but it no longer threatened to engulf him.

At that moment he sensed that he was nearing the hill he'd fallen down. He slowed. He would not go hurtling over the side twice. The drop was a good ten feet ahead.

Checking behind for signs of pursuit, Jiro found only a barren landscape and the fog, which concealed the burning wreckage of their ship. No sign of the rogue Malsain.

Exhaling, Jiro jogged over to the edge and peered down the hill.

His father was gone.

Chapter 3

Jiro half-hobbled, half-slid down the hill, sending showers of rocks cascading to the dead rhino boar.

"Dad!"

Skidding to a stop against the boulder where he'd last seen his father, Jiro scoured the area, digging in the piles of rock, fearful his father might've been buried. Had he been attacked? Crawled away? The few streaks of blood left behind offered no answer.

"Dad! Dad!" Every time Jiro shouted for his father, he cringed internally, terrified the rogue Malsain might hear him.

Perhaps the Malsain had gotten here first and attacked Daichi, but Jiro rejected that fear. The Malsain hadn't had time to pass him, attack, and carry his father away before Jiro had arrived. His father might have hobbled away, even with a broken leg, but where and why? He knew Jiro would return!

He'd clearly gone somewhere, willingly or not. But in which direction? What if his father was in serious trouble and Jiro failed to find him in time?

A desire to crumple to the ground weakened his legs. He needed his father to return. Make everything okay again. Get rid of the rogue Malsain. Find a way to get them safely off Herne.

But thinking like that wasn't helpful. He reached for his father's maxims again.

A calm hunter is a safe hunter.

He had to get his emotions under control.

His brother had always been good at maintaining calm in any situation. Noboru had told Jiro countless times that a clear head allowed one to think better. What would his brother do in this situation?

If only his brother was here to help. Jiro had wanted Noboru to come on his first hunting trip. After all, his brother had taught him to shoot and track—

Track! He knew how to track. Why hadn't he thought of that first?

That's why you have to remain calm. Push the fear to the back of your mind.

Returning to the bloodstains that marked his father's last location, Jiro fought down his fear and examined the evidence. There were no signs he'd been dragged off. And he'd expect a lot more blood if an animal had attacked. His father wouldn't have left voluntarily knowing he'd return. Had he heard the explosion and tried to come after him? Had they passed each other in the fog? Looking back up the hill, Jiro doubted his father could've made it back up with his leg broken.

There was also no sign of a struggle. His father had a rifle and knife and would've defended himself from an attacker or predator.

If his father had left for some reason, he would've left a message, but there was nothing. Unless… he'd buried it with rocks descending the hill. Jiro dropped to his knees and shoved rocks out of his way with his good hand, looking for such a message, but came up empty.

He was back to square one, trying to decide where to go looking for his father. His wrist-comp would be great to have right now with its surface map, but he'd left it on the ship. His father insisted they keep technology to a minimum while hunting.

From what Jiro recalled, wilderness ended at the ocean several miles to the south. The landscape to the west was rocky and barren. Maybe a few caves for shelter, but his father would have had to search blindly for them, something he would never do. No, he would've headed for the forest. It made the most sense. He could find food, water, and shelter in the forest.

Assuming he had chosen to go of his own volition. If not… Jiro forced away that thought again.

Scanning the top of the hill one last time, he was relieved not to see the Malsain there. Out of alternatives, he headed east.

With the winter sun offering scant heat, he was glad when the rocky landscape gave way to forest. The trees, even with all their leaves fallen, provided some barriers against the cold wind. He scanned for blood or other signs of disturbance among the foliage, mushrooms, the occasional rotting log, or flowers filling the forest floor. It was difficult finding signs in the fog, so he forced himself to move slowly, inspecting trees and brush as he passed. The lack of blood gave him a small measure of relief.

Around midday, Jiro spotted bootprints on gray-green moss growing along the base of a tree. Too small to be his father's.

Someone else, then.

If those belonged to the rogue Malsain, his father was in great danger. Though they seemed a little small even for the Malsain.

He raised his rifle, scanning for more prints. His instinct was to pick up the pace. If the Malsain was after his father, he might need help. But his father's second maxim surged to the front of his thoughts: A patient hunter is a successful hunter.

Running recklessly after his father or whatever it was he tracked could end badly. He might lose the trail. Run into a trap. He'd wanted to show his father his tracking skills. Proving them right now might mean their survival.

Further signs materialized—broken twigs, flattened mushrooms, bloodstains on a trunk that caused his heart to skip a beat. The chitter of a squirrel caused him to flinch, wildly scanning for his father or the Malsain, then chastising himself for jumping at nothing.

A short distance ahead, the trees paused at an old riverbed, roughly ten feet across. As Jiro got closer, he discovered the riverbed wasn't completely dry. A small stream trickled down the middle. As good a place as any to refill his canteen. He was down to the final couple of swallows.

He knelt down, setting the canteen aside so he could first wash his hands and face. The icy water chilled the fingers of his left hand, his right remaining limp in his lap, but he ignored it as he realized how much dirt and grime had stuck to him during his fall earlier. He didn't have much time to waste, but he needed a moment to collect himself, and he reasoned his father might need the water.

A squeal farther upstream jolted Jiro. A woolly rhino bristled thirty feet away. Its thick front horn reminded Jiro of a stalagmite. The rhino, rare in this part of Herne, stomped the ground and snorted. It had likely been hunting for roots or tubers when he had disturbed it.

Before he could think how to respond, it charged. He raised his rifle, straining to hold it straight with his left arm. He failed, his shot wide, as the rhino stampeded toward him.

No time for another shot.

He forced himself to his feet and ran. He dove back into the trees. Pain flooded his right arm when he hit the ground. The rhino raced past him down the riverbed and out of sight.

Lying on the cold, hard ground for a few minutes, his vision swam from the pain in his arm. It took several deep breaths for the pain to subside to a dull throb.

His father had been right. They should have stuck with hunting a sloth. How could he have been so unaware as to not notice the rhino in the first place? He could hear his father scolding him for being too self-absorbed.

Jiro used his rifle as support to climb to his knees, then back to his feet. The taste of blood filled his mouth; he'd bit his tongue when he'd landed, but it wasn't bad. Dirt and twigs covered his clothes and his just cleaned hands. Should he even try to clean them again? At this point, he'd settle for having a full canteen.

Returning to the stream, his stomach lurched as he spotted his canteen—crushed canteen. He started to scream, but cut himself off. He didn't need to alert anyone or anything else to his presence.

Instead, he carefully scanned his surroundings for the rhino or any other danger. Concluding that he was alone, he knelt and re-washed his hands. His canteen busted, with its built in auto filtration, he could no longer purify his water. But he had to drink. Stay hydrated. If he got sick from unfiltered water, he could get a shot when he got back to the ship. So he drank.

The water chilled his teeth. He swallowed. Cold water was refreshing in a way no other liquid could match.

After a couple more gulps, he climbed to his feet, crossed the riverbed and picked up the trail again. As he did so, he debated how much farther to go. His father couldn't have traveled this far with a broken leg. If he'd been fleeing something, he would've found shelter earlier. Logically, Jiro knew he must've missed some sign in the fog. All the time Noboru had spent training him to track had been for naught. Yet Jiro's gut told him to keep moving forward. He tried to come up with a reason for the feeling, but he couldn't. Forward just seemed right.

To the southeast, out of the fog, appeared a camp built into a modest cave. The sight of it caused him to freeze in his tracks.

A couple of fat logs stood on end like chairs next to the remains of a fire pit in the campsite. A few small animal skins adorned the cave entrance. Then Jiro spotted his father, lying on the ground, legs splayed out. His father's wrists were tied to a stake behind his head.

Jiro's knees weakened momentarily, before his father's chest rose and fell with ragged breaths. Alive but unconscious. A prisoner.

A Malsain emerged from the cave. This one possessed a darker green hide than the one he'd seen around their ship. Jiro doubted two Malsain just happened to inhabit the same unpopulated moon, so this one must be a rogue, too. The top of its head had also been painted red. Welts covered it's torso, as if someone had repeatedly burned it with pokers. A short-barreled shotgun hung in a sling from the Malsain's hip. And a hatchet hung from the belt at its waist. The Malsain likely had more weapons hidden on it or within the cave.

How was he going to fight the Malsain when he couldn't shoot with his left hand? How would he free his father?

Before Jiro could devise a plan, the Malsain who had blown up his ship waltzed into camp.

Chapter 4

The pair of Malsain talked animatedly, the yellow-green one pointing repeatedly out into the forest. To Jiro's fearful mind, each word was a reference to him. How long until they started searching for him? Would they kill his father before or after the search? They hadn't carried him to their camp to mend his leg after all. Of course, if all they wanted to do was kill him, why not do it where they found him?

As if to contradict that thought, the yellow-green Malsain pointed a weapon at Daichi's head. Jiro's breath caught in his throat, but before he could react, the dark green Malsain stopped the other.

Biting his lip, Jiro stifled a shout. He had to act. But how? What? He'd failed at every turn today. Another misstep would be fatal.

Rushing into the camp, light rifle firing, appealed to him. It was the simplest solution. Also the most likely to doom them both. A move borne of panic. He could barely hold the rifle steady with his left arm, much less aim. And he'd need two quick, accurate shots—not likely in his present condition—or the Malsain would return fire. And he couldn't count on them missing.

Logically, he knew a successful rescue depended on a good plan. The sooner he developed one, the better his father's chances, and his own. Which meant retreating so he wasn't spotted while he figured out what to do.

He felt like a coward skulking away. To mollify himself, Jiro carefully inspected the ground before each step to avoid making the slightest sound to give himself away. Once he'd put a safe distance between him and the Malsain, he headed south, unsure what to do, but knowing he needed a better weapon or something to even the odds against two adversaries.

Noboru had taught him to survive; skills learned from their father and his father before him. Thanks to his brother, Jiro could find water, build a campfire, or create a lean-to shelter. Perfect, if he needed to hide from the Malsain until rescue arrived, but of little help to his father.

With his wrist-comp, 3D printer, and supplies, he could've made a light grenade. Or used a mini drone to lure one or both Malsain away. All of that had been stored on their ship, but he'd not been carrying any thanks to his father's ban on technology while hunting.

Why did his father insist on that? He was the chief technologist on the Space City council!

Daichi worked with the Space City scientists to turn their latest R&D projects into practical applications that were produced for use by all of Space City. He ensured the latest technologies were in the hands of personnel in the field. Yet he wanted nothing to do with those same innovative technologies when hunting. He refused to allow wrist-comps—preventing Jiro from sending an emergency signal to the southern lodges—because they could be used to call up a 3D map of Herne in order to quickly locate any animal they wished to pursue.

Cheating! he called it. Why did he love and embrace new technology in every other aspect of his life except this?

Up ahead, a growl caused Jiro's heart to skip a beat. Going stiff as a rusting tin-man, he searched the trees and fog. What he wouldn't have given for that 3D map right now! A second and third growl followed—playful, young growls. Cubs.

But where there were cubs, a mother was sure to be as well.

Jiro ducked behind a nearby fir tree. More growls from the cubs drew his attention to a small cave. Panther cubs wrestled with each other. From this distance they looked like *panther albus*, or white panther, a sort of cross between a lion and a panther. The cubs were not much larger than twenty pounds. The mother on the other hand, she'd be much larger. Double the size of a lion. Their near-white fur helped partially camouflage them in the fog. Thankfully, it hadn't snowed recently.

No adults visible. Yet.

He scanned in every direction, meticulously checking the trees. Once he felt reasonably sure of the mother's absence—perhaps retrieving food for her cubs, though not too far away—a crazy idea crossed his mind.

"Koketsu ni irazunba koji wo ezu," he whispered.

To take the saying literally was stupid. If he was wrong about the mother, and perhaps even if he wasn't, he might end up cat food. Still, he needed a crazy idea to get rid of the rogue Malsain. Only a few hours of daylight remained. He wasn't sure why the Malsain hadn't killed his father yet, but he wasn't taking chances they'd wait past dusk.

Slipping the rifle strap over his head, Jiro crept toward the den. The cubs, consumed with proving who was toughest among them, remained oblivious. They bit and tackled, growling as if each were the most dangerous creature alive. In other circumstances, Jiro might have enjoyed their innocent bravado.

Instinctively, as he crept forward, he reached for the lucky saber tooth, only remembering once he didn't find it that it had been lost earlier during his fall. His ears started to burn at that memory. But there was no help for it now. He could've used that luck, but it was gone.

Inside ten feet, he charged. He was upon them within the span of a few breaths. The cubs scattered at the last moment, but Jiro snagged one by the scruff of its neck.

Countdown initiated.

The cub squirmed, paws and head flailing to get at him, but Jiro gripped it firmly behind the neck as he ran north. When the cub realized it couldn't escape, it whined piteously.

I'm begging to be eaten.

Reason insisted he toss the cub and abandon this insane plan. But was this crazier than taking on two rogue Malsain alone?

An angry roar, this time definitely not from a cub, filled the forest, assuring Jiro that, yes, this was crazier than taking on a pair of Malsain. And holding the cub with his one good hand prevented him from wielding the rifle.

No more calm. No more patience. He was all in.

Another roar of fury was followed by a third. Closer now. And from slightly different directions behind him. At least two adults in pursuit. He wanted to toss the cub aside, hold up his hands and say, just kidding. No harm done. Let's all go our separate ways.

Back tingling in foreboding, Jiro spotted the cave. The Malsain had drawn their short rifles. He hoped the fog obscured him.

Lady Luck wasn't on his side. That's what he got for losing his saber tooth.

A moment later, they started shooting. Tree bark exploded on his left and right. Before he reached the clearing around their cave, he tossed the cub, with every ounce of strength he possessed, at one of the Malsain, before ducking for cover behind a tree. Successive laser blasts shattered the side of the tree behind him.

Screams and hisses filled the air as the frightened cub bit and scratched at the Malsain, who tried to knock it away.

The white panthers materialized out of the fog.

Not two.

Three.

They bared fangs. Jiro unslung his rifle and propped it on one knee to steady it. But the three panthers raced past him, straight for the cub and the shocked Malsain.

More rifle fire filled the air, and a panther howled in pain. Jiro scrambled up and turned to shoot, but the rogue Malsain had already fled their camp, one panther in pursuit.

A second panther grabbed the cub by the scruff of the neck and limped from camp, its rear left leg bleeding. Guilt punched Jiro in the gut, but he couldn't have exactly asked for their help to save his father's life.

The third panther sniffed his father's bare legs, the pants torn away around his knees. Jiro whipped around the rifle and fired over the panther's head. It spun toward him, crouched and growling. He fired again, not bothering to aim. Fortunately, with the cub retrieved, it was no longer interested in fighting. It fled after its companion. And he was relieved the cub had appeared unhurt by his stunt. He hoped the adult panther's injuries had been minor.

Panting, Jiro rushed to his father's side. "Dad! Dad!" He dropped the rifle and grabbed one of his father's shoulders, shaking him. "Dad, are you okay?"

Slack-jawed, his father remained unconscious.

"Dad, wake up." His words came out as a half sob. Had he waited too long? "Please!"

There were no other obvious wounds. His father still breathed.

At that moment, Jiro remembered Noboru telling him their father kept smelling salts on him whenever he hunted. Had done so ever since a hunting accident long ago. Jiro stood and scanned the camp. His father's brown pack rested against the wall just inside the cave.

Retrieving it, Jiro dumped the contents on the ground. He snatched up the first aid kit. Inside was a bottle of smelling salts, just as Noboru had said.

"Thank you, brother," he whispered.

Unscrewing the cap, he held it up to his nose and sniffed. An overpowering wave of ammonia hit his nostrils, causing him to lurch back. His eyes watered. It was as if he'd drunk a dozen sodas in an instant, flooding him with energy. Potent stuff.

One whiff of that would wake anyone. Except his father didn't twitch when Jiro waved the bottle beneath his nose. Fighting to control his terror, Jiro tried again. This time, his father's head rolled to the side. After a couple heartbeats, his eyes popped open. He gripped Jiro's arm until it hurt, wide eyes disoriented. He groaned.

"Dad, it's me," Jiro said. "You're safe."

He glanced around, searching for the Malsain. No sign of them. But for how long?

"You have to go. Get away!" Daichi said. "There's a rogue Malsain."

"Two actually."

"Leave me. Escape."

"I can't. We have nowhere to go."

"Get back to—"

"The ship was destroyed. Can't call for help. The Malsain will return soon. We need a place to hide."

He recapped the smelling salts and replaced it in the first aid kit, which he stuffed with his father's things back in the pack before slinging it over his shoulder along with the rifle. Ignoring protests, he grabbed his father's arm and pulled. Despite using only his left hand, lances of pain surged through his injured right arm. He gritted his teeth, refusing to cry out.

"Lean on me." Jiro placed his father's left arm over his shoulders and they hobbled from camp.

His father couldn't make the steep climb to the north, nor had Jiro spotted any possible shelter to hide them. He was not about to head east toward the Malsain, so that left south. Back toward the white panthers.

As they made their escape into the forest, Jiro chuckled to himself. "Koketsu ni irazunba koji wo ezu." To catch the cub, he had entered the tiger's den.

Chapter 5

Progress slowed.

Daichi slumped into Jiro, struggling to maintain his balance. His left foot barely touched the ground, but each step elicited a grunt. Those exhalations worried Jiro more than anything. His father had always borne pain in grim silence, a trait Noboru and Jiro attempted to emulate. The broken leg must be worse than was apparent. He had to find some way to send a distress signal.

After he found shelter for his father.

"Do you know a good place to hide?" Jiro guided his father southwest, hoping to avoid the white panther den. "A place the Malsain won't find us?"

After a few more steps, his father replied, "The Malsain destroyed the ship?"

"Incinerated."

Daichi wheezed for several more paces, his injuries exhausting his strength. With each step, his father slumped a little more, sending jolts through Jiro's wounded arm. Jiro closed his eyes and turned his head to the side, away from his arm as if not looking might ease the pain.

"There's an outpost," his father said finally.

Hope coursed through Jiro. Noboru had never mentioned any outposts. Were there other hunters around? A majority of hunters preferred the comforts of the southern lodges, but there could be some who liked the isolation of the north like they did.

Jiro waited for his father to elaborate. When he didn't, Jiro prompted him, "What outpost?"

"For emergencies."

"Where?"

"East."

Of course it's East, Jiro thought, stifling a groan. *I'll just rendezvous with the Malsain and we'll all go together.*

His father collapsed, dragging Jiro down. Jiro tried to brace himself and hold his father up, but the weight dropped him to his knees. His father fell face first to the ground.

Jiro's arm flared in agony and his vision swam. For a second all thought vanished. He gasped and moaned, wishing the pain away, longing for unconsciousness so he wouldn't feel it. Finally, the agony subsided enough for him to recover his senses.

His eyes flew open. "Dad, are you okay?" He grabbed his father's arm.

Daichi made no effort to rise.

"Dad, we've got to get you up. We need to find shelter."

"Can't."

"What?"

His father slowly rolled over onto his back. "I can't go any farther."

"I'll help you," Jiro said, reaching again to help his father to his feet.

Daichi swatted listlessly at Jiro's hand. "Not with that arm you won't. You'll have to go on alone."

"No!" Jiro shook his head adamantly. "I'm not leaving you again."

When he had found only blood stains where he had left his father earlier, he had feared he'd never see him alive again. And when he'd come across his father tied up in the rogue Malsain camp, he'd thought his fears had come to fruition. Now that they were back together, he could not bear to split up. He didn't want to leave his father alone. If the Malsain weren't tracking them, they would be soon.

"No choice." His father's face was pale and slick with sweat. "My leg. Something's wrong."

His leg was swollen and discolored, as if from internal bleeding.

The admission made Jiro sick. They had no way to stop that. "What can I do?"

"I need help from a doctor, Jiro," Daichi said. "You can't carry me, and the outpost is too far."

"I could try—"

"No, Jiro," his father insisted with what little strength he had left. "You have to get to the outpost and call for help. If you don't leave now… I may die from the injury."

The admission chilled Jiro. It was like a taboo had been spoken. It was one thing for him to fear for his father's safety while he lay unconscious in the custody of the Malsain. It was quite another for his father to admit mortality. Jiro blinked back tears suddenly welling to the surface. This was his fault. He'd caused all of it.

He scanned for a place to hide his father, but nothing looked promising. He could build a lean-to, but it would be difficult with one good arm. Plus, he'd have to hope the Malsain didn't spot it before he returned. Unless—

"Dad, let's get you over to this tree."

Slipping his arms under his father's, Jiro half lifted half dragged him. Each tug made him feel faint, his right arm throbbing, but he gritted his teeth and pulled his father to the base of a wide tree trunk, similar to a maple. He propped his father's head on his pack. After that Jiro gathered vines and uprooted small bushes, hiding his father. An effective camouflage. Especially with the fog limiting visibility.

He didn't like separating again, but there was no other choice. Not if he wanted his father to live.

"Will you be alright?" Jiro was still afraid to leave, afraid that if he did so he might not find him again this time.

"Go," his father said.

Jiro had one last idea. He retrieved the pain pill bottle from a pocket and emptied a couple into his hand. "Dad, take these." He forced the pills between his father's lips.

His father swallowed. Jiro opened his father's canteen and placed it to his lips. Daichi gulped the water down, then opened his mouth a second time. Jiro poured a little more in, which his father also drank.

When his father didn't open his mouth a third time, Jiro asked, "Do you want more?"

"Please go, Jiro," his father said.

Jiro took a couple of swigs from the canteen to give him a couple of extra seconds. The white panthers' cave was southeast, and he hoped they didn't come prowling, but he had nothing else with which to ward them off. Had he done a good enough job covering his father so the Malsain wouldn't find him?

These worries ate at him as he reached for his rifle. He hesitated, his hand inches from the weapon. They only had one. His father was defenseless, while he could at least run. And he had his knife. He placed the rifle against the tree by his father's head. "I'll be back soon, dad. I promise."

"No," his dad said, stern eyes peeking out from the foliage that covered him. "Take the rifle."

"You can't protect yourself, and I can barely wield it with my left arm."

"Take the rifle," his father repeated. "That's an order."

Unable to reply or disobey, he retrieved the rifle. But he set the canteen in its place, along with the knife. The only thing he could do for his father now was find the outpost.

Actually, there was one other thing he could do. He retraced their steps north.

Chapter 6

About halfway back toward the Malsain cave, having erased their tracks as best he could, Jiro turned east. On the march, he scanned the forest for trouble, wishing he had the wrist-comp with him to identify heat signatures on a map of his surroundings. The light fog had remained steady throughout the day, and now that the sun plummeted toward the horizon, the fading daylight made it harder to differentiate his surroundings. He slowed down to avoid rushing headlong into a Malsain's shotgun.

A bird squawked from its nest overhead, as if to warn him away. He crouched lower, certain the alarm would draw the Malsain. Unfortunately, the only way to silence the bird was to shoot, which was not only difficult to do at present, but it would also draw the Malsain more surely than the birds' complaints.

Mini drones with tranquilizer darts. That's what he needed! Once they got home, he'd suggest those to his father.

The ground rose steadily as he hiked. With no trails to follow, he repeatedly had to zigzag around clumps of trees and bushes until the way forward was blocked by a swift-flowing river twenty feet or more across.

Approaching the shore, he knelt and dipped his hand in. The icy water shocked his fingers. The river looked deep, but that might be deceptive in the fading light. Either way, the last thing he needed was to drown or freeze to death as the temperature dropped. And he lacked dry clothes to change into on the other side.

His best option was to follow the river until he found a way across. Upstream or down?

A wrong choice would extend his father's suffering and increase the risk that he wouldn't survive. Either of them, really.

The fog obscured so much. He closed his eyes and listened for signs of pursuit, tuning out the river current. He ignored the rustle of wings as a bird took flight.

No unusual noises. The Malsain weren't close. Yet.

With nothing to guide him, he chose upstream, reasoning that downhill was too much like taking the easy way out, which for the moment felt like a death sentence. The uneven slope was filled with dips, tree roots jutting out of the ground, and loose stones that slid underfoot. Five minutes passed, then ten, with no way across the river. He started to doubt his instincts. He was wasting time, putting his father in greater danger. As he was about to turn around, he spotted a large tree log spanning the river. He nearly laughed out loud in relief, but caught himself.

He jogged over to the wide trunk, grinning, and quickly tight-rope walked to the far side. Much faster than wading across.

The crack of a snapping limb split the forest behind him. Instinctively, he dropped to a knee, using the fallen log as a shield. The river's far shore was barely visible in the twilight. Was it the Malsain or just some animal?

He couldn't see anything moving, but he also lacked the time to wait. Nor did he want to get into a fight with a Malsain.

Rising from the fallen log, Jiro turned to head on as the tree behind him ruptured. He ducked, heart racing. A second blast rocked the fallen trunk. Shards of bark flew in all directions. A few pieces nicked him.

He didn't wait for a third shot.

He ran.

There suddenly seemed to be movement in every direction, giving him the sense that he was surrounded. The darkness and fog so obscured his vision that he felt like Izanagi running through the underworld with monsters encircling him. He wished he had a hat to throw on the ground behind him from which a grapevine would sprout to distract the Malsain. A childish desire, but in that moment he would have taken an old folktale if it helped him escape.

Seconds later he topped a rise. Down a short hill ahead was the outpost, a round building not much larger than a single-room cottage. Out front was a large black box which probably held a generator.

At the front door, he found a security panel that required finger prints. Hoping for his father's foresight, he slammed his open right palm onto the panel. A dizzying burst of pain in his arm made him weak all over, but the door mercifully opened. He gave silent thanks that his father had entered him into the outpost's security log, probably at his mother's insistence.

Overhead lights near a glass ceiling switched on automatically as he entered, momentarily blinding him. He shielded his eyes and blinked rapidly, letting them adjust. Then he rammed the butt of his rifle against a black button on the door and it closed behind him. The Malsain would not get through that locked door easily.

The outpost held a small kitchen in the back-right corner behind an overturned cot. Next to the kitchen stood several shelves filled with supplies inside a locked steel cage that ran from floor to ceiling. The glass ceiling was covered by steel bars. Along the left wall, a simple wooden table held the emergency comm computers, three in total, but one look at them left him stunned.

"No. No, no, no. No!"

The smashed, blackened computers lay in a garbage heap along with shattered glass from part of the ceiling.

He groaned.

The rogue Malsain. They had found the outpost. Unable to fit through the bars covering the glass ceiling, they'd likely dropped an explosive of some sort to destroy the comm equipment. It made sense that they would want to prevent visitors from sending out distress calls.

Thankfully, the Malsain had not simply destroyed the outpost as they had the ship. Probably because of the stocked shelves inside the locked cages. Boxes and cans of emergency food rations and other supplies filled the shelves. It gave him a small measure of satisfaction that the Malsain had failed to break in to loot the place.

A long gray pole with a stop-sign-sized emitter dish at the back of the shelves caught his attention.

Is that what I think? he wondered.

He moved to the cage doors—locked by another handprint pad— and spotted the letters LCS on the emitter dish. Grinning, he placed his hand on the pad, then exhaled in relief when the lock clicked and a door slid open.

He pulled the door wide, then rushed to retrieve the emitter. His father had saved them! The Laser Communications System was a project completed two years ago that allowed the packaging of data onto laser beams, which could be transmitted to a receiver. Laser beams greatly increased the amount of information that could be transferred versus what radio waves sent. The LCS had drastically improved communications between Space City and the alien races on foreign planets. Now, it would save their lives.

Shotgun blasts pounded the door, spurring Jiro to action. On the shelf next to the LCS was a wrist-comp. He switched on the wrist-comp and got a loading screen.

"Come on. Hurry." It wouldn't take long for the Malsain to find a way in, now that they were motivated to stop him.

Thirty seconds later, with the emitter set up, Jiro signaled a mayday and emergency evac into the LCS app. He sent it to all of the lodges in the south. A single burst of white light shot from the emitter through the glass ceiling and fog. If it worked, the message should reach its destination in the next ten seconds.

From the rear of the outpost rolled a softball-sized silver device. A grenade! The Malsain had tossed in a grenade.

He grabbed his rifle and ran for the door, hammering the emergency release with his fist. At the last second, as the door slid open, he recognized the trap and dropped to his knees. Another shotgun blast was followed by pellets slamming into the steel cage. They would've caught him in the chest if he hadn't ducked. He scrambled through the open door on both knees to the shielded generator.

The grenade exploded, rocking the outpost.

Chapter 7

A cloud of smoke poured out of the outpost and washed over Jiro as he crouched behind the generator. His ears rang from the blast. Moving over to the generator's left edge, he peeked out. Buckshot pellets pounded the generator. He raised his rifle as best he could, guessing where the Malsain were and returned fire. The rifle kicked and he nearly dropped it. More buckshot rocked the generator and he slid back behind it. A third round struck the outpost wall behind him, causing him to shield his head. A fourth and fifth blast battered the generator.

If he remained pinned down here, the Malsain would soon surround him.

Gambling, he scrambled back inside. He punched the emergency button and miraculously the door slid shut before another shot shook it.

Only a single, flickering light remained on inside the outpost. The steel cages were blackened and bent; one door hung from its top hinge. The shelves inside the cage had all toppled over onto each other, dumping food and supplies everywhere, ruining most of it. The mini fridge in the kitchen lay on its side, door slung open, contents splattered on the floor. All that remained of the LCS was shrapnel imbedded in the walls. Had the message been sent in time?

That thought made him laugh deliriously. All this work to free his father, trek here to the outpost, send a distress call, and he might die before rescuers arrived.

To keep himself from going crazy, he moved back to the kitchen. A concussive blast shook the outpost door. He dove behind the mini fridge for cover. He waited for the door to fall. It held. But for how long?

To his surprise, no more shots followed. Everything went silent. He remained behind the fridge, waiting. What were the Malsain up to? He glanced up at the glass ceiling, figuring they might try to get up there. And then he remembered the grenade they'd tossed in. It had come from the back. He spun around, looking for where they could've tossed the grenade.

There. At ground level. A hole in the back wall. Cut wires hung from the wall above the hole, with their ends dragging along the floor. The Malsain must've cut the wires to clear the hole. Perhaps trying to use it to create a larger opening. He needed to fill it before they tossed in another grenade.

As he looked around the room, he realized the little fridge was about the only thing that might work. Setting aside his rifle, he crouched down in front of the fridge, placed his left hand against the door, pushing it shut. He proceeded to shove it back toward the rear wall. If he'd had two good arms it would've taken seconds to complete. But even with one he managed to slide it back.

When the fridge struck the back wall he rushed back to retrieve his rifle, then returned and sat in front of the fridge, back pressing it against the wall. He waited, with only his heavy breathing for company.

Once more he wondered what the Malsain were planning. He couldn't hear them moving around outside. Nor up on the roof. There hadn't been any more shots. He sat in agonized silence, body tense, waiting for the Malsain to make a move.

A loud roar overhead shook the outpost walls. He covered his ears, fearing it was some Malsain weapon powering up to destroy the outpost. Several blasts dented the door inward. Whatever the Malsain now had at their disposal would soon penetrate the door. If not destroy it entirely.

But the next round of rapid shots came from automatics, and none struck the outpost. After a minute the roar died. Surely the Malsain hadn't given up. Had they run out of ammo already?

A faint silhouette appeared at the edge of the glass ceiling. He tensed, realizing the Malsain must've just climbed to the roof to attack. He immediately propped his rifle on the fridge to help him steady it as he crouched to aim, preparing to shoot the second he saw a target—hand, foot, torso.

"Is anyone in there?"

He frowned. He didn't have his tradutor to translate alien tongue, and if the Malsain happened to know English—extremely unlikely for a rogue Malsain—it wouldn't sound close to what he'd heard. This voice sounded human.

A flashlight turned on, momentarily illuminating a large man with a full beard, before it pointed down and half-blinded him. "Is anyone in there? We received your distress signal."

Sighing in relief, Jiro waved a hand in the air. "I'm here. Did you see the Malsain?"

"Fled," the bearded man replied.

"Where are you from?" Jiro asked.

"Space City Hunters."

Recognizing the code, Jiro clicked the safety on his rifle before racing to the door. Six men in camouflage gear, spread out in front of the outpost, all turned rifles on him. Beyond them, more men with rifles deboarded a tour ship. Others pursued the Malsain into the forest.

"Are you all right?" The bearded man jumped down from the outpost roof to the ground.

Jiro nodded, his relief fading. "We have to get my father."

"Where's he at?" the bearded man asked.

"In the forest. He's got a badly broken leg."

"Don't worry. We'll find him. Are you okay?"

"Think my right arm's broken. We have to get to my dad."

"Come on." The man motioned for Jiro to follow him to the ship. "We've got a doctor on board. We'll pick up your father."

On board the tour ship, a doctor examined Jiro's arm. A small fracture. The doctor assured him that it would heal just fine. He put Jiro's arm in a sling and gave him a shot of nanobots to begin repairs.

The tour ship took off and minutes later, they recovered Daichi, unconscious, but alive. After a quick examination the doctor assured Jiro they had the tools to care for him at their lodge. In the meantime, he had painkillers. Jiro wanted to stay at his father's side, but the doctor forced him out, telling him he needed to sleep.

The ship picked up the hunters who had pursued the remaining Malsain, before returning south. There, Daichi was rushed to a clinic for treatment. Jiro spent several hours pacing the clinic lobby, despite the urging from the staff that he get some rest or eat. They would find him as soon as his father awoke. But he refused to leave until he knew his father was fine.

At some point in the middle of the night, a nurse finally brought Jiro back to his father. Daichi slept, and the nurse instructed Jiro not to wake him. Seeing his father at last, with assurances his old man would be alright, Jiro slumped into a chair by the bed. His burdens at last slid from his shoulders. They had survived!

He tried to rest, but his mind replayed the day's events. He flushed a little at the thought of telling Noboru that his first kill had come from chasing a rhino boar off a cliff and falling after it. The memory of their ship blowing up sent a shiver back down his spine. And all the day's horrors. He thought he might've lost his taste for hunting here. Especially the way his father wanted to hunt.

Jiro chuckled. "For all your insistence that we not use technology for hunting, you kept what we needed in the outpost. I was angry with you for not letting me have any, but at the end when we needed it most, you had a little bit available."

It seemed silly to talk to his father when he was asleep, but now that he had started, he couldn't stop. "It does feel good knowing all that I accomplished."

The point of the hunt had been to prove to his father that he was a man. Measure himself against saber-tooth cheetahs or rhino boars. His father had understood the need to challenge oneself.

He had thought he had.

He had not.

"I get why you hunt without technology. Because what if it failed? Could we still survive without it? On our own."

Jiro grinned. "Today we did."

Diplomatic Relations

Chapter 1

"Arielle, the day is over. Get out of here."

Startled from her reading, Arielle looked up to see only Kana in the empty classroom. The aging, blue-skinned Azzaro instructor, gave her a mock reproachful stare. When had her classmates left? Her wrist-comp read 17:13, prompting her to jump to her feet, tossing her diplomats 101 textbook into her backpack.

"Guess I should've set an alarm," Arielle said, as she rushed for the door.

"I doubt you'd have heard it," Kana said. "Enjoy your holiday weekend."

Arielle had heard similar refrains from her mother and instructors back at the Space City Preparatory Academy countless times. It was easy for her to become so engrossed in whatever she was doing that she ceased to notice the rest of the world.

Out in the hall, Arielle hurried for the Lore Center's exit. After the long week of diplomat training, she'd wanted to escape the city as quickly as possible. She was finally traveling to the Triplet Geysers. She'd heard about them all summer, and this was her last chance before her summer training program on Sundara ended and she returned to Space City for her final year at the academy. She was not going to miss this. If she avoided any serious delays, she could be out of Tanarille in less than thirty minutes.

As she burst out the front door of the Lore Center, Arielle nearly plowed into the back of Dirk Fischer. He jumped, but when he realized it was just her, he flashed a broad smile that revealed perfect white teeth.

"Hey Arielle," Dirk greeted, his cheeks dimpling. "Are you visiting the Otoch monuments this weekend? Everyone I've talked to is going. Want to travel together?"

The invitation caught her off guard. She returned her best smile as her mind scrambled for an excuse. She wanted to travel alone to unwind and explore. To be completely herself in a way one can only do alone.

"The monuments are quite spectacular." He ran a hand nervously through his spiky blonde hair. "And the Triplet Geysers are erupting, too!"

"I'm already headed there. Leaving as soon as I swing by my room. Bag is all packed. But I'm hiking over. I'm sure you'll want to fly."

Instead of agreeing with her, his smile expanded until he positively beamed. "I love to hike. I'm ready to leave now." His smile turned cautious. "That is, if you wouldn't mind my joining you?"

No. No. No. Her weeklong plans, like a ship caught in a tempest, were sinking. He could've asked anyone else, and they'd likely have been thrilled for the company. "Yeah, uh. Okay."

"Great! I'll meet you in ten minutes by the Hasab."

"Yeah."

He practically skipped down the steps. She wanted to stomp, throw a tantrum; jump up and down until she got her way. Childish she knew, but that didn't lessen the urge. Instead, she trudged toward her hut, resenting the two suns in the sky that shone as brightly as Dirk's face had when she agreed to go with him. It shouldn't be so bright and cheerful out when she felt like cold, pouring rain.

The Lore Center campus, located in the southern portion of Tanarille, was the oldest school on Sundara. Many of the pale blue stone buildings on the campus were dated back more than one thousand years, including the simple huts near its heart that served as student quarters. Over time, the campus had expanded outward, surrounded by newer buildings, like the rings of a tree trunk. A majority of the Lore Center's students lived in larger dorms along the edge of campus.

Arielle considered herself fortunate to receive a simple hut near the center. How many generations of scholars had lived and studied in her hut? She liked to believe that a portion of their knowledge remained within those walls, rubbing off on her through osmosis. A couple of times over the summer, she had even considered trying out an Ouija board to see if she could channel their help to get through a particularly difficult test.

She entered her hut wanting nothing more than to collapse on her bed. She hadn't the energy for a hike *with* someone. She couldn't set her own pace. She'd have to talk. And worse, she'd need to carefully consider everything she did in front of him.

It was exhausting.

After retrieving her pack, Arielle plodded toward the Hasab, a water fountain near the front of campus. As she walked, she considered excuses for begging off the trip. Twisted ankle. Her best friend just broke up with her boyfriend. She couldn't really cry over that, which was crucial to making a guy uncomfortable. Or—she *could* tell him it was her time of the month. Yes! He certainly would accept that excuse. He wouldn't ask any questions either, just squirm, mumble, and rush off.

Worked every time.

Yet when she found Dirk sitting on the fountain ledge, dark green pack slung over his shoulders, he leapt to his feet. The smile returned, flashing pearly whites. She had to admit he had a good smile.

She sighed. She couldn't back out and hurt his feelings. She'd just have to make the best of the company.

"While I was waiting, I plotted out a route." Dirk pointed at his wrist-comp. "Should reach the Hatsu waterfall tonight. It's a great place to camp."

"Thanks," she replied. *He had planned out a route? Might as well just beam us straight there. When will we explore if we keep to a set path and schedule?*

As they ambled toward the edge of campus, Dirk said, "Hard to believe the summer will be over next week."

"It's flown by," Arielle agreed.

The diplomat training had been amazing. The renowned Tanarille Lore Center hadn't disappointed. They had worked countless hours this summer, but it was worth it. Between the program, her final year at the academy, and the Foreign Service exam she'd take next summer, she was pretty much guaranteed a position in a Space City embassy somewhere. It was highly unlikely she'd get Sundara for her first post; everyone wanted to come here. But Niveum might be a real possibility.

Tanarille, like the Lore Center, had expanded greatly over the course of its history, with dark blue stone structures growing in size the further out one traveled. Depictions of Azzaro deities and heroes were carved into the walls of most buildings near the city's heart. As they traveled outward, the structures lightened in color and changed in complexity as the Azzaros had learned to advance their architectural prowess. Abstract architectural designs replaced mythological carvings.

The Azzaros had also chosen to weave the city through nature, keeping as much of the natural flora and fauna as possible, which meant new buildings varied wildly from those nearby in order to reduce the harm to the environment. Some homes were carefully concealed by trees, vines, caves, and in one strange case, grass. There was even one which had a front door behind a waterfall. The owner had installed a shield that could be raised to divert the water around the entrance to allow one to enter or exit without getting soaked.

These architectural choices also made Tanarille appear smaller, like a rural town rather than the great sprawling city it was.

A tantara rang through the city from horntets, the Azzaro equivalent of trumpets. The tantara signified the top of the hour. 1800 hours, and they were just leaving the city. If only she'd left class earlier.

Thanks to his map, we'll probably make up that time on the way, Arielle thought darkly.

Dirk checked his wrist-comp, which he had velcroed to his arm. "We should reach the Hatsu around midnight."

Through clenched teeth, Arielle said, "Dirk, will you do me a favor?"

"Sure."

"Can we forget about what time it is for a while?" The annoyance was thick in her voice.

"All right." He frowned in confusion.

Her goal this weekend had been simple. Leave behind her studies, not worry about the upcoming school year that was so critical to her future plans, and free herself from everything else that dictated her day-to-day activities. Time was a leash to one's responsibilities. She needed a respite.

Foothills surrounded Tanarille, which led to the Muyal mountain range to the north and were absorbed by a forest to the east. The Triplet Geysers were to the northeast, beyond the forest.

A single road curved through the foothills, following the bends. Arielle decided to set the pace so that she could ignore the road… and Dirk's map. She didn't follow a straight line either, allowing the flow of the hills to carry them right or left as they would, as long as it was away from the road. She also detoured when she spotted interesting flowers, searching for new ones for her collection.

Dirk followed without comment, his posture relaxing, apparently willing to let her lead.

Within a short time, they left Tanarille behind, and despite Dirk's presence, the stress drained away from Arielle. She breathed deeply, the air sweet and fresh.

Star blossoms crowned a few hills; the bright orange flowers smelled sweet like spring rain, and had been the first on Sundara in her collection. A little farther on she fell onto a Purgias patch when, topping a hill, she had stepped in a small hole and tumbled down the far slope. She came to a stop amid the dark purple flowers that were soft as a baby's skin.

"Are you all right?" Dirk had asked as he charged down the hill after her.

He offered her a hand, but she chose to lay there for a few minutes to enjoy the caress of the Purgia. She had never lain on a more comfortable bed. She took deep, calming breaths. How long had it been since she hadn't felt compelled to get something done?

Dirk sat on the hill and studied the forest. After a few seconds, he checked his wrist-comp, probably ready to get moving. To stay on schedule.

His impatience exasperated her. He was one of those people so focused on the goal at the journey's end that he missed all the little wonders along the way. Hoping to give him a glimpse, she sat up, plucked a single Purgia from the ground, and held it out to him.

He accepted the flower and sniffed it. "Smells good."

"Feel the petals," she urged.

He ran a finger over the flower. "It's nice." He glanced at his wrist-comp once more.

"Just go," she huffed, climbing to her feet and pointing in the general direction of the Hatsu, like a mother ordering a child to bed.

He recoiled and rose as well. "What's wrong?"

"You obviously want to get to the waterfall. Don't let me keep you." She couldn't enjoy the scenery while he acted like a sheepdog herding her.

He made no move. "I won't leave you behind."

"No, go." She stabbed ahead once more. "I want to wander a bit. I can't enjoy all this with you hovering."

"I'll relax. I'll put my wrist-comp away." To prove it, he stuffed the device into his pack. "We can take as long as you want."

But she was in no mood to be mollified. She had wanted to be alone. After the long, grueling summer, she needed the peace of time alone, out in the middle of nowhere with no one or thing to disturb her.

"I need time to myself. If you won't go, I'll… I'll…" She looked around, trying to decide where else to go. "I'll turn around and return to campus." Might as well if she couldn't have the quiet she desired. If she couldn't relax, what was the point?

The hurt look on his face, as if she had whipped him, took a little of the heat out of her, but not enough for her to recant her demand. She did soften her next words. "Look, just for tonight. I'll catch up at the waterfall and we can continue on in the morning. Please."

He nodded. He offered a smile, but couldn't hide the hurt in his eyes. "I'll have camp set up when you get there."

"Thank you," she said.

He proceeded without another word, headed for the road that weaved through the hills deeper into the forest. She felt guilty for being so abrupt. To distract herself, she focused on searching for other flowers until he was gone from sight.

And sighed in relief.

Chapter 2

Dirk scolded himself as he marched along the road to the waterfall. He'd thought his careful planning would please Arielle. He'd packed a tarp to sleep under in case of rain, though it wasn't in the forecast. He'd brought extra food and supplies in case they ran into any trouble. The route on his wrist-comp would ensure they didn't get lost and miss the Otoch monuments. He'd even marked the closest towns they'd pass along the way in case they had any emergencies.

Instead, his efforts had agitated her. Even his attempts to show interest in the flowers had upset her. He'd agreed they were pretty, but somehow that was the wrong answer. She'd expected a different response. Girls were nebulous, so difficult to understand.

He wished that she played in the Academy Games. Out on the field, he always felt at his best. Scaling the rocks or weaving through the forest, scouting for the opponents' defenders and either sneaking past or shooting them; he instinctively knew which. He'd never make any of tonight's errors—whatever they'd been—in the Games. But Arielle didn't play. He had to win her interest on a field where he didn't know the rules, and his instincts were failing him.

Though they were in the same year at the academy, they'd never interacted before. And then on the first day here in the Diplomat program, he'd happened to sit next to her.

"Who can tell me what a diplomat is?" Kana, their first diplomat instructor, asked the class.

Dirk was exhausted, having barely slept in the three days since they landed on Sundara. He had all summer to explore the city, but he'd still tried to see every major site those first few days, leaving him only four to five hours of sleep a night. Now, as their Azzaro teacher discussed diplomacy basics, he wished that he'd put off one or two landmarks for next weekend.

"A diplomat manages relationships," Kana informed the class. She had a soft-spoken voice that neither dominated attention, nor withered away into hiding, but rather conveyed a sense of helpful confidence. "The number one goal of any diplomat on a new planet is to get to know the people and learn their perspectives."

"Are we discussing foreign diplomacy or dating tips?" A hushed voice asked him.

Startled by the question, Dirk turned to see Arielle, a beanpole of a girl, holding a bowl of steaming coffee in both hands.

He smiled.

"You will not be solely focused on government," Kana continued, "—but also businesses, scientists, artists, musicians, and many other figures, building relationships through shared ideals and goals."

Arielle snorted. "Translation: date around. A lot."

He choked off a laugh and wished he could think of a clever reply, but then the moment was gone.

"This summer you will take a foreign language class." Kana held up a hand to forestall a protest from one of the students. "No. Using tradutors for translation isn't good enough. To truly understand another culture, you need to understand its language."

"Guess she doesn't mean Spanish or French," he suggested.

Arielle arched an eyebrow at him. "I bet you don't know either of those."

"Oui."

She shook her head. "Everyone knows that one. You're not fooling anyone."

"If you want to succeed this year." Kana pointed at a screen behind her with today's headlines. "You'll need to keep up with current local events. A good diplomat listens, analyzes, and uses everything at hand to solve problems."

"Good luck," Arielle told him over her coffee. "If listening is a requirement, you boys are already handicapped."

Since that day, Dirk had routinely had lunch with Arielle. But never alone. Always in groups. They didn't share any classes, and keeping up with daily studying had left little free time. He'd invited her on a couple of tours over the summer, but each time she'd had an exam or project to complete. She seemed pretty wrapped up in her work most of the time. Inviting her to the Otoch monuments for this final holiday weekend had seemed a brilliant idea, but it was off to a bad start so far. He just didn't understand why.

It occurred to him that while she had joked that first day about the similarity between diplomacy and dating, maybe some of the techniques would prove useful. One of the keys in establishing diplomatic relationships was to observe and listen. What had he learned about her to this point?

She lived at home with her parents on Space City, rather than in the academy dorms. That meant an hour of travel to and from the academy each day. Was that her own choice or her parents?

Arielle also had an older brother, François Delven, and younger sister, Camilla. She had four or five years between her and either of them, and that was the extent of his knowledge about either.

He was now well into the evergreen forest, an endless string of Christmas trees. Despite the lateness of the day and one sun dipping below the horizon, the sky remained as bright as midday. The breeze that tickled the hair on the back of his neck remained warm. Up ahead, the flow of the Analane River beckoned.

Retrieving his wrist-comp from his pack, he opened the map and grunted. He'd wandered farther south than intended. He could follow the Analane north to a bridge. If he was lucky, he might rendezvous with Arielle there and this time ask her more about herself.

He pressed on toward the river, hoping to try his luck. Upon reaching the shore, he found a patch of Icelets. Similar to rosebushes with stems covered in thorns, the Icelet's petals were long, thin cylinders that resembled icicles, giving it a frozen over look; quite beautiful, especially among all of the Christmas trees.

Arielle had eyed each type of flower they'd passed in the foothills outside Tanarille. Maybe she'd appreciate having one. Retrieving a small knife and a spare shirt from his pack, He moved over to the Icelet bush and cut off a stem, taking care to avoid pricking his fingers on the thorns. The bud had four long petals hanging down. He gently wrapped the flower in the shirt and placed it in his pack.

Hoping the flower would mend things between them, he rushed upriver until he reached the main bridge spanning the Analane.

Consisting of three long tree trunks lashed together, the bridge provided the sole means of crossing the waist-deep river. Arielle would have to cross here. But as he waited, he started to worry that she might have already passed by. He had detoured out of his way a good distance.

There were no signs of her passing, but after twenty minutes of waiting she didn't appear out of the forest. He bit his lower lip, debating what to do. He might wait here for hours without knowing for sure if she was ahead or behind him.

An idea illuminated his imagination. He could hurry to the Hatsu waterfall, and if he didn't find her there, set up camp. He'd arrange the Icelet where she'd find it. A nice little gift upon arrival.

Casting a last look over his shoulder, he crossed the bridge. It took him two more hours of hiking in the twilight to reach the waterfall.

The air was noticeably cooler and damp around the pool at the fall's base. Mini rainbows hung from the waterfall like ornaments, while insects hummed in harmony with its constant roar. He chose an open spot between three pine trees for a campsite. It surprised him not to find other campers, but most travelers heading to the Otoch monuments would fly. Ten-hour hikes were largely a human pastime.

After hanging the tarp between the trees, he unrolled his sleeping bag and sat to eat. For tonight, he'd packed a pair of luan sandwiches—the meat, a local favorite in Tanarille, reminded him of smoked ham—and a purple melon. He ate, enjoying the chirping of birds as they settled for the night. It had been a couple years since he'd been on a good hike, not since his last trip to Herne, the summer after his first year at the academy. He'd gone on a weeklong hike with his best friend, James Hardin, and a few other guys. They'd planned to return last summer, but Dirk had broken his right leg during the Academy Games semifinals match. The guys had gone again this year, but he'd received acceptance into the Sundara Summer Diplomacy program. A part of him regretted missing the hike with the guys, but he could never have passed up on this program.

Nor this shot with Arielle.

And now to figure out how to present the Icelet to her.

He walked around the area, searching for a cool place to set the Icelet. Some Janthems, a common, light red wildflower, grew along the shore. Picking a half dozen, he tied them together around the Icelet with a string from his pack. He placed the bouquet against a small log on the edge of camp.

He sat on his sleeping bag for a few minutes, waiting, then began to second guess the arrangement. It was too plain. Too simple.

As he debated what else he could do with the flowers, he headed over to the waterfall to refill his canteen. There was a narrow, rocky path behind the waterfall. It was wide enough to walk along without fear of slipping off.

That was the spot.

But just the Icelet. He separated it from the Janthems, which he tossed into the waterfall. The Icelet he leaned up against the back wall on a bed of moss.

Perfect.

Arielle still hadn't arrived. She wasn't kidding about wanting to take her time. Had she perhaps gotten lost?

Hoping she'd arrive soon, he retrieved his wrist-comp and studied their route for tomorrow. They'd pass through the Kaan passage, probably around midmorning or lunch time, depending on their start. The remaining time to the Otoch monuments was between five and six hours.

"No fire?"

Arielle approached, shoulders relaxed; a satisfied smile brightened her face. She also held something in her hand.

"Too warm." He rose to his feet. "Plus, it's not the same when the nights are a perpetual twilight." That had also taken him a bit of getting used to at the start of the summer. It could be one or two in the morning and still look like early evening. After several days of spotty sleep, he had purchased some used, heavy curtains to darken his dorm room at night.

As she got closer, he realized she carried an Icelet in her hands. It had double-buds with eight icicle petals in total.

"What have you got there?" he asked, hoping she didn't hear the disappointment in his voice.

She held up the flower. "It's an Icelet. I've been looking for one all summer. It's going in my collection."

"Collection?"

She nodded as she pulled a sleeping bag from her pack and spread it out on the ground a few feet away from the tarp. "I have a scrapbook where I seal flowers that I've come across. Started it with my mother when I was six. I've collected over two thousand species. Working on my fifth book."

The Icelet would've been the perfect gift, if she hadn't also found one. His probably wouldn't make the book.

She walked toward the pool. "It's a lovely waterfall."

A couple of frogs croaked, back and forth as if in conversation.

"Mhmm." He wished he had left the Janthems with his Icelet. The bouquet might've looked better than the Icelet alone. Still, maybe she'd like it. Even if it didn't make her collection. "There's a narrow passage behind it."

"Really?" She turned back, eyes gleaming.

When he nodded, she ran to the waterfall. They ducked behind the crashing water, moving across the rocks toward the middle.

"Oh, look at that." She stooped to pick up the four-petaled flower. "Another Icelet. I wonder how it got here?"

Not only was it smaller than the one she'd found, it seemed paler. He found he couldn't answer her question. Instead, they leaned back against the rock wall and studied the blurry landscape through the water.

She smelled the flower, which made him smile, though he still couldn't speak up. He tried to think of something cool or clever to say, but the silence grew until breaking it seemed impossible. Everything about this evening had gone wrong.

A yawn escaped him. Embarrassed, he quickly covered it up with a hand.

But she had already noticed. "Past your bedtime?"

He blushed.

"I'm teasing," she said, smiling. "Probably should get some sleep. It's late."

They returned to camp and she sat on her sleeping bag, removed a large book from her pack, and slipped the Icelet inside, along with the one she'd brought with her. He felt a grin spreading across his face that she had included his.

"There's plenty of space underneath the tarp," he said. "I've got mine on one side... in case, um, just in case it rains."

She smiled as she returned the book to her pack. "If I did, my grandmother would roll over in her grave. I can just hear her going on about how it's inappropriate for a young woman to share a tarp with a boy she wasn't married to. She'd probably be scandalized enough that I'm this close to you. Silly, I know, but I'll be fine. If it does rain, we'll revisit the offer."

It took him more than an hour to drift off, but not because of the twilight.

Chapter 3

Arielle woke early. Sundara's primary sun peeked over the horizon, though thanks to its second sun, it was bright enough to be midmorning. The sunshine helped her wake quickly, no lingering grogginess. Dirk still slept, a little drool running down the side of his mouth. She smiled, rose quietly, removed soap, a rag and towel, and a fresh change of clothes from her pack, then marched behind the waterfall to wash. The far side of the waterfall ended in stone, giving her enough privacy to feel comfortable stripping down to clean herself up.

The cold water invigorated her. Last night's peaceful hike here, combined with a good night's sleep, had drained away her weariness and stress from the long week of study and work. She regretted snapping at Dirk the previous night, but she'd needed time alone. Now she felt refreshed and ready for the day's hike. And even his company.

Feeling clean, and starting to shiver a little, goosebumps rising on her arms, she dried and dressed before returning to the little campsite to roll up her pack. As she approached, Dirk was just sitting up, eyes wide and unfocused.

"Morning, lazy bird." She returned her old clothes and cleaning supplies to her pack and started rolling up her sleeping bag.

"Morning," he mumbled.

After tying up the sleeping bag, she rummaged through her pack for cheese, bread, and pyrn slices. The golden, syrupy fruit, native to Sundara, had filled up more than its share of her diet over the summer. Pyrn pies, ice cream, oatmeal, and anything else she had seen with the fruit in it. She had packed five for the trip alone, which made her feel like a glutton.

By the time she'd finished breakfast, he had packed his own stuff, except for the tarp, which she helped him take down and fold up.

"Which way are we headed?" she asked.

He arched an eyebrow. "I thought you didn't like planned routes?"

"Oh, I'll still detour," she assured him. "I'm hunting more flowers for my collection."

"Right, you mentioned last night you've got five books of flowers?" He led the way to a series of rocks across the shallow river south from the pool. They hopped from one rock to the next.

"Everywhere I go, I search for new flowers. I've already collected Star Blossoms, Janthems, Purgias, Jellies, and a number of others on Sundara. I still need to find a Mooncup before we return to Space City."

"Haven't heard of that one."

She had only seen one in a picture. "They're large, light yellow flowers with a pale bud in the middle. A single flower will barely fit onto one page in my scrapbook."

"That's quite a collection," he said.

"My mother wanted me to be a botanist, which is why she started the collection with me."

"So why did you apply for the Diplomat program?" he asked.

She tripped over a root. He grabbed her shoulder to help steady her.

"Thanks," she mumbled, face heating. To cover her embarrassment, she rushed on. "I'm hoping to help Space City expand its educational reach to some of the more primitive alien races we encounter. There are many children on foreign planets who don't get the kind of education we take for granted. And at the same time, who knows what we may learn from them along the way."

"Improving school for kids. That's pretty cool," he said.

"Yeah," she agreed. She couldn't be a botanist as her mother had hoped, but she might inspire others to do so. "What about you? Why do you want to be a diplomat?"

He grew serious and for several minutes they continued on in silence. Up ahead, the mountain they hiked across passed close by another. The Kaan passage was a narrow strip between the two.

When he spoke, he was measured and far more serious than she could ever remember from him. "My father worked as a diplomat on Gleeson, during the Malsain Civil War."

She had read about that war during history class. It had been especially violent, with the Xanthou tribe fighting against the Malachite. The estimate of Malsain killed in the war was between forty and fifty million. By far the deadliest in Gleeson history.

He grimaced. "Dad worked tirelessly with the Malachite, begging them to let him initiate peace talks between the two tribes. Instead, they demanded Space City ally with them against the Xanthou. They threatened to kill us if my father didn't convince the council to send weapons and reinforcements.

"During that time, I witnessed countless Xanthou executed—old men and women with few teeth left in their mouths and no strength left to harm any Malachite, even terrified children too young to understand what was happening. The Malachite didn't care. They killed them all because they were Xanthou.

"Unfortunately, the Xanthou leaders weren't any better. They killed and tortured Malachite just the same. Men, women, children, anyone they could capture."

Arielle was horrified, unable to comprehend such cruelty and devastation. How could he have lived through all of that and want to become a diplomat?

"My father never gave up through it all," Dirk said, fists clenched. "He fought for three years, even after the Council wanted to walk away. All embassy personnel returned to Space City. But he refused to evacuate.

"Finally, members of both the Malachite and Xanthou governments, sick of endless bloodshed, reached out to each other. After careful coordination, they managed a peaceful overthrow of the leaders waging the war. My father worked with the new leaders to form a treaty that has held for the last six years."

"Why didn't your father send you home?" she asked, appalled that anyone would allow their children to witness genocide.

He nodded, as if this was a question he'd answered many times before. "During that time, when everyone else left, he sat me down and told me about his grandfather, who raised him. A Nazi soldier during World War II. My father had listened to his grandfather brag about committing those same atrocities. Kill men, women, and children solely because they were Jewish. The old man would laugh about it, claiming he was making the world a better place. Dad kept me there because he wanted me to know the hatred and barbarism that every living being, human or alien, is capable of. And that the only way to stop it is for good men to stand up against it.

"After that, I decided that I had to follow in his footsteps. Not that he forced it on me. He would have encouraged me no matter what I wanted to study. But after observing his courage on Gleeson and hearing him say how important it was for *us* to be good men, I had to choose that same path. I saw Malsain my own age, their lives destroyed simply because they were born with the wrong skin tone, or eye color, or some other arbitrary marker. And I don't want to ever see it happen again if I can stop it."

Arielle didn't know what to say. Suddenly, her own reasons for becoming a diplomat seemed like shadows compared to his, and she told him as much.

He stopped in his tracks and shook his head. "Never think that. There isn't a ranking system for helping others. You want to improve the lives of others. That's all that matters."

His affirmation felt good. She was glad that he had asked to join her this weekend. She had learned what drove him. Could she have shown such fortitude as his father had in such a situation? She wanted to believe so, though fear and doubt nagged at her.

For a while they hiked on in quiet contemplation, reaching the foot of the mountain and entering the Kaan passage. The reddish stone cliffs on either side rose hundreds of feet, making the passage feel much narrower than reality. A weight clamped around her chest which made it difficult to breathe, as if she were suffocating. She wanted to retreat and find another route, but this was the fastest way.

"Oh, crap," he gasped as they passed around a bend in the passage.

Her pulse quickened in shock and dread. Blocking the way forward was a massive pile of dirt and rocks from a landslide. Her feet tingled with a desire to run, flee the passage before they were buried under a similar avalanche.

"This is terrible," he shouted, throwing his arms up. "This will set us back hours."

"Hush," she hissed, eyeing the clifftops nervously for more falling rock. She grabbed his arm, pulling him back.

"We'll find another way," she whispered, a tremor in her voice.

"But we'll have to detour south to Kaahrim," he complained.

She punched him in the arm. "Do you want to bury us alive?"

His eyes widened in realization, and he glanced upward.

"Let's go," she said, and was grateful when he said nothing further.

They moved quickly, though it took all her restraint not to run. The air thickened around them, like quicksand, as if the passage was trying to slow them long enough for a second rockslide to trigger. She knew that was simply her fear playing tricks on her. Strange, the ability of the brain to take one's fears and make the body feel it as if it were real and tangible. That knowledge didn't lessen her unease.

It took twenty grueling minutes to reach the entrance and escape the Kaan passage, but once they had passed its leading edge, she found herself able to relax. She breathed deeply.

He typed on his wrist-comp. After several seconds, he said, "It's going to take us close to two hours to reach Kaahrim. Another two to backtrack beyond the passage. We're going to be cutting it close."

At the moment, she didn't care. She was just relieved to be in the open. They'd figure out how to make up the time.

*****

Kaahrim was a small town nearly as old as Tanarille itself. Some of its citizenry claimed it was older. The town buildings were mostly constructed from the same dark blue stones as the heart of Tanarille. The citizens lived in simple stone huts similar to Arielle's own on the Lore Center campus. Even the largest buildings were no more than two stories. And the roads were little more than glorified hiking trails.

As she and Dirk entered Kaahrim, they were stopped by a wach—an Azzaro equivalent of a police officer.

"Welcome to Kaahrim," the wach greeted. An older man, his blue skin was rough and pock-marked. He didn't smile, apparently all business. "May I see your identifications?"

She was glad that she had brought her tradutor to translate. The wach spoke too fast for her to follow.

"Sure." Dirk pulled his Tanarille ID badge from his pack and showed it to the wach.

Arielle slipped her hand into the small pouch in her pack where she kept her ID and found it empty. Surprised and alarmed, she adjusted the pack to look inside. She always kept her ID there. What had she done with it?

"Heral, do you have your ID?" the wach asked, eyeing her up and down as if to memorize her features. Heral was the Azzaro equivalent of ma'am.

"Yes, it's here somewhere," she assured him, and began to dig in earnest.

"What are you two doing here?" the wach asked.

While she searched her pack with growing apprehension, Dirk explained to the wach that they were traveling from Tanarille to the Otoch monuments for the weekend. He added that they were students and had come this way after finding the Kaan passage blocked, forcing them here. While he spoke, Dirk typed up something on his wrist-comp.

By the time he had finished, she had searched her entire pack. No ID. She could've sworn she'd double-checked for it yesterday morning.

"Heral, do you have your ID?" the wach asked again. He sounded guarded despite Dirk's explanation.

She knew it was bad to travel anywhere on Sundara without a local ID. They'd been drilled many times by the instructors on how important it was that they always have their Tanarille ID on them.

"I'm sorry," she said. "I seem to have misplaced mine."

"Show him your Space City ID," Dirk suggested.

Yes! She immediately grabbed her wrist-comp and pulled up her Space City ID.

"No." The wach waved dismissively. "You must have your Tanarille ID. Who are you?"

"I'm Arielle Delven, as my ID says," she replied.

The instructors had warned them that most wach refused to accept foreign identifications. Everyone was expected to carry an Azzaro-issued ID. But surely he'd understand. They weren't doing anything suspicious.

"I don't believe you," the wach said.

"We'll go back," Dirk offered, stepping between the wach and her. "We made a mistake. We'll go back and get her ID."

"No." The wach shook his head and pulled a rifle from his back. "Come with me."

She cringed, eyeing the rifle uneasily.

"Please," Dirk begged. "We'll go. We're just students from the Tanarille Lore Center."

"No." The wach gestured further into Kaahrim with his rifle. "You will be held until we confirm your identities." He looked coldly at them, as if they were lying.

Arielle's stomach churned. How could she have been so stupid?

Chapter 4

Dirk rose from the wooden chair, Arielle a half second behind him, as a Kaahrim official entered the narrow holding room. The official wore a few turquoise gemstone rings on his fat fingers and smiled like a deep-sea diver who has discovered pearls. His eyes seemed to calculate their value as he sized them up.

"I humbly apologize for your detainment," the official said.

He was followed by another wach with a fake smile, no rings, and holding their packs.

"Unfortunately, it's protocol for anyone traveling without proper identification." The official shrugged. "I am Nohchil Rassa. And you?"

Dirk spoke quickly, trying to sound like someone who takes charge and is listened to. "Dirk Fischer. When will we be allowed to return to Tanarille. We've done nothing wrong."

"I understand you're diplomat students at the Lore Center?" the Nohchil asked. "Here from Space City?"

"Yes, sir," Dirk replied.

Still smiling broadly, Nohchil Rassa gestured for the wach to hand over their packs. "We checked your packs for security purposes." His expression indicated his assumption that they understood the necessity for such precautions.

Dirk smiled to hide his anger. According to Azzaro law, the Nohchil had the right to examine Arielle's pack since she was traveling without proper identification. But they had no right to search his. They had clearly done so hoping to find something of value. From Rassa's greedy eyes, it appeared he had succeeded.

Dirk searched his pack. His wrist-comp was missing. "Where are our wrist-comps?"

Nohchil Rassa's smile never wavered. "I beg your pardon, but until we can confirm your identities, we cannot take risks."

"How can I confirm my identity if you won't let us contact the Lore Center?" Arielle asked, missing the plural in the Nohchil's statement. "We're students. We pose no risk."

The wach gave Arielle a cold look and placed a picture of a girl on the table in between them. The girl was human, had long, dark wavy hair, and carried a duffle bag. The blurry image made it difficult to distinguish her facial features.

"What were you doing here?" the wach asked Arielle.

"That's not me," she replied.

Dirk gaped. They couldn't be serious. While the image was tarnished, the girl looked nothing like Arielle.

"You were here a month ago." The wach pointed an accusatory finger at her. "At the same time a device was stolen from Kaahrim."

"I've never been here before," Arielle snapped.

Dirk put a calming hand on her arm. "Please, call the Lore Center. They can confirm our identities. And that we haven't been here before."

Rassa's eyes danced at that remark. Dirk guessed Rassa knew they weren't involved, yet was proceeding with this charade anyway. His companion, however, was in earnest. Yet if the Nohchil knew Arielle wasn't the girl in the picture, what was he hoping to accomplish?

"I know you have a cover," the wach growled. "These identities are fakes."

"This is crazy." Arielle threw her hands in the air.

"Captain Bilo, why don't you give me some time with them," Rassa suggested. "I'm sure I can convince them to cooperate."

Through narrowed eyes, Captain Bilo studied them. Dirk's skin crawled under his gaze. Finally, the wach nodded and stormed out.

"Please, sit." Rassa gestured for the two chairs. He sat on his side of the table.

Relieved that the captain was gone, Dirk did as he was bid. Arielle joined him.

"This is all a mistake," Dirk said, willing Rassa to believe him. "We're just students."

Rassa smirked. "I believe you. I even think I can help, but it's not without personal risk. Perhaps a small favor will help me prove your innocence."

"What risk?" Dirk asked, unable to believe this turn. "It's nothing for you to contact the Lore Center."

Rassa ignored the question as he raised two fingers, held closely together. "A small thing."

Dirk could only shake his head in disbelief. The Nohchil was trying to extort them.

"We're innocent, no matter what that man thinks." Arielle stabbed a finger at the door.

"As a neighbor to Tanarille, we've tried to work out an agreement with the Lore Center so that our students can attend on scholarship." From Rassa's tone, Dirk gathered the Nohchil believed this should obviously be the case. "Such an arrangement would mean a lot to Kaahrim, and should earn enough good will to convince Captain Bilo to work with the Lore Center to figure out the truth."

Dirk blinked, unable to believe what he was hearing. "The Lore Center *will* confirm our identities."

Rassa shrugged. "As the captain suggested, you may have created false identities as cover for your thefts. And a good thief could easily fool the Lore Center."

"We're only diplomat trainees," Arielle protested. "Whoever this girl is, I'm not her. We don't know or work with her."

"And beyond that, why would the Lore Center negotiate with us?" Dirk asked. "Surely you have your own people who can do so."

The Nohchil pushed on undeterred. "You have training from the Lore Center. Surely you can persuade them as to the importance of increasing the relationship with their closest neighbor."

Arielle crossed her arms. "So, what? You accuse us of a crime we didn't commit, and we're supposed to help you out so you'll drop it?"

The Nohchil's face sobered. "From our standpoint, you're both liars who've stolen from us and are likely back to do so again. And if you won't work with me, I'll have to hand you back to Captain Bilo for further questioning."

Dirk wanted to put his head in his hands.

"I want to place a call to Space City," Arielle said. "You've seen my ID on my wrist-comp. Per the terms of the Space City treaty with Sundara, you must allow us to contact our superiors."

"No."

A chill ran through Dirk.

"Excuse me?" Arielle asked, face reddening.

"No," the Nohchil repeated. "But now that I think about it, help with scholarships to the Lore Center really isn't the best use of your situation." Rassa rubbed his chin. "A trade agreement between Space City and Kaahrim on the other hand…"

Dirk's mouth dropped, at a loss for words. He hadn't expected that request.

"Space City already has a trade agreement in place with Sundara," Arielle said, frowning.

Rassa waved dismissively. "That agreement is controlled by Tanarille. Kaahrim needs its own agreement."

Dirk understood now. Nohchil Rassa had ambition. He had suspected Rassa knew they were innocent. Now he realized the Nohchil had trumped up this whole thing. He had convinced Captain Bilo that Arielle was the thief in order to use them for his own ends.

Carefully considering his response, Dirk spoke slow. "Based upon my understanding, the Space City embassy is responsible for reaching trade agreements with Sundara. We don't work for the embassy. And the embassy won't work with individual cities." He almost added *or town*, but stopped himself. Rassa would likely take offense to his referring to Kaahrim as a town.

This time Nohchil Rassa pursed his lips. "I guess we have nothing further to discuss then." He turned to go.

Dirk wanted to yell at the Nohchil, threaten him that neither the Lore Center nor the Space City embassy would take kindly to his detaining students over something as simple as a missing ID.

"You want to work with me," Rassa said as he opened the door. "You don't want Captain Bilo to return."

It took all of Dirk's willpower not to throw his pack at the closed door. Instead, he paced the back wall, wondering just how long they'd be here.

"You should go," Arielle said, slumped in her chair, staring at the floor.

"What?" Dirk paused, staring at her in confusion.

Her fingers pressed her temples as if she had a headache. "You have your Azzaro-issued ID. They can't hold you. You can get away."

He moved to the other chair, sitting on the edge of it and leaning toward her. "Absolutely not. I'd never leave you like this."

"I was stupid. This is my fault. You shouldn't be punished."

He reached out a hand for her shoulder, then hesitated. "I'm staying here with you. Besides, you heard them. They think my ID is a fake. They'll never let me go."

"I'm sorry I got you into this."

"This isn't your fault." He shook his head. "This is Rassa's fault. He wants to use us."

She laughed harshly. "Thanks. You're a good friend."

Through the window of their holding room, he saw Captain Bilo returning with two burly, scowling wach, both armed with rifles. Had Rassa sent Captain Bilo? Or had the captain grown tired of waiting?

Terrified of what might happen next, Dirk decided to confess to her in case he never got another chance. He stared down at his lap, his fists clenched on his knees. "Arielle, I… uh." His voice quavered. Every muscle in his body tensed as he struggled with exactly how to say it. "I, um. I like you. I have all summer, and been trying to tell you."

She didn't respond.

He looked up to find her open mouthed. Her face had reddened. He felt hot himself.

"I didn't know," she said. "I hadn't thought."

"I know it's bad timing, but I had to tell you before… before…" he couldn't make himself finish. He waited for the door to open and whatever came next.

"I'm sorry," she said weakly. In her eyes, he could see her answer. He looked away, wishing he'd said nothing. He'd only made this worse.

The door opened. Captain Bilo entered with manacles and chains and ordered his men to bind them.

Chapter 5

"Let him go," Arielle shouted, pulling at the cuffs that bound her to the table.

Two wach hauled Dirk from the room, his legs pumping to keep up to avoid being dragged. The barrel of one wach's gun was pressed against Dirk's temple.

"We'll recover the device you stole," Captain Bilo growled. "One way or another." He followed his men out.

"You can't do this," she yelled at the closing door. When no one re-entered, she fought with her chains, desperate for the strength to rip herself free. Eventually, she collapsed into the chair. She was a torrent of emotion. Fear of the captain. Anger with herself. Hatred at Rassa.

Overwhelmed by Dirk's revelation.

How could he have thought now was a good time to drop that bombshell?

And the girl in the photo. Whoever she was, Arielle hated her most of all. It was her theft that had put them here. Had gotten Dirk hauled off to what? If Captain Bilo really believed they were lying, what might he do to get the information from Dirk? And would he stop when Dirk failed to deliver? For a terrifying moment, Arielle feared that she might never see Dirk again. He might have been the last friendly person she'd ever see. And he was here because of her.

Tears welled up in her eyes. She slumped back in her chair, unable to do more than worry about what the captain was doing to Dirk, or what he might do to her later. Her wrists ached. She realized the cuffs had cut into her when she'd been struggling to get free, leaving stains on her wrists.

Sometime later, Nohchil Rassa sauntered in carrying a sheaf of papers.

"What are you doing with Dirk?" Arielle demanded, though it sounded far too shrill.

Rassa said nothing as he sat, a malicious grin curving his lips. The smile infuriated her.

"Why are you doing this?" She wiped her eyes, embarrassed that he should see she'd been crying. "We've done nothing."

"I know."

The admission shocked her. Slack-jawed, she sat, unable to respond.

"Nonetheless, that won't help you get out of here. Either of you." Rassa leaned forward and pushed the sheaf of papers in front of her, a pen on top.

She stared at the papers, struggling to read them. Her skill with the Azzaro language had progressed, but she wasn't fluent. "What is this?"

"An agreement. It's the only way you'll ever get out of here."

"What agreement?" She stared at the pen, afraid to touch it, as if it was covered in poison.

"You and your friend agree to work for Kaahrim for five years."

Her blood chilled. "You want us as slaves?"

"If you're convicted of stealing that device, you'll be imprisoned for life."

Arielle sank in on herself. Five years or life here?

"With your training, working for Kaahrim will be easy," Rassa said. "You'll put your diplomatic skills to work on our behalf."

She frowned. "If you use us for diplomatic negotiations, what's to stop us from revealing our situation to others?"

Rassa pointed at the papers, his smile never wavering. "Those papers are a confession. An admission of guilt as an accessory to the theft."

Her hands started shaking so she clasped them together.

"Besides, you won't negotiate directly with anyone. You both will train others here, and we'll consult with you when needed."

At least Dirk would be all right. That didn't change the reality. The thought of signing a document that enslaved them sickened her. She wanted to rip the papers to shreds, yet what alternative did she have? Wait here and hope someone locates them?

"May I read over the papers?" she asked. "I'll need some time."

Rassa nodded, rising. "Sure. I should point out that Dirk is in Captain Bilo's hands until you sign. And let's just say he's not a patient man."

A shiver ran through her. She fought the urge to immediately sign, as Rassa clearly wanted. This had all been his plan from the beginning. Once she'd been arrested and he'd seen her likeness. It was probably him who suggested to Captain Bilo that she looked like the girl from the picture. He had likely suggested the wach remove Dirk in a rough fashion, to cause her to panic and make a rash decision. His comment now about what the captain was doing with Dirk. He was manipulating her.

But she wouldn't allow it.

Instead, she forced herself to read the documents. And he didn't rush her, not wanting to tip his hand. He slipped out, likely hoping her worry for Dirk would eat at her until he got what he wanted.

Progress through the papers was slow. She had trouble with many words, guessing at their meaning. While the document didn't reveal what was stolen, it did make clear that the device was vital to Kaahrim security. It stated that she and Dirk had aided in the theft as accessories. As part of a plea deal, they agreed to provide information that could lead to the capture of their co-conspirator and recovery of the device. In exchange for their cooperation, their sentence would be reduced to five years of service to Kaahrim.

Reading that last bit made her tear up again. She'd never been accused of a crime in her life. Seeing her name on a plea bargain, and knowing that signing it meant spending the next five years imprisoned here. It would ruin her life. Her time at the academy would be over, her career prospects sidetracked so badly she'd never recover. And her family. Friends. Five years without seeing or talking to any of them.

She couldn't sign this.

She had no choice but to sign.

If she signed it her life, hers and Dirk's, were over for the next five years. But if she refused, their lives would likely last a lot less. If they were no use to Rassa, he didn't seem the type to just let them go.

But if she was going to sign, she wasn't going to take the terms as written. She picked up the pen—her diplomatic training kicking in—and made notes in the margins. She wrote clarifications for herself and considered possible revisions to the document. Rassa wanted a negotiator, and he was getting one starting now. She was going to minimize the damage in every way possible for herself, but more so for Dirk.

By the time Rassa returned to check on her, she had devised her plan of attack.

"Have you come to a decision?" he asked.

She straightened in her chair. "I've made some revisions."

His smile grew as he resumed his seat. "Please, proceed."

"First, I propose that in exchange for my service, Dirk be released. He doesn't deserve to be punished. I forgot my ID. He's done nothing wrong."

Rassa's smile evaporated. In fact, he looked disappointed, as if he'd hoped for a smarter response from her. "We have no intention of losing his services. And you forget. Your charges aren't for a missing ID, they're for theft of vital local government property."

She had expected him to dismiss her first request, so she had made it easy. He couldn't let Dirk go because he'd come back with the weight of Space City at his back.

Rather than give him time to reconsider this negotiation, she rushed on. "I'd like to set specific goals we can help Kaahrim accomplish. If we reach those goals, you agree to reduce our service time." She chose the term service time instead of sentence to appease him. It was the last thing she wanted to do, but it was in their best interest for the moment.

He nodded. "That can be arranged, but I will set the goals you both must reach."

She pretended to study the document for a few seconds, as if making these terms up as she went. "If the woman involved in the theft is caught and the device returned, our service time is reduced by one year."

He waved dismissively. "I already know you offer little help there. And your sentence is life if you don't agree. Five years is already a bargain."

Biting her lip, she forced herself not to respond to the reminder that he knew they were innocent. She focused on the papers, breathing deeply until she'd calmed enough to continue. This last part was the most important of all. And she couldn't let him see how important it was.

"The Sundara treaty database. We'll need access."

He considered this for a moment. "Why?"

"We need to review all existing treaties to see what we can exploit or add to in order to accomplish your goals. That's much easier than starting a new treaty."

He stared at her, saying nothing. No expression, but his eyes probed her face. She fought to remain still, keep her expression neutral. Sweat beaded her forehead. The silence stretched between them. It took every ounce of resolve she had not to look away or shrivel under his piercing stare. What was he waiting for?

"Very well," he said at last.

She nodded, anxious not to show the hope he'd suddenly given her. She placed her pen on the signature line. He licked his lips, eyes bright, clearly pleased he'd gotten her to agree, never realizing he'd already given her the key to their freedom.

As she started to write her name, the door burst open and in stormed Instructor Zelo, head of the Diplomat Department.

"Sign nothing," Instructor Zelo ordered.

She dropped the pen, sighing in relief.

Outraged at the intrusion, Nohchil Rassa jumped to his feet. "What are you doing here? Who let you in?"

"Never mind that." Instructor Zelo held out a signed paper to Rassa. "You will release Arielle Delven and Dirk Fischer to me immediately."

Rassa grabbed the document. As he read, his lip curled in a snarl.

"Unchain this girl," Instructor Zelo ordered. A wach from the hall hurried in to do as ordered. "And bring me Dirk. Now!"

The wach unchained Arielle and she rubbed her wrists, the little bits of dried blood flecking off. Instructor Zelo grabbed her arm and led her toward the door.

"We're not done here," Rassa snarled after them, but he now reminded her more of a dog barking behind its fence at passers-by.

Dirk stood in the hall, arms restrained by Captain Bilo and another wach.

"What is going on?" Captain Bilo demanded.

Instructor Zelo removed another signed document from a pocket in his shirt, which he handed to the captain. "I have an order signed by the Tanarille council and the head of the Space City embassy. You're to release these two students into my custody."

The captain took the paper, frowning. After reading the document, he nodded. "Let them go," he told the wach. Unlike Rassa, he made no threats. For all his earlier anger, he accepted the order without question.

Instructor Zelo led them out front of Kaahrim hall, the town's government office. A dark gray, sleek helicopter waited for them, and Instructor Zelo ushered them inside. The interior possessed leather seats, a stainless-steel control stick and throttle, and a mini-computer on the dash with GPS, climate controls, and music options.

In the passenger seat sat an Azzaro woman dressed in a casual green dress. Instructor Zelo introduced her as his wife, Tiru.

"How are you both?" Tiru asked, brow furrowed with concern. "You're not hurt?"

"Thanks so much for coming to get us," Arielle replied. "How did you know?"

Instructor Zelo had climbed in and was already lifting off. "We received a warning from Instructor Kana. Seems Dirk sent her a message before you were detained."

Arielle looked at Dirk, surprised. "You beat me to it?"

"Beat you? You had a way to get us free?"

She nodded and proceeded to relate everything that had happened. When she got to the part about the request for access to the Tanarille treaty database, Instructor Zelo gave her a 'smart girl.'

Dirk gave her a perplexed look. "How would that help us? It's just a database for recording and reviewing treaties."

She grinned, pausing to see if he'd figure it out. And after a couple of seconds he blinked, eyes widening. "Adding treaties?"

"Exactly. Or reviewing old ones. We could add in a line and an alert so that the requested change is immediately delivered to the Tanarille Diplomat Agency for review. If we did it right, our names would be included."

Dirk whistled. "Clever. I'd have never thought of that."

"It was a brilliantly simple idea," Instructor Zelo said. "And don't worry, Rassa's actions have the attention of the Tanarille council. He's going to answer for this."

Arielle sighed, staring out the window at the passing landscape.

"How are you both enjoying the diplomat program?" Tiru asked.

Dirk looked at Arielle, waiting for her to respond first.

"It's been wonderful," Arielle said, hoping to impress the instructor and his wife. "Everything I had hoped for when I applied."

"And what's your focus?"

Arielle answered and they talked about what she needed to do to become an education-focused diplomat. Some things she had already learned, but Tiru gave her several insights she had never considered. By the time they reached the Otoch monuments, the Azzaro couple were sharing past stories from their careers as diplomats, before they retired to Tanarille and Zelo took a position at the Lore Center.

"You should apply for a position here at the embassy," Tiru said once they'd landed. "After you graduate."

"I'd love to," Arielle said wistfully.

"Seriously," Tiru urged. "Let's talk next week. I'll introduce you to some people you should know before you leave."

"Thank you!" Arielle couldn't believe her luck. "I will."

"Good." Tiru nodded once as if the matter was decided, then grabbed her husband's arm. "We need to find our son and grandchildren. Let us know if you need a ride back."

"We will," Arielle promised.

Hundreds of people had gathered around the Triplet Geysers, making it difficult to find a close spot to view the eruption. The geysers resembled three whirlpools carved into the ground with thick yellow rings surrounding them, followed by hot springs. The smell of rotten eggs filled the air, and the swarm of people didn't help matters.

The Otoch monuments served as a backdrop surrounding the geysers. The Muyal mountain range to the north had given way to a vast plain covered with hundreds of four story step-pyramids with flat tops. In the heart was one enormous pyramid, a few hundred feet tall and massive in scale.

"Did you know the Otoch monuments were once the imperial seat of Sundara?" Dirk asked. He seemed rejuvenated. "The emperors ruled here for a thousand years before the rise of Tanarille and a republic."

Arielle had heard this before, but let him babble on. They found a place to watch the eruption from a bridge between two of the pyramids. They were a good distance back, but standing on the bridge gave them an unobstructed view.

Near the expected time for eruption, most of the people gathered fell silent in anticipation. Everyone waited as a faint rumbling began deep underground. Water came shooting up from the three wells in the ground, twenty feet into the air before crashing into the hot springs. The geysers reflected light from both suns, creating three separate rainbows that crisscrossed. Everyone cheered and whistled. The eruptions went on for a full five minutes, as if buoyed by the crowd, before dying back down for another month.

Arielle turned to Dirk and what she saw silenced her. Glowing around his head was a Glory—a faint series of circles: green, yellow, orange and red.

Couldn't be.

On Earth, Glories surrounded only one's shadow.

But on Sundara, maybe as a result of having two suns, Glories were always seen surrounding the heads of others. They didn't appear regularly, however. The Azzaro had long held a superstition about sighting a Glory.

At that moment, as Dirk basked in its glow, Arielle couldn't dismiss the superstition.

Chapter 6

"What?" Dirk asked, noticing Arielle staring at him. Gaping, in fact.

The question startled her and she colored. She shook her head and looked away. "Nothing."

But he could tell from her expression that something was off. Did he have something in his teeth? Or his hair? He ran his tongue over his upper row of teeth, then the lower. As he did so he turned as if to survey the Otoch pyramids. He ran his hands through his hair, but didn't feel anything in it. Hopefully, he'd gotten whatever it had been.

"What now?" she asked when he turned back.

He shrugged. "I don't know. Want to take a pyramid tour?"

"Sure. After all it took us to get here, seems like we should get a little more out of the visit."

"I'll say."

On their way to a temple entrance, he spotted a few pale orange flowers growing along the base beside the pyramid. With as many people as there were around, it was amazing they hadn't been trampled. Perhaps she would like one.

A twinge of pain shot through him as he remembered her rejection from earlier in the day. He shoved that down, not wanting to ruin things. After all they'd been through today, they didn't need to rehash that subject.

"Come here for a second," he said, and led her over to the flowers. "Do you have one of these in your collection?"

"Mooncups!" She beamed, dropping to her knees to smell the flowers. "It's the last flower I hoped to find here on Sundara, but I'd given up hope I'd find one."

164

The yellow petals cupped a cream-colored bud, the whole flower as large as a sunflower, though with much smaller stems. And resting on the bottom lip of the pyramid was one Mooncup, its stem broken. Obviously recent because the flower looked fresh.

He picked up the flower, offering it to her. "Didn't you say you wanted one for your collection?"

"Thank you!"

Her smile lit up her face, and he thought she had never looked more beautiful. For a moment they regarded each other silently. An awkward tension started building between them, so he turned away, studying the line into the pyramid. It wasn't too long.

"Dirk."

He turned back and she kissed him. It took him by surprise. He froze. She placed her hands on his shoulders. He wanted to reach out and touch her, but didn't know where to place his hands, so he let them fall to his sides.

When she pulled away, he wanted to draw her close again, but hesitated.

"This will never work once we're diplomats." She bit her lip. "We'll both be at the mercy of the Council in our diplomatic assignments."

Perplexed, he asked, "Why did you—?"

She blushed. "You'll laugh."

Impulsively, he reached out for her hand. It was soft, except for the electricity that shot through him, quickening his pulse. "I promise I won't."

"Earlier, during the geyser eruption, I saw a Glory behind your head." She paused, searching his face for laughter. He squeezed her hand in encouragement, and she continued, "I'm sure you know the Azzaros' superstition about observing a Glory behind someone's head?"

He shook his head. He'd learned a lot about Azzaro customs, but that one he'd missed.

"They believe Glories only appear behind the head of your true love."

All he could do was smile.

"You think it's foolish," she said, turning away.

"No." He pulled gently on her hand, so that she turned back to him. "I'll take any reason for your interest."

They kissed again.

When they separated this time, her face was aglow.

"What do you want to do now?" he asked her.

She considered for a minute. "How about visiting the Otoch Palace?"

He nodded. "I'm game for a tour."

Indebted

Chapter 1

"I'm sea diving today," Cade lied. He stripped off his t-shirt and tossed it into the giant clamshell serving as his dresser.

"Again?" Gro's gills flared, and his lime-green scaled fins flattened. The Murgin's over-sized eye cluster drooped. "Diving's for Mugies!"

Which was exactly why Cade chose it. Because only the Murgins' little ones wanted to sea dive. Gro would feel ridiculous going. Cade was spending his summer break from the Space City Academy with Gro on his home planet, Araxia. The place was pretty cool; the Murgin lived in underwater cities. But Cade had already been here for three weeks without managing to sneak away for the five minutes it took to register. That was changing today. It was his real reason for visiting, though he couldn't tell Gro that.

"Let's ride the jets instead." Gro's native tongue sounded like a chittering squirrel, forcing Cade to concentrate hard on his tradutor.

Cade grabbed his wet suit from the clamshell and started changing. "Tomorrow. I promise. You don't have to sea dive with me. I can get around myself."

Gro fell back into his night pool, his four legs hanging over the coral lip. "Fine, I'll hit the jets alone." But Cade could see the relief on the Murgin's face that he didn't have to join in a Mugie activity.

"Good. You need the practice. You're slow as manatee."

Gro's mouth opened wide, for a moment resembling a fish out of water. "You couldn't beat me racing the jets if you practiced every day for a year."

"Train hard today," Cade said with mock solemnity as he zipped up the wet suit. "It'll be more satisfying when I crush you." Diving mask in hand, he hobbled out of Gro's room and downstairs, hating that his limp belied his words. It was an ever-present reality check.

"The only thing you'll do is inhale my jet stream," Gro shouted after him.

Cade didn't reply as he exited Gro's home, stepping out onto the sea-shelled streets of Amadii, the capital of Araxia. The city, smelling heavily of salt, resembled a cross between a giant reef and the inside of a beehive. The homes and other buildings were all made from specially manufactured bioluminescent coral that provided much of the city's light, since it was too deep in a trench to get much sunlight from Araxia's sun. Sponges, seagrass, conch, and green, lettuce-like seaweeds—all of which had been ironically adapted to survive out of water—decorated most of the homes in Amadii.

The Murgin had once lived in a hybrid land/shallow ocean style on Araxia until an asteroid had nearly wiped them out. The survivors fled deep underwater, building cities surrounded by artificial atmospheres throughout the planet's oceans. When he first arrived, Cade had been tempted to ask Gro why the Murgin, still possessing gills, bothered with the artificial atmospheres to keep water out. But the question felt inappropriate.

Cade moved as fast as his crooked left leg allowed, disappearing into the crowded streets before Gro could change his mind. He hated lying to his friend, but today was the last day for registration in the Tefnot. If Gro's parents somehow found he was entering the sub race, they'd stop him. Too young, they'd say. They'd call Aidan, who'd agree. It would be hypocritical of his older brother, who'd started racing after their parents' death. Aidan entered and competed in just about any race, no matter how dangerous. But Cade was too fragile with his bad leg. Not that Aidan called him such, but his treatment made the sentiment clear.

The Tefnot was the one race in which his leg didn't prevent him from competing. A week-long race across the Puakai ocean in subs. He'd spent the last year practicing for the race in the sims, getting comfortable with how the Murgin subs operated, as well as the route through the Puakai ocean. This was his chance to prove to Aidan that he was a racer, too.

The champion's purse of one million pearls wouldn't hurt either.

The Tefnot registration office was located on the east side of Amadii near the Estate District. Unlike the rest of the city, the Estate District was filled with water maintained at surface pressure so special breathing equipment was not required, and the homes were built both horizontally and vertically. As Cade reached the translucent line separating the district from the rest of the city—like standing before a giant aquarium tank without the glass—he slipped on his diving mask and air hose. Then he stepped forward into the water.

Sprawling bioluminescent coral mansions filled the district outward and upward, so that it was a lot like wandering through New York City, except instead of towering skyscrapers, there were row upon row of the mansions as far upward as he could see. Numerous aquatic creatures—orangefins to neon flatheads to exotic bloodfish—swam around the district, giving the Murgin elite the illusion of living closer to the surface. Cade caught a current, which carried him upward past colorful artificial barrier reefs.

Cade exited the current around the fourth level of mansions, swimming toward the registration office. Red, stalactite-like seaweed covered the residences. An underwater fountain, at least three stories tall, emitted golden bubbles, which spread out like a narrow fizz ceiling above one estate; the bubbles rose toward other parts of the district.

The entrance to the mansion had another water barrier that enabled Cade to step out into the dry lobby. Large fans on either side of the narrow entrance hall blew warm air that dried him. The hall gave way to a great room decorated with expensive imports from all over the universe. Valm rugs with intricate patterns from Ourania covered the floors. Sky blue crystal vases from Sundara rested on stands on either side of a grand banister. Tables made from palm trees from Niveum held golden candlesticks, pitchers, and other expensive ornaments. And the heads of a saber-toothed cheetah, a rhino hog, and a panther albus—all likely hunted around the southern lodges on Herne—adorned the walls.

In a corner of the entrance hall was the registration desk for the Tefnot. Behind it stood a large-lipped Murgin watching a hologram replay of last year's Tefnot race.

After a moment's pause, Cade coughed to get the Murgin's attention. "Excuse me, sir. Are you in charge of registration for the Tefnot?"

The Murgin looked him up and down, sneered, then turned back to watching the race. "The entrance fee is ten thousand pearls."

Stiffening at the cold reception, Cade retrieved a bank data chip from his pocket, placing it on the desk. A few seconds passed before the Murgin, eye-cluster wrinkling together, bothered to glance at the bank chip. Once he did, the Murgin picked it up with webbed hands as if it were covered in sludge and deposited it into a scanner to verify its authenticity. When the chip was confirmed, the Murgin huffed and tossed it back to Cade, who quickly deposited it in his pocket.

Once he finished registration, Cade still had to find a sub. The registration had cost nearly everything he had. With what little he had left over, a derelict sub might be his only option. Maybe he should reconsider hiding his plans from Gro. His friend could fix anything.

"Name?" the Murgin asked.

"Cade Martin, resident of Space City."

The Murgin traced lines on a clear glass screen behind the desk. "Qualifying races this year?"

Cade's breath caught. "What do you mean? The only requirement for entering the Tefnot is the registration fee and a sub."

The Murgin snickered, clearly believing the world had returned to the way he liked it. "You have to win at least two races during the current year to qualify for the Tefnot. Now get out of my scales." The Murgin waved for the door.

Cade couldn't believe it. He'd studied both the Tefnot rules and the registration criteria extensively. The only requirement was the entrance fee. There would've been no way for him to travel here during the school year without Aidan finding out. *Visiting* a friend during the summer was one thing. Missing school was quite another.

"Any upcoming races before the Tefnot?" Cade couldn't keep the edge out of his voice. A part of him wondered if the Murgin was making up this requirement.

"Seare!" The Murgin shouted. A second Murgin, tall and blubbery, emerged from a room at the back. "Seare, please remove this algae eater from the premises."

Cade started to protest, but Seare lumbered forward menacingly, disinterested in his arguments. Cade retreated briskly, head held high in defiance, but Seare was surprisingly spry. The Murgin grabbed Cade's shoulders as he attempted to dodge free, hauled him to the mansion entrance, and tossed him out into the water. The only thing Cade had time for as he flew into the water was to hold his breath.

After a few seconds floundering, he pulled his mask back over his face and sank. Registration closed at the end of the day. There was no other way for him to sign up. He'd been imagining telling classmates of his victory in the Tefnot when he got back to the academy. He'd be the envy of everyone. No one would pity him for his bad leg anymore.

Instead, he was in for another year as a nobody.

Or as a target.

*****

Exiting the Estate District, Cade removed his dive mask as he plodded through the crowded streets, jostled by Murgin hurrying about their business. A few shouted "Mugies to the kiddy pool" or "you're holding up the school," as they pushed past him. He couldn't muster a reply. He paid no attention to where he was headed. What did it matter? He'd failed his dream, the one thing he needed to do.

A familiar face appeared in the crowd ahead. It took him a few more steps before he recognized Ansa. Aidan's girlfriend. What was she doing here?

In her early twenties, Ansa possessed long, smooth legs presently on display thanks to a pair of mid-thigh shorts. Her skin was nicely tanned and her lips curled seductively. The v-necked shirt she wore dipped low, revealing the tops of her—

"Cade!"

His eyes darted up to her face. Green eyes glared at him along with pursed lips. His cheeks burned, and he chastised himself for being so obvious. It was embarrassing. And she was Aidan's girlfriend at that. Cade wanted to beg her not to tell Aidan, but he couldn't make himself speak.

"I didn't realize you were here," Ansa said, approaching.

173

"Staying with a friend for the summer," Cade replied, wishing he could sink through the seashell street into the ocean; end his humiliation.

But she smiled at him as if the moment before had never happened. "Cool. So, what are you up to?"

He mulled a few likely stories, but decided against lying. He'd never find another way to register in the few hours left. "I wanted to register for the Tefnot. Turns out you have to compete in qualifying races first."

Her thin eyebrows rose. "The Tefnot? You're as reckless as Aidan."

He flushed once more at the mention of his brother. "I wanted to prove I could win a big one like Aidan."

She snorted. "How were you going to pay the entrance fee?"

He hoped his cheeks weren't reddening again. "I saved up the money working at the arena last year."

"Not ten thousand pearls, you didn't."

"I had some saved up already."

She rolled her eyes, crossing her arms as she did so. "Try again."

"And if I don't? What're you going to do? Tattle?" The words were out of his mouth before he even had time to process them, but it felt good to lash out.

The pleasure only lasted a breath before Ansa started tapping one foot. Her eyes narrowed. "You think I need help to handle a sixteen-year-old with an attitude problem?"

Something about her stance, and the look on her face, gave him pause. Another wrong answer, and he thought she just might give him other reasons to feel sorry for himself.

"Okay, okay. I borrowed from Aidan. But I would've paid him back."

"He let you borrow the money?"

"No…"

"Cade Martin, I didn't know you had it in you." She shook her head, then pointed down a side street. "Well if you're not doing anything, I was headed to lunch. Hungry?"

He wasn't sure if that meant she'd keep his secret, but he was starving. Gro's mom had cooked fried eel for breakfast, but that had been before he'd traipsed all over the city. "I'd love something."

"I was headed to my favorite little spot."

Ansa led him through the crowd to a small café. The place had a dozen mangrove tables, only a couple of which were occupied. The smells of shrimp, fish, and other seafood infused the air, making his stomach rumble.

They took a seat in the corner. The waitress stopped by, and Ansa ordered Emperor crab legs and a beer. Cade chose Araxia ringed shark with a lettuce seaweed soup on the side.

"Aidan would've killed you throwing away his money on a race." Ansa sipped her beer.

Cade shrugged. "I'm not throwing it away if I win."

She smirked. "The Tefnot is the toughest race in the universe. Anything is fair game."

"I know that," he said, irritated that she wasn't taking him seriously.

"No, you don't." She shook her head. "Most racers I know won't enter. Too many *accidents* every year."

"Aidan would do it."

"So you want to be stupid because your brother is?" She took another swig of beer.

He huffed, wishing he hadn't come after all. She didn't understand. Aidan would. At least he would've after the race.

"Look, it's dangerous." She pursed her lips and stared at him as if contemplating. "*But* if you're determined, I may have a way you can enter."

The waitress dropped off their entrees.

"How?" Cade asked, ignoring his plate.

"I have a few connections." Ansa broke an enormous emperor crab leg—easily two feet in length and a little thicker than a banana.

"Can you reach them this afternoon? Registration closes today." He gripped the edge of the table, wanting to leave now. They could eat later.

"Eat first. Then we'll talk." She removed a strip of crab meat and stuffed it in her mouth.

He nodded, exhilaration flooding through him.

The piece of shark on his plate was covered in a dark sauce. The steaming seaweed soup looked like cooked spinach and seagrass in a broth, but it was surprisingly savory. The dark sauce on the shark reminded Cade of blackening seasons that set his mouth on fire, forcing him to gulp down water. He loved it!

A few more of the spicy bites and his nose started to run, forcing him to dab at it with his napkin. Perhaps some of the soup would cool his mouth.

About halfway through the bowl of soup, he started to feel drowsy. He shook his head, trying to clear it. He'd stayed up late with Gro last night, but he hadn't been this tired when he awoke. He'd felt good. He took another bite of the shark, hoping the spiciness would energize him, but his eyelids grew heavy. He had the sudden impulse to lay his head on the table and sleep.

No! Not in front of Ansa. Pushing himself to his feet, he leaned on the table for support. "I think. Man, I'm suddenly exhausted."

She reached across the table and placed a hand on his, her expression concerned. "Are you okay?"

He didn't know the answer, but he was sure he needed to lie down. He wasn't sure he could make it all the way back to Gro's, but maybe fresh air would clear his head. Or he could buy a caffeine shot somewhere. "I think I'm going to—"

He pointed out the front door. As he turned to go, his knees weakened. He wobbled. Ansa was on her feet instantly, moving to his side. He tried to push away her helping hand. He could walk on his own. But as he stepped toward the exit, he tipped sideways onto her. She grunted under his weight, but steadied him.

"I'm sorry." Cade was embarrassed, but found he lacked the strength to straighten. Something was wrong.

"Let me help you." She led him out the door onto the front steps, telling the waitress to charge her account for the food on the way out. "This way." She guided him around the corner to a pair of chairs beside the café. "Sit down. Rest."

He plopped into the chair. He tried breathing deeply. His last thought was that the race organizer or his guard must've done something to him on his way out of the mansion.

Chapter 2

Cade lurched upright in icy shock as water poured over him. He gasped and sputtered, reaching with both hands to wipe his face, but his right arm was halted by a manacle. Why was his arm chained? To a bed.

A tall, rippling Murgin stood over him holding a grime-covered bucket. "It's time to work."

"Who are you?" Cade asked, trying to understand what was going on. They were in a small, windowless room. How had he gotten here? "What is this?"

The Murgin stepped closer, his eye cluster dropped down to face level. Pus leaked from two of the eyes. Cade flinched away as the Murgin pulled a key from its pocket and removed the manacle.

"Just to keep you out of trouble," the Murgin said.

Cade stared at his dripping clothes. He remembered becoming dizzy and Ansa helping him outside. Something was wrong. Was this a hospital? There was no medical equipment, and it was way too quiet.

"Follow me." The Murgin turned, grabbing the empty water bucket from the end table and marching out the door. A white dresser was the only other thing in the room.

The open door had three heavy locks, two of which looked brand new.

"Hey, what am I doing here?" Cade asked.

The Murgin didn't answer. Cade followed him to a simple hallway, past three other doors and outside to a fish farm. Well, not exactly outside. A clear dome enclosed the farm, covering several acres of space, and ocean water surrounded the dome. Definitely not a hospital. Well above the farm, he could make out the lights of

"

Amadii. The fish farms, for there were many surrounding them, were removed from the city itself.

The fish farm held a large pond, with water spinach growing in turquoise frames dotting the surface. Waist-high mangroves surrounded the shoreline. There was also a small shed off to the right of the property, and an undefined building at the rear.

"Is Ansa here?" Cade saw no signs of anyone else. "Did she bring me here?"

For a response, the Murgin strode to some mangroves. "Clean up the dead branches and leaves from the shoreline. Dump them in the mulch pit." The Murgin pointed out a dumpster-sized bin against the nearest dome wall. "After you've cleared the entire shoreline, trim the mangroves."

Cade gaped. "Um. I don't know what is going on, but I'm not doing that."

The Murgin picked up a broken mangrove limb from the shoreline, about as thick as his thumb, and snapped Cade in the face with it. The limb cut Cade's jaw and he yelped. A trickle of blood dribbled down to his chin.

"Slaves don't question." The Murgin waved the limb in warning. "And address me as Master Isk."

A roiling sickness filled Cade's stomach. He clenched his fists to fight off fear. "I'm no slave. You've no right—"

The Murgin flicked his wrist once more. Cade barely got up a hand to block the blow. The limb cut a welt in his forearm, causing him to inhale sharply.

"Right? You're the one with no rights." The Murgin stared him down. "I bought and paid for you. *I* have every right."

"Bought from whom?" What had happened after he'd passed out?

This time the Murgin caught the side of Cade's neck with the branch. "I am Master Isk to you."

Cade started to protest again, then thought better of it. He didn't want to be struck again by this crazy Murgin. None of this made sense. He debated running for it.

As if reading his mind, Isk pointed at the house. "The door locks automatically. Only I can open it."

The response made Cade immediately search the surroundings again. The dome appeared smooth with no openings.

Isk gestured at the shoreline with the limb. "Get to work."

Perhaps he could simply buy his freedom. He felt in his pants pockets, but the bank chip was gone. Had it fallen out? Had whoever had sold him taken it? Had Ansa taken it? She wouldn't have done any of this. She was Aidan's girlfriend. But what had happened to her then?

"Master Isk," Cade said cautiously. "This is a misunderstanding. I'm from Space City. Please, let me contact my brother, Aidan. He could reimburse you."

Isk raised the limb again. "Stop wasting my time!"

Nervous energy hummed through Cade. Slavery was illegal on Araxia. Had been since the Murgin formed an alliance with Space City. At the moment that didn't seem to matter.

Rather than spend more time drawing the ire of Isk and getting struck, Cade walked to the pond's edge and collected debris. He couldn't fight the big Murgin. He'd left his wrist-comp at Gro's. He could test out Isk's assertion that the house possessed an auto-lock, but even without it, he couldn't just swim to another farm or up to Amadii. Too far away and without the proper equipment his body couldn't handle the pressure. He was stuck here.

Once he had an armload, he carried it to the mulch bin. He took his time dumping it so that he could stare out through the dome. Another fish farm with a dome abutted this one. Two Murgins, an Azzaro, and a Malsain worked at various tasks. Cade considered waving his arms and trying to get their attention. Could he get a message to them?

One of the Murgin strode up to the Azzaro and struck him, knocking him to the ground. The Azzaro stared up fearfully at the Murgin.

"Get back to work," Isk ordered.

Cade tossed the rest of the debris in the bin and marched back to the shoreline. Did all the fish farmers own slaves? How did they get away with it?

As he worked his way around the shoreline, he eyed the entire landscape outside the dome. Fish farms surrounded them, all with workers, many of whom possessed cuts and bruises as if whipped and beaten. It wasn't right. Someone needed to do something.

The rest of the afternoon, as calculated by the 32-hour clock on the back of Isk's house, Cade cleared debris. After that, he retrieved hedgers from the shed, along with a cart he found in there, which he used to wheel the trimmed mangrove limbs to the mulch bin. The shed was filled with numerous other tools—hammers, saws, netting, and traps. He contemplated using the hedger or a saw as a weapon, but even if he managed to gain the upper hand—no easy task with the Murgin keeping a constant eye on him—he still didn't know how to get into the house if it was locked. Or contact anyone to help him. And for now, he didn't want to irritate the Murgin while he was trapped here.

Around hour twenty-eight, Isk called him over. "Put up the tools and wash in the pond."

With that, the Murgin strode to his house, opened the door, and entered. He didn't unlock it as far as Cade could tell. The auto-lock had been a lie then.

Deciding to test it, Cade hurried over to the door, holding his breath in hopes that the Murgin wouldn't come out. There was no obvious lock around the door. When he reached the door, he grabbed the handle and rotated. It didn't budge. Isk must've locked it from the inside.

Still no closer to an answer, he returned the tools to the shed before wading a couple of feet into the pond among the sea grass, until he reached an edge where the bed dropped away. He eased his way closer and stared down into the dark, cold water. He could see numerous fishes, penned in by walls that disappeared into a void. It was like the fish hovered above a vast precipice. He shivered.

A short time later, Isk returned and shoved him back inside. Isk did nothing special to open the door. Cade glanced at the inside of the door, but there was no obvious lock mechanism. So if it did auto-lock, how did it know when to unlock?

"I'll be by with food shortly," Isk said as he ushered Cade into the room he'd woken up in.

The blankets on the bed still looked wet from earlier. He'd have to try to hang them up, maybe over the headrail and dresser.

"The dresser has clean clothes." Isk closed the door behind him. The three locks clicked one by one. Cade waited a few seconds, then tiptoed over to the door to confirm it was locked.

Chapter 3

A sharp sting to his ear caused Cade to double over in his paddleboat. His hands rose to cover his head.

"I don't tolerate laziness." Isk waved a pair of clippers meant to cut spinach.

They were in separate paddleboats harvesting the water spinach. The paddleboats were steered with a pedal system designed for a Murgin's four legs, not Cade's two; his left not helping much at that. Isk either didn't notice or didn't care; he only grew agitated every time Cade couldn't do something as fast as he liked.

A trickle of blood ran down Cade's ear and fell to his shoulder. Just one of a growing number of cuts and bruises he'd sustained at Isk's hands. The attacks came randomly, frequently, and without warning, compelling Cade to work far away from Isk as much as possible. But there was only so much room to steer around the spinach frames.

Hoping to avoid another strike, Cade grabbed the spinach frame and pulled the paddleboat over against it. He clipped the largest spinach leaves, depositing them in a knapsack attached to the paddleboat. He took care not to drop any in the water, which would draw another beating.

"It's all I can do to survive," Isk grumbled. "Growing spinach and raising fish. All day every day. I buy a slave, and the cursed fool wants to lay about and eat my food instead of working."

Cade leaned forward over the spinach, dodging the next swipe he knew was coming. When Isk got in a complaining mood, the beatings increased. Two weeks in and he already knew Isk far better than he ever hoped to.

More blood from his ear spotted his arm, and if he wasn't careful, would start staining the spinach, too. "I need another tool from the shed." That would buy him a few minutes to get cleaned up.

"You're already taking a break? We need to finish the spinach by midmorning, or you'll be out here during lunch. You want to eat, you need to gather your share."

Cade muttered under his breath that he wouldn't *need* a break if it wasn't for Isk.

In the shed, he found a dirty old rag on a shelf in the corner, which he could rinse off in the fish-gutting sink and use to clean his ear. He hoped the cut wasn't bad enough to warrant stitches. As he picked it up, a tiny flash of light glinted off metal from the back of the shelf. A small knife, like a scalpel. He picked it up and caught a whiff of fish guts. It was too small to wield effectively as a weapon. But perhaps he could use it to pick his door locks?

The clothes he'd been given lacked pockets, so he set the knife back on the shelf. He carried the rag over to the sink. He ran the rag under cold water, before dabbing at his ear with the grimy cloth. He winced.

The cut continued to seep, so he squeezed his ear, pressing the rag hard into the cut and held it there, which elicited a groan. He squeezed his eyes shut for a count of thirty. When he let go, the cut bled again. But Isk didn't keep a medical kit around. So he tore off a strip of the dirty, now partially bloody rag and tied it around his ear.

Knowing he better not stay much longer, he returned the rag to the shelf and regarded the knife. Perhaps he could retrieve it at the end of the day. Then he had a better idea. He could hide it in his shoe!

"Cade?"

He spun around. Isk stood in the doorway, a large gutting knife in hand. Cade inhaled sharply.

"Our fish haul is needed earlier than expected. We need to take care of it now." Isk held out his webbed hand to Cade, expecting something. For a second Cade thought Isk had spotted the knife behind him and was asking for it. But Isk gestured for his spinach clippers, which Cade had left on the counter.

"Works for me. I'd rather fish anyway." Cade grabbed the clippers, but as he turned to hand them to Isk, the Murgin stared at the shelf where Cade had been a moment before. Isk's expression hardened as he strode forward and grabbed the knife.

"What were you doing with this?" Isk growled, brandishing it and the fish-gutting knife. "Thought maybe you'd try to stab me with it?"

"N-No! Of course not. It was already there."

The Murgin stepped closer, forcing him up against the counter. Cade nearly fell back into the sink.

"You must think me a fool! I never leave my tools out. Never! What were you planning? Stab me when I wasn't looking?" Isk jabbed at Cade's right cheek, nicking him.

Cade's hand flew to cover his cheek as he leaned farther back, feeling the faucet dig into his back. "No. I wasn't."

"Liar!" Isk was leaning over him; his two pus-filled eyes leaked onto Cade's chin.

Cade wanted to point out that the knife was old and rusted. Not worth much. But his throat felt constricted.

"If I catch you with a knife again, I'll gut you in this sink. Now get the nets."

And with that Isk stormed out of the shed.

Chapter 4

Cade scrubbed the counter and sink in the shed, washing the fish blood and guts down the drain. His hands were stiff from the icy water. The farm's heating system had broken down two days ago, meaning no warm water. Everything was the temperature of the deep ocean. It also meant freezing nights with only a small blanket. And cold food.

Only a couple days remained until the Tefnot kicked off. A race that he was supposed to be in. At that moment he would've settled just for being warm again. To take a hot shower. Or an extra blanket. Even a small fire beside the pond. But none of that was possible.

Thanks to Ansa.

He'd resisted that conclusion at first, but the more he thought about it, who else could it have been? Maybe someone in the restaurant. They could've put something in his food. But what were the odds Ansa had happened to take him to a favorite restaurant that decided he'd make a good slave?

But if it was her, how had she done it? Drugged his food? He'd been sitting right there and hadn't seen anything.

As he left the shed and headed toward the house, he glanced over the pond, and it struck him for the first time that he could be working here for the rest of his life. Cleaning the pond, catching and gutting fish, tending to the spinach until his hair turned gray and he died. If he lived long enough for his hair to turn gray anyway. For days, he'd maintained hope of rescue, but Gro had no idea where he'd gone and no one knew he'd run into Ansa. All he had to look forward to were Isk and beatings for company. And to make things worse, Isk would outlive him. Murgin had longer life spans by a good forty or fifty years. It made him want to tie something heavy around his waist and sink into the pond, just to have some sort of escape.

"Get in here if you want your food," Isk barked from the back door.

Cade trudged into the house and to his room. Isk locked the door behind him as he did every night. His plate on the end table held thawed needletop fish patties—still cold—and soggy sea grass. Same thing he'd been given twice a day since the heating system had broken. The first day he'd ignored it, but his hunger had soon overridden his distaste.

After forcing the meal down, he crawled into bed, knowing Isk would soon turn off the lights. And he wanted to warm himself the best he could with the blanket.

He'd barely gotten himself situated in bed when the lights blacked out. But this time it was accompanied by a click. Cade turned to look at the door, thinking it sounded like a lock. For a few heartbeats he lay there staring at the door, half afraid Isk would re-enter. Not a good sign at this time of night.

He waited for his eyes to adjust to the dark. The door remained closed. Perhaps he'd imagined the noise. But what if he hadn't? If the door was unlocked, this might be his one chance to escape.

So he rose from the bed and tiptoed to the door, breath caught in his throat as he listened. Everything was dark and quiet. He reached for the door handle and pulled. The door cracked open, revealing a darkened rest of the house. Had Isk gone to bed or had something else happened? He hoped for the latter. Why had his room unlocked for no reason?

He eased the door open. He peeked out, an excuse already rising to his lips in case he spotted Isk.

"One more month," Isk said from a room down the hall. "I've had good hauls lately."

Who was he talking to? And why was he talking to them in the dark?

Fear told him to close the door before Isk discovered him. But he forced himself to take a tentative step forward.

"You haven't had a profitable month in two years, and the price of needletops is plummeting," a Murgin said. "And now your power has been cut off due to lack of payment."

"I'm growing spinach, which will bring in extra funds. I'll pay them in a couple days. And I've plans to add pincers to the pond later this year." There was an edge of desperation in Isk's voice that Cade hadn't heard before.

The other Murgin laughed at that. "You'll need a lot more than spinach and pincers to save your farm."

"Please," Isk begged. "I'm close—"

"You've got two weeks," the Murgin overrode him. "After that we're foreclosing."

Foreclosing? Cade wondered what that meant for him. He decided he didn't want to stay long enough to find out. He took a few steps down the hall, but froze when Isk swore. Had he been caught? He tensed, prepared to run. But when Isk didn't emerge from the room, Cade couldn't decide whether to push on or retreat.

"Hello?" Isk's voice sounded drained.

"Isk, we've got everything arranged for your brother's commemoration," a new Murgin said.

Cade realized that Isk was video conferencing, despite a lack of power to the house.

"That's great news, Teze," Isk replied with little enthusiasm. "What about the reserved entry for the race? Were you able to sell it?"

"Not yet."

"What about a racer? Anyone I can hire to race instead?"

"Anyone interested in the race has already registered. For everyone else, it's too dangerous."

Isk laughed, a little deliriously.

"I've got a few extra Murgin I can check with," Teze said, with an obvious note of doubt in his voice. "Anyway, it'll be good to see you at the opening ceremony."

"Yeah," Isk said. "Great."

A second later, the door ahead was yanked wide and Isk stormed out into the hall. The Murgin froze when he saw Cade, and they both gaped at each other.

"The power..." Cade said.

"Where do you think you're going?" Isk took menacing steps toward him.

Cade's sense of self-preservation kicked in and he pivoted, pointing back at his room. "Everything went dark. My room unlocked."

"And you thought you'd take advantage and try to escape?"

Cade backed away. "No, I just thought you'd need help."

Isk grabbed his arm and shoved him back toward his bedroom. "You were trying to escape. I'll just have to chain you to the bed again. And no meals tomorrow."

The force of Isk's momentum nearly knocked Cade over backward. The effort of maintaining his feet prevented him from trying to break free of Isk's grasp. But as Isk forced him back to his room, Cade's desperation kicked his mind into overdrive.

"Wait!"

To his surprise, Isk paused.

"The Tefnot. You have an entry in the race."

Isk's expression darkened and he resumed dragging Cade into his room, grabbing manacles from the wall.

"Let me race for you," Cade suggested. "The prize is one million pearls. You can pay off your debts."

Isk snorted. "Like you could win."

Cade allowed himself be pushed to the bed and shackled so as to not draw Isk's ire.

As the Murgin headed for the door, he added, "You'd end up dead, and the money I've invested in you will be wasted."

A fair point, but he wasn't giving up. Better to die in the race than live out the rest of his life as a slave.

He exhaled. "You've got two weeks until you lose the farm. Do you know any other way?"

Isk hesitated, one hand on the door. He said nothing, but he also didn't leave. Cade pressed on, sensing he had but a moment to convince Isk.

"I'm a great racer. That's why I came here, to race in the Tefnot. If I win, you'll have more than enough to pay off your debts. Maybe even expand. All I ask is my freedom."

"I don't have a sub," Isk said.

Cade frowned. "What about your brother? He was a racer?"

"His was destroyed. Last year's race. Him in it."

"What about the Murgin you spoke with earlier? If they're willing to hold a spot for you, maybe they'll lend you a sub?"

"Like they'd trust you with any sub that belonged to them."

"They don't have to. Tell them you've decided to race. I'm just there to help you."

Isk stared across the hall for several silent seconds. Cade held his breath. He was out of arguments. If Isk didn't accept this, the chance was over.

"Hmph." Isk left the room, pulling the door shut and locking it. The door didn't unlock again that night.

Chapter 5

Cade felt like a colt set free to run as he followed Isk toward the Estate District. Isk trudged along silently. It occurred to Cade that he could easily escape. He knew how to find Gro. And while he'd lost his brother's money, Aidan would forgive him... eventually.

But if he ran now, he might never get another chance to compete in the Tefnot. And due to Isk, he was registered to race now. He had his shot. He couldn't pass this up. All he had to do was win and buy his freedom.

As they reached the water barrier to the Estate District, Cade slipped on his dive mask, then stepped through. The warm water felt great after days without power on Isk's farm, like stepping from a snowstorm into a hot bath.

The District was far more crowded than the last time he'd come. It seemed a lifetime ago. There were Murgin everywhere. Racers, trainers, race officials, fans, and many of the mansions advertised racing merchandise, turning into temporary businesses to capitalize on the Tefnot. It seemed to be a universal fact. Wherever there was a race, sport, or any other competition with fans—anywhere in the universe—you'd also find merchants selling shirts, caps, mugs, and a host of other memorabilia.

The lift current had a long line. Cade made his way toward it, but Isk, impatient, grabbed his arm. "We're swimming up."

Cade wanted to argue he was too slow a swimmer, but Isk was already swimming upward, pulling Cade along with him. With his four legs, Isk propelled the both of them. The extra effort didn't seem to bother the Murgin, and they quickly reached the race mansion. As they neared the entrance, Isk tossed him out of the water to land on the floor with a thud that drew a groan from him. He narrowly avoided colliding with a dark green Murgin, whose fingers were adorned with clams. On Araxia, clams were actually quite rare and prized. The richest Murgin in Amadii had gotten that way as clam merchants, catching the mollusks and turning them into jewelry and other expensive trinkets.

When Cade landed at the Murgin's feet, it sneered, eye cluster wrinkling, before moving off. Cade realized that he had now been tossed both out of and into the same mansion. How many people could say that?

Isk led the way into the great room of the mansion, which was every bit as crowded as outside. A rotund Murgin approached.

"Isk, it's great to see you." The Murgin grabbed Isk by the arm and dragged him forward. "I'm thrilled you're racing in Ilo's honor."

Isk nodded and mumbled something Cade couldn't hear, except for the name, Teze. Isk suddenly looked less than thrilled to be here. In fact, if Cade had to guess, Isk would love nothing more right now than to be home working. Was it the racing or the crowd Isk didn't like? Or both?

"We've got everything set up for your brother's commemoration," Teze said. "And your sub is ready."

"I've got help that will attend to my needs during the race." Isk gestured to Cade.

Cade gritted his teeth, but remained silent.

"Yes, fine," Teze said, not even bothering to look at him.

"Isk, where's my money?" another Murgin asked, approaching out of the crowd. This one was even larger than Teze, and reminded Cade of a giant slug.

Isk puffed his chest out. "Laza, I will pay you when I win."

Laza grunted, bulk quivering. "When you reach the finish line, if you make it, I'll take your farm as payment. But don't worry, I'll still let you work on it."

Isk clenched his hands, arms twisted but stiff like warped wood.

"Cade!" Pushing through the mass of people came Aidan with Gro in tow. Aidan practically launched himself at Cade, wrapping him in a bear hug. Cade struggled for breath. Aidan's long blond hair, soaking wet, tickled Cade's nose, causing him to sneeze.

Standing behind Aidan, Gro wore an expression of relief, as if Cade's disappearance had been all his fault.

"I knew I'd find you here, what with the Tefnot going on," Aidan said as he let Cade go. "Where have you been?"

It was such a relief to see Aidan again, and Gro, that Cade couldn't even speak.

Aidan squeezed him once more, than stepped back. "What happened to you?"

"I..." Cade wasn't sure how to answer the question. He wanted to tell Aidan the truth. But telling the truth now would mean no racing. It also meant revealing what he believed Ansa had done. For some reason he suddenly wasn't ready to, though he couldn't explain his reluctance.

"What is it?" Aidan asked, cocking his head a little at Cade's silence.

"He's racing with me in the Tefnot." Isk stepped forward and looked ready for a fight.

Aidan gaped at Cade. "What is he talking about?"

Gro gave Cade a look of awe at the news.

"Isk needs my help," Cade answered, feeling his face going red, both from the lie and from anticipated embarrassment at what he knew Aidan would do next.

Aidan crossed his arms, head shaking. "No way. You are not racing in the Tefnot."

Before Cade could respond, Isk shoved Aidan back. "He belongs to me and I say he races."

"Belongs?" For a moment Aidan seemed so surprised, he just stood there, eyes wide. For a span of two breaths. Then his brow darkened. "I don't know who you are, but Cade is a citizen of Space City. He *belongs* to no one."

"Excuse me," Laza said, squeezing his bulk in between Aidan and Isk, forcing them away from each other. "Isk, do you have a contract for the boy?"

"Yes."

"Not for long," Aidan shouted. "I will alert the Space City embassy of this slavery violation."

A conch shell struck Aidan in the back of the head, wielded by Teze. Aidan collapsed to the ground. Unable to believe what just happened, but desperate to make sure his brother was okay, Cade dropped to his knees to check on Aidan.

"Isk, I'll make you a deal," Laza said. "This man and the boy in exchange for a two-month reprieve on your debt."

"Aidan, are you okay?"

He didn't move. Cade rolled him over, finding his brother unconscious. But there was no blood on his head. Tears rushed to Cade's eyes.

"Seare," Laza yelled.

The burly guard emerged from a nearby room with three other Murgin of equal size in tow.

"Take these three and chain them up," Laza ordered, pointing out Cade, Aidan, and Gro.

"Wait." Isk stepped forward, shielding them from Laza's men. "I don't care what you do with the older one, but I need the boy for the race."

Laza nodded, and Isk moved aside. Laza's men moved in.

"No!" Cade jumped to his feet to fight off Laza's men. Gro slid to his side, helping him to shield Aidan, but the much larger guards easily shoved them aside, sending Cade sprawling. Despite the number of other Murgin in the building, most pretended not to notice the conflict. The only awareness they displayed was to hurry on about their business a little faster.

Cade rolled over to see two Murgin dragging Aidan's limp form away, while the third seized Gro.

"Stop!" Cade scrambled to his feet and turned to Isk. He was the only one here who might help. "We need them."

"What?" Isk stepped back from them, as if worried this was about to go bad and he wanted to distance himself.

Cade pointed at Gro. "He can fix anything. If we end up needing repairs—and we will, it's the Tefnot—he can do them. And my brother, he's a racer. A better one than I am. With him we're sure to win."

"You can have the Murgin," Laza muttered, gesturing for his man to let Gro go. "The other one stays with me."

Isk shrugged at Cade's pleading gaze. But Cade wasn't going to let this go. He charged after the guards, until a punch to the gut doubled him over. While he gasped for air, arms wrapped around his torso, pinning his own to his sides, and lifted him off his feet. He gasped, struggling to breathe, the fight knocked out of him.

"Get them in a sub," Laza ordered. "Seal them inside if you have to."

Cade hung limply in Teze's arms, desperate to get to Aidan, but his body wouldn't respond. As Teze carried him toward the rear of the mansion, Isk and Gro followed, his friend slumped over, clearly cowed, the last guard at his back. Cade wished Gro would run; escape and alert the authorities. Find someone who could free them. But he followed meekly.

"Gro, go to the Space City Embassy. Tell them what's happened." Cade struggled against his captor. Teze squeezed tighter, like a snake suffocating its victim, until Cade thought he might be sick.

But as Gro eyed the front entrance, weighing the chance of escape, the guard shoved him forward.

"Don't even try," the guard said.

Chapter 6

Cade barely had time to slip on his dive mask before Teze lugged him bodily out the rear of the mansion and back into the water. The mansion had been built close to Amadii's atmosphere bubble, giving them an unobstructed view of the dark ocean surrounding the city. There were no signs of life outside the atmosphere barrier, just a seemingly endless expanse. It was one of those moments that illustrated to Cade just how small he was; how big this world was, and really any world, by comparison.

And he was about to venture into it for the first and possibly last time. Take a sub and race through it. Who knows what he might find? A thrill of anticipation rippled through him and immediately mutated to guilt. How could he be excited about a race with Aidan held captive? He was doing the right thing, as Gro had said. Racing was his best chance at helping Aidan. But he couldn't shake the nagging sensation that he was acting selfish; rationalizing what he wanted to do at his brother's expense. What would Aidan do if their roles were reversed? A part of him insisted that Aidan would be right here making the same decision. But he also felt that might not be an honest assumption.

The Grand Dock was a massive underwater station, which resembled an enormous dam with row upon row of ports from which the major fishing subs launched. Today, the entire city had gathered, crowding the docking ports on every level. Being underwater, if he called for help it would only be muffled. And if anyone thought it strange that Teze was hauling him around like a prisoner, they showed no outward sign.

Teze hauled Cade to a sub that resembled a tank-sized sailfish minus the long, pointed nose. Artificial gills allowed the silver-blue sub to pull in oxygen from the ocean. Cade barely had time to take it in before he was forced through the hatch inside. Teze crawled in after him.

The interior lacked much space. The curved walls were composed of a single, continuous touch screen that served as the interface. There were two chairs toward the bow, a small bathroom in the stern, and a single rack that served as a makeshift galley. It held mostly canned fish or sea plants.

"I guess you want Conn?" Gro asked as he and Isk squeezed through the hatch and passed Teze. The sub's hatchway also had a water shield, allowing Cade to remove his dive mask. The Murgin didn't require such a device, but many other alien races participated in the Tefnot, so subs with the feature were common.

"Do you even know how to steer a sub?" Cade hurried to the right front seat, a little in awe. This was a sub, a S-3RL Shrike. A real classic, though this one hadn't been properly maintained. It was criminal that someone had allowed it to fall into such disrepair!

"Do you?" Gro asked.

"Over a hundred hours simulation time."

"I'm so relieved you're not a Mugie at this," Gro muttered as he hopped into the other seat. "Please don't kill us." His fingers moved rapidly over the wall screen in front of him, running a functionality scan to ensure everything was in good shape.

His job done, Teze slipped out, slamming the hatch closed. Through the starboard side viewing screen, Cade could see Teze guarding the hatch in case they tried to escape. But Cade had given up on that possibility. It was too late for that. Now, he turned his attention to familiarizing himself with the ship's control screens.

Isk milled about awkwardly behind them. The Murgin might as well be useful, so Cade pointed at the starboard wall. "Isk, double-check the fuel tanks to ensure they're full." He hoped Teze had taken care of the sub since they were commemorating Isk's brother, but he wouldn't put it past Laza to set them up to fail.

A smack across the back of the head sent Cade tumbling forward.

"Hey!" Gro half-rose from his chair, but then thought better of it.

"I'm the one giving orders," Isk said. "Don't either of you forget it." He turned and stalked toward the food rack.

As Cade righted himself, Gro sank back into his seat and busied himself with the ship readings, head bowed and shoulders hunched inward. "Gas tanks one hundred percent. We're straight board."

Cade knew that last bit meant the major hull openings were shut, so they were ready to dive. An obvious statement since the sub only had one opening and they were already underwater, but Gro was clearly more excited than he was letting on, despite the threat from Isk. Cade's own adrenaline pumped through him like gas through an engine.

Race officials gave the signal for all racers to prepare to dive. Cade activated the sub's engine. It hummed softly, reminding him of crickets in summer, but was quickly drowned out by the roars of the larger subs. His senses twitched with the volume. He'd been waiting for this moment for over a year. He pinched his cheek to prove to himself that he was actually here. And with a little luck over the next week, they'd have their freedom and he'd have bragging rights when he returned to the academy for his second year.

The countdown began. "Ten. Nine. Eight."

He held his hands ready, counting down himself. They would enter the Nanet Trench first, with its smooth, open waters. They'd have to avoid attacks from other subs straight out of the gates, which he'd prepared for, then follow the Nanet all the way to Kathon, the end of the first leg.

At "One," he executed a dive. The other racers dove as well and shot forward like Olympic swimmers at the start of a heat.

"I'm going to sweep the baffles," Gro announced.

"What's that?" Isk asked, returning with an open can of Needletop fish.

Gro grabbed a short broom from under his chair with two of his legs and offered it to Isk. "Actually, can you sweep the baffles? I need to run sonar to ensure nobody is behind us." With both arms he continued to type away on the wall screen.

Isk looked around the sub, a confused expression on his face. But he took the broom, heading toward the back of the sub. Cade stifled a laugh, not wanting Isk to lose his temper at the prank.

"Look at those boomers." Gro pointed at the much larger subs that had pulled ahead; Cade had activated a video feed on the front wall, like a windshield. He felt most comfortable steering the sub that way.

The boomers were whale-sized subs with crews as large as six, creating an advantage over the smaller sailfish subs. The sailfish accelerated faster and were more maneuverable, but couldn't match the boomers top end speed once they got going. For a weeklong race across an ocean, Cade was going to have to get creative to keep up.

And suddenly the sub pitched wildly to starboard, throwing them. It was accompanied by the deafening sound of metal grinding on metal. Cade hit the front wall and toppled to the floor. Something had hit them from behind. The cabin lights pulsated red as a siren blared. The sub's nose dipped. Cade scrambled to his feet to steer the sub back to zero bubble, otherwise known as level.

"We've been hit," Isk announced redundantly as he pushed himself up from the floor between the seats.

"A boomer," Gro confirmed, typing away on a monitor on his side of the sub. "Someone's trying to knock us out early!"

"I thought you swept the baffles!" Cade couldn't believe they'd already been hit. They'd barely left the dock.

If Gro answered, Cade didn't hear him. The sub groaned as it sank, the controls unresponsive. The engines were offline. As the other subs pushed ahead, Cade tried to restart the engines.

"Running diagnostics," Gro said. In addition to his hands, he began to use two of his feet to tap away on the wall screen at floor level, his head bobbing up and down to monitor what his hands and feet were doing.

A few other subs sank around them, all of the sailfish variety; run over and marooned. The rest entered the Nanet Trench.

"Looks like all the damage is superficial," Gro said, darting toward the engine compartment, also known as the box, next to the escape pod in the bottom middle of the sub. "We were lucky."

"Superficial?" Cade threw his hands up in the air. "The engines are dead. How is that superficial?"

"Not dead. Just got knocked over the head. They're woozy. Give me a second to manually reboot."

Cade growled at the horrible translation of the problem and at himself for his lack of knowledge in that area. He should've learned to do ship repairs, too, instead of spending all his time racing in the simulation. He and Isk were about as useful as Flobs at the moment.

Up from the Nanet Trench swam a school of fish. The school closed quickly, as if fleeing something. Cade studied the trench behind the fish, expecting to see some larger predator in pursuit. The faint outlines of the remaining subs were disappearing into the distance, but that was it. Then Cade realized the school wasn't fleeing.

The fish—roughly the size of his hands clasped together—bore down on one of the other stranded subs.

Cade watched curiously, wondering what drew them. The fish closed in around the sub, completely covering it. They pulsed, as if anxious for something. Or fighting over something.

"Have either of you ever seen anything like this?"

Isk moved up beside him, staring at the screen a second before his eyes widened. "We have to go. We have to get out of here."

"What is it?" Cade asked, the Murgin's reaction chilling him.

Doing a one eighty, Isk shouted at Gro. "Get the engines running. Immediately."

An escape pod shot upward from the fish-covered sub. Once clear, it careened back toward the docks. The racers had fled without even trying to repair their sub. Cade couldn't believe it. Abandoning ship meant they were done. Disqualified.

The school of fish broke away. In their wake was an unrecognizable husk. Broken pieces sank into the trench. If Cade hadn't seen the sub before the fish had attacked, he'd have never known what the remaining scraps had been.

"They ate a sub. Through metal." His voice rose a little high for his own liking.

"Hornteeth," Isk whispered, his hands beginning to shake.

The fish charged another sub, while more swam up from the trench. These, Cade realized, were headed straight for them.

"Hornteeth?" Gro shouted from the escape pod. "There're no hornteeth around here!"

"I'm telling you, those are hornteeth," Isk said, expression wild, though Cade couldn't tell if it was from anger or fear. Probably a bit of both.

Gro made what could only be described as a screech.

"Cade, get ready to undertow it!" his friend yelled.

Dropping into his seat, Cade's hands hovered over the engine controls screen. His eyes darted between them and the rapidly closing hornteeth. He itched to activate the engines and floor it.

"Almost ready."

Before, all he could see was that the fish were a dull gray. Now, Cade could make out the bulbous eyes. A series of thin appendages—which made him think of a turkey tail—stuck out from their rears. And curving down from their mouths were two tusks like a walrus.

"Gro!" Cade shouted as the hornteeth clamped onto the sub. A sound like hail clanged all over the sub. He jumped up from his seat, feeling like he was in a shark cage and unsure if it was strong enough to hold.

"Now! Start the engines!" Gro slammed his arms on the sub floor, pointing for Cade to get them moving.

With a swipe on the control screen, the engines roared to life, drowning out the pounding. Cade accelerated and the sub sprang forward. He activated the exterior hull sensors. Many of the hornteeth hung on in spite of the speed. There was nothing to clear the rest of the creatures off the hull. But now that they were moving again, he had no wish to give up.

"What do I do?" he asked.

"Broach?" Gro asked.

"Too long to reach the surface." Cade activated sonar to scan for other threats.

"We should return to Amadii," Isk suggested.

"That would mean quitting the race," Gro said. "Wait." He pointed out a green line flowing like a river along their viewing screen. "The ocean current."

"Quitting is better than dying." Isk squeezed the back of Cade's chair.

"Trust me," Gro said.

Cade angled northwest. He knew ocean currents were too slow. They couldn't possibly knock the hornteeth off, but he was desperate for any solution. The hull sensors showed a number of the creatures still attached to the sub.

"Get into the current," Gro said as they neared the green flow. "Weave in and out on either side."

Cade followed Gro's instructions, merging into the current, dipping sharply to port, then banking starboard back into the current and out the other side, before repeating. To Cade's genuine surprise, each time they entered the current some of the hornteeth were ripped free. Despite the slow current, the cross-flow was sufficient to knock the creatures loose. Within a few minutes, they'd cleared the hull.

"Damage?" Cade asked, dropping into his seat with a sigh of relief.

Gro had taken the other seat and was already shifting through the ship's computer. "A number of minor hull breaches. I've sent nanos to fill in and seal, but that means running at sixty percent power for the rest of today's leg. Tonight we can get a new hull coat in Kathon."

Antsy about leaving the current, lest more of the hornteeth attack, but knowing they needed to follow the Nanet Trench, Cade redirected the sub. They'd have to push hard to catch up.

"Those hornteeth, how can they eat through a sub?" Cade had never seen anything like it and hoped to never do so again. There were many large aquatic beasts that could ram a sub and break it, but eating through a metal hull was a new one.

"No, head that way." Gro pressed a finger to the viewing screen. The Nanet angled left, but Gro pointed straight at the right wall of the trench.

"What?"

"There's a tunnel straight ahead. It'll be a tight fit, but that'll put us in the Wyna Trench. It's a more direct route." Gro stabbed at the screen again, enlarging the view. "There."

Cade gaped at the narrow mouth of a cave. "Are you kidding?" He couldn't believe Gro had suggested such a move. It would take a steady hand to guide the sub into it. A very steady hand. "How far?"

"About a mile, then it opens up. Then another twelve to the Wyna."

For a minute Cade hesitated, debating if the risk was really worth it this early in the race. This wouldn't be their only opportunity to make up ground, though there'd be just as many opportunities to lose even more.

"Do it." Isk spoke, his earlier cowardice forgotten, as if they were back on the farm. "Catch up or there will be no dinner rations."

Biting his tongue, Cade slowed the sub. He really didn't think this was a good idea, but he followed the direction anyway.

His breath caught in his throat as they approached the cave entrance. He pulled up a second display showing the sub's outline and the cave's walls, allowing him to monitor clearance. If he hit anything, they'd probably die down here.

The hairs on his arms stood up. He sat rigid, afraid to make more than the slightest movements, as if staying immobile kept them safe. The tunnel walls contracted upon them, reducing the margin for error.

"Why are you going so fast?" Gro asked, a tremor in his voice.

"We're at one tenth power," Cade replied. "If I slow any further we'll be parked." His nerves screamed to get out of this tunnel now, but it was too late to turn around, so he pressed forward, focusing on smooth, stable control. Fortunately, Isk kept his mouth shut.

They crept forward until Cade thought he couldn't steer anymore. He was about to ask Gro to take the controls so he could walk away for a moment—he was drained and needed time to breathe and turn off—when the clearance monitor showed the tunnel gradually opening. Before long they could visibly tell the tunnel was widening, allowing Cade to exhale, the tension draining from him. He increased their speed and made minimal adjustments, which became easy again now that they weren't partnered with the threat of destruction.

When they finally reached the tunnel's mouth and exited into open water, Cade jumped to his feet. "Gro, take over."

He walked toward the rear of the sub, breathing deeply, skin tingling. He'd done it. He'd gotten them through. They were still in the race, and with the hour saved, they'd be back within striking distance of the other racers. He still had a chance to win and rescue Aidan.

Chapter 7

"There's a storm brewing on the surface." Gro didn't look up from his navigation. He simply noted the change and kept on working.

"Guess it's a good thing we're down here," Cade answered.

After departing Kathon yesterday morning, they'd had an uneventful day. The same couldn't be said for all the other racers. Two subs had never left port, most likely victims of sabotage. Another three had crashed during the start to the leg. The original field of twenty-four had dropped to fourteen.

The second leg was three days in the open ocean, allowing the boomers to push ahead. They hadn't seen anyone else since midday yesterday. During the night, Cade and Gro had taken shifts so they could each rest while powering on toward Tyne—Isk had refused to take a shift nor wanted to learn to operate the sub on the fly.

"Torpedo!" Gro shouted, pressing his hands against his screen.

"What?" Cade leaned over to see Gro's screen. "From where?"

"At our six. 3K."

Cade steered hard, causing the sub to yaw wildly to starboard. A thump was accompanied by a shout from Isk behind them.

"There." Gro pointed at his screen. Three subs popped up behind them. He scrambled out of his seat and darted toward the rear of the ship.

"Where're you going?" Isk demanded.

"To drop scraps."

With the engines already running at ninety percent, there really wasn't much more Cade could do. There was nowhere to hide the sub. The torpedo was closing in. Based on current speed, they had maybe thirty seconds to impact.

Gro dropped into the box while Cade pivoted his gaze between the viewing screen and the box. Waiting. The torpedo was gaining on them. The three subs trailing them had spread out. And there was nothing he could do.

"On my mark," Gro shouted from the box.

"Cade, be ready," Isk commanded, as if Cade hadn't heard Gro.

"Evade, *now*!" Gro cried.

Cade steered. The sub jerked. On screen, a dozen other points appeared, as if by magic, as the sub angled starboard. The torpedo hit the scraps, exploding and sending a shockwave that shook the vessel, but caused no damage.

Cade whooped. "You did it, Gro! The torpedo is gone!"

The Murgin cheered, but before he could climb back up, three more torpedoes appeared, one from each of the subs.

Cade gaped.

"Uh, Gro. Got any more scraps? Three more incoming."

Gro swore.

"Why are they firing at us?" Isk marched up to see the radar for himself. "Surely, this isn't allowed."

"They aren't racers," Gro replied. "Most likely smugglers waiting to ambush isolated subs. Particularly small ones like us."

"Do something. Fix this." Isk glared at Cade as if this were all his doing.

Cade pushed the sub to one hundred percent acceleration, knowing as he did so that it wouldn't be enough. And out here in the open, no amount of fancy maneuvering would avert their fate.

Tears sprang up in his eyes. He blinked them back, but Isk had already noticed.

"This is no time to cower like a Mugie. What are our options?"

Cade just stared blankly at him, unable to come up with any solution. So Isk grabbed him by the shoulders and hurled him across the floor. Isk marched toward him, looking bent on beating him to a pulp.

Then Gro was standing between them. "We have to abandon ship. There's nothing more to do."

Isk clenched his fists as he regarded Gro. "You don't want to interfere."

But Gro turned and pointed at the escape pod. "You can either attack us and die, or get in the escape pod."

When Isk said nothing further, Gro grabbed Cade's arm and dragged him to his feet. Cade didn't resist, though a part of him wanted to go down with the ship. Like captains of old on Earth. It was more dignified than being a slave on Amadii, though he would die knowing he'd consigned Aidan to that fate.

Gro forced Cade down into the pod, which didn't have much room for the three. Cables, rods, and other parts Cade couldn't name lined the escape pod. Gro slammed the lid shut overhead and activated a new radar on a small screen. "We've got to wait until right before impact."

"What?" Cade asked, eyes bulging. "We'll be caught in the blast."

"The escape pods are heavily reinforced. We'll be fine. We can't let them know we've escaped."

Cade dropped to a crouch, leaving it all to his friend, hoping he knew what he was talking about. Gro watched until the torpedoes were on top of the sub. Then he ejected the pod. Cade closed his eyes, unable to believe their race was over. He hadn't even made it halfway.

The pod dropped like an anchor. Overhead, the torpedoes struck the sub, but there was no explosion. The ship and torpedoes remained clustered together on radar. Had they all been duds?

Frowning, Cade stood and opened a viewing screen on the ceiling. The torpedoes had latched on to the sub. Seconds later, the sub sank after them. Gro let their pod sink as well to avoid alerting their attackers. He didn't even send out a distress beacon. They couldn't do so without giving themselves away.

The other subs approached slowly, like predators circling, waiting for their quarry to die.

As the escape pod sank, Gro gave it short bursts of power, just enough to guide them out from beneath the sinking sub. Seconds later, they hit bottom and Gro powered everything down, leaving them in darkness.

They waited, listening. Everything was muffled. Was that the sound of engines? No. The other subs couldn't have spotted them. Gro had done too good a job. Except there hadn't been an explosion, so there was no reason for pieces of the sub to be falling away from the rest.

Something clamped on to either side of the escape pod, giving it a little shake.

"What do we do?" Gro asked, voice cracking.

Cade shook his head, then realized Gro wouldn't see him in the dark. They began to rise, their escape pod lifted by whatever had found them. "They know we're here. Might as well power back up."

A few seconds later, the interior lights came on. The viewing screen in the ceiling re-activated, revealing a sub overhead. A hole was opening in its bottom. The escape pod was being lifted into the sub, a birth in reverse. Cade wished they had some sort of weapons to defend themselves with, but they hadn't counted on being hijacked.

The hatch opened, along with a door up into the sub. Bright light from the sub blinded him, forcing him to shield his eyes, but he could see the outlines of multiple figures above.

"Would you like to come aboard, Cade?"

He dropped his hand, recognizing the feminine voice. For a few seconds, a dark figure was surrounded by a ring of light, like an eclipse. His eyes adjusted to the light, revealing Ansa.

"It was you." Cade clenched his fists, trying to come to grips with the fact that she had attacked them. And it had been her before. This proved it. "Why are you doing this?"

"What? Rescuing you?" She offered a hand to pull him up. Two large Murgin and a Malsain were with her, all with dark expressions.

"Rescue? You hijacked us." Cade struggled to pull himself up into the sub, wanting to confront her face to face, but couldn't reach high enough to lift himself; the Malsain grabbed him by the shoulders and easily pulled him into the sub, much to his chagrin. The Malsain held a short rifle and its forked lizard tongue tasted the air, ready for violence. While Cade hesitated, one of the Murgin moved behind him and handcuffed him.

Ansa stepped forward, a gloating smile on her face, and patted him on the cheek. "We can get a good price for your sub, even one in as bad a shape as that one."

Gro and Isk climbed up on their own, adding insult to injury for Cade. The Murgin quickly cuffed both of them as well, though Isk struggled and shouted to be released.

"And before? That was you, wasn't it? Drugged me and sold me as a slave?" Cade leaned forward, face a snarl, but the Malsain pointed the end of its rifle at his chest, halting him.

"What can I say? You're worth good money. Will be again." She turned and walked away as if he were dismissed.

He wanted to charge after her, to make her understand what he'd gone through. What he was going through. And Aidan. "Aidan's now a prisoner thanks to what you did."

She kept on walking. No pause. No hesitation. She didn't even look back.

Chapter 8

"I'm a Murgin. You can't sell me," Isk shouted. With his hands handcuffed behind his back as he stood down in the escape pod, he was all bluster. "And you can't sell Cade. You sold him to me."

Cade debated pointing out that Isk had had no qualms about Laza trying to take Gro as a slave back in Amadii, but there was no point. Besides, he couldn't help but enjoy Isk's current position. It was a small silver lining to this madness.

Ansa simpered. "I'd say that's good business savvy, selling a slave twice. His master included the second-go-round." After connecting their sub to hers for towing, she'd returned to get the access codes from Isk to turn off the GPS so no one could track them. He'd gladly handed them over, hoping to curry favor with her, before he realized she intended to sell him, too.

"You're getting maybe fifty thousand pearls for the sub and us?" Gro asked her.

"Close enough," she replied.

"What if we doubled it?"

Cade gaped at Gro, wondering where he was going with this. His parents didn't have that kind of money lying around or they'd be living in the Estate District.

Ansa rolled her eyes. "You haven't got twenty."

"We will after we win the Tefnot," Gro said.

She motioned for the Malsain to put Cade and Gro back in the escape pod, as she turned to walk away.

Gro struggled against the Malsain, who shoved him backward. "We can win if you help me with some performance modifications while we complete this leg."

"No!" Cade scowled, unable to believe what Gro was suggesting. "Upgrades during the race are illegal." And he wanted to win the race, not fix it.

"Do you want to get Aidan back from Laza or not?" Gro asked.

"I can still win the race and rescue Aidan without cheating," Cade insisted. But even as he said the words he knew that was likely a lie. They'd lost a lot time when Ansa attacked them and had already been a good distance behind. "That is if Ansa stops screwing us."

She returned, eyes flashing, her nose scrunched up. "You should stop blaming others for your troubles."

"You are the *source* of my troubles!" Cade shouted.

"And yet you've done nothing to stop me. If you won't take the necessary steps to defend yourself properly, that's on you. You're responsible for you."

He huffed, unable to come up with a response.

She reached out a hand and squeezed his arm. "I've got a crew to employ, and this is business," she said, as if it was supposed to make him feel better.

He jerked his arm away and nearly fell back into the escape pod in the process; he collided with the ship wall and steadied himself. As he did so, he studied Ansa's sub. It was nearly double the size of their own and littered with crates and random device parts.

"I'll tell you what." Ansa turned to Gro. "Make it two-hundred-and-fifty thousand and you've got a deal."

The Malsain turned on her. "This is a bad idea. We should sell them to our usual buyer." The hiss of the Malsain's own tongue behind the tradutor's translation emphasized his words.

Ansa whipped out a gun and pressed it against the Malsain's chest before he realized what she'd done. "Maybe I should sell you, too. Hmm?"

The air around all of them was suddenly thick, as the Malsain regarded her coldly. After a few tense seconds, the Malsain backed away.

Ansa turned back to them. "Do we have a deal?"

Cade gritted his teeth, wanting nothing to do with her deal, but Gro spoke up. "We have to… for Aidan." Cade swallowed and nodded.

Ansa chuckled. "The funny thing is, selling you got us the money to repair this sub, which allowed us to ambush you, and now sell you and your sub back to you." Cade hated the amusement in her voice. "Is that irony? Cause if not, it sounds like it should be."

Before he could come up with a reply, Gro spoke up. "Let's get to work."

*****

An hour before the start of the next leg, Gro, with the help of Ansa's two Murgin, wrapped up modifications to their sub. They'd worked all through the night while Cade got the sub to Tyne and docked. The Malsain had brought Ansa's sub covertly from a distance.

While waiting, Ansa had made Cade, Gro, and Isk sign a contract stating that she was an investor in their team, with her payout being twenty-five percent of the race winnings; Isk had argued that this was his sub, not Cade's or Gro's, but Ansa insisted they all sign. And now that they'd made the illegal modifications, they couldn't accuse her of anything. Not to mention that winning was Cade's only means of freeing himself or Aidan.

As Ansa and her crew made their way to the hatch, she patted Cade's arm one last time. "Good luck."

He growled, focusing on the ships control screen to avoid looking at her. She stood over him a moment before departing. Gro came up to join him, dropping into the other chair, whistling.

"Cut out the whistling," Isk snapped. "I hope you were competent with your upgrades. I don't want them to cost me the race."

Gro leaned forward, peering over the path Cade had chartered while he'd been busy with the modifications. "With the power I've added, we'll win the Tefnot. I'm sure of it."

"And if we do?" Cade asked. "You realize we now owe Ansa a quarter of what we promised to Laza in exchange for our freedom? Aidan's, too."

Gro sobered. "I solved this problem. It was the shark closest to the city. Now you have to win the Tefnot. Then we figure out Laza." He began to redraw segments of the path Cade had plotted out for them, likely finding shortcuts.

"I'll deal with Laza and Ansa," Isk said. "Just win the race."

Cade ignored the false bravado. There was nothing Isk could do to get them out of this situation. Only Gro would be of help. He was lucky to have his friend here with him. Cade hadn't anticipated how much more there was to winning the Tefnot beyond simply racing. Without Gro, he wouldn't have made it far from the starting line. He might not have even made it onto the sub. Now here they were, among the final racers in the Tefnot, and it was all thanks to Gro's efforts.

The race leaders received the go-ahead and started forward. A thirty-second countdown commenced, giving them a head start before the next line was off. Willing the clock to run faster, it was all Cade could do to sit there and wait while the other subs opened up a lead. Even with three days left, every second mattered. Every meter those subs travelled made it that much harder for him to win. Or to get Aidan back.

"Go, go, go!" Gro slapped the arm of Cade's chair.

"Quit slacking off and wasting our precious time," Isk shouted, as if it had been Cade's fault the others had a head start.

Pushing the engines to full throttle, Cade steered the sub ahead. As it accelerated, he could feel the increased power, almost as if Gro had tripled their engines. Despite the increased speed, by the time they got to start the leg, the leaders had opened up a large enough lead that it took Cade a full two days to catch up.

When they were about a half day's journey from Amadii, a giant net wall appeared ahead, stretched for miles across their path. Enormous signs on the netting warned them.

DANGER!

DIVE

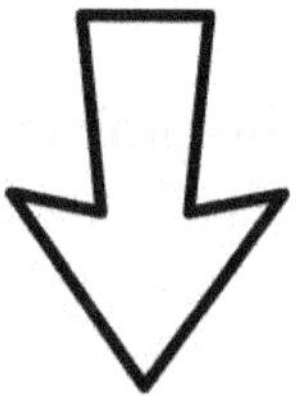

Wondering what could be behind the net wall, Cade plunged the sub into a jagged, tangled landscape, filled with strange stone arches and barriers. It looked like an ancient city that had crumbled and sank into the ocean, though they were nowhere near land. Cade decelerated to twenty-five percent power.

Passing around a bend, they spotted another sub skewered on a jagged mound beside a narrow hole it's pilot had tried to slip through. An escape pod dropped from the sub. On the emergency band, the downed sub was sending out a distress call.

The wreckage forced Cade to veer far to the right, seeking another way forward; the larger subs would've needed a larger passageway. He could see them on radar ahead, and from their slow pace, they were still in this maze. Unfortunately, the sonar couldn't show them a route through.

As he steered them ahead, he marveled at large pillars and stone edifices that looked artificial one moment, natural the next depending on the viewing angle. He guessed there had to be some ancient Murgin something here, city or otherwise, but time and seawater had worn it down. Assimilating it.

"What was this place?" Cade asked.

"The Coventina," Gro replied, face grim. "It was the greatest city on Araxia before the asteroid strike more than a thousand years ago. Like an island paradise. But it was close enough to ground zero that the shockwave sunk it."

"Wow." As he studied the landscape, Cade began to pick out structures that reminded him of some of the homes on Amadii.

Passing around a last line of gnarled rocks, Cade realized why the larger subs were still going so slow. They weren't still trapped in the maze.

They were under attack.

Isk croaked.

Cade's mouth went dry. Whipping in a frenzy around the other subs were dozens of enormous beasts that resembled giant eels with webbed fans around their heads. The creatures rammed the subs. One large sub, dark without power, sank toward the ocean floor, an eel wrapped around it, squeezing.

"Emergency dive!" Gro screamed.

Cade steered sharply downward. With the increased power from the upgrades, it took only a few seconds to reach the sandy bottom. He quickly powered down, hoping the beasts wouldn't notice them. They sat in silence, unmoving. A shadow passed overhead.

Cade didn't dare to breathe. Or move. He was terrified any noise would alert the creatures to their presence. The rest of the subs were in disarray. They floundered, escape pods firing off in rapid succession. Cade caught something about Eelsin Dragers attacking. But how would emergency crews provide aid without becoming the next fodder? It wasn't long before all the subs had crashed to the ocean floor.

"What now?" Gro whispered.

Transfixed by the destruction, Cade shook his head. What could they do without becoming the next victims?

With all the subs down, the Eelsin Dragers lost interest in them; they'd defended their territory, crushed these metal invaders. The creatures milled about for a short time overhead, before finally drifting off.

"Do we go?" Isk asked, voice quiet for the first time Cade could remember. "They're gone, right?"

Gro shrugged. "I don't know. We might draw them back. Maybe we should wait for emergency personnel?"

Two other subs powered up and rose. Large subs with numerous dents.

"Let's get out of here." Cade brought their systems back online. If the large subs thought the way forward was safe, he wanted to stick with them. They couldn't lose ground at this juncture.

As they passed over the downed subs—one split completely in half and flooded—escape pods began to shoot up. Cade counted, relieved when one ejected from the broken sub. But as they reached and passed the final downed sub, its escape pod hadn't been deployed. He double-checked the number of pods overhead versus downed ships, confirming there was one too few.

"Gro, contact that sub." He pointed it out while he simultaneously reduced speed.

Gro opened a direct comm link with the other sub. "Sub seventeen, are you okay?" No response. "Sub seventeen, are you in need of assistance?"

Cade zoomed in the display window and discovered a gaping hole in one side of the crashed sub. If anyone was trapped inside, they'd need help now. Rescue crews wouldn't arrive fast enough.

"Sub seventeen, are you in need of assistance?" Gro repeated.

A hoarse voice finally responded. "We're in our escape pod, but something is blocking us. We can't fully eject."

"I'm setting us down next to them." Cade initiated the descent.

"No!" Isk grabbed Cade's arm roughly, stopping him. "We have to catch up with the other subs. They'll be fine until rescue crews arrive. Escape pods come with more than enough air for them to wait it out."

But Cade felt sick at the thought of abandoning the trapped racers. "We don't know that. They need our help." He tried to pull his arms free, but Isk's grip tightened.

"We have to win to save ourselves," Isk said. "Are you willing to lose your brother to help them? Because if we don't get that money for Laza, I guarantee you'll never see your brother again."

Cade grimaced. He wanted to win this race. Wanted it badly. So that he could make things right with Aidan. But if he left these trapped racers to die, nothing would ever be right between them again.

"Ask their status," Cade said.

"Sub seventeen, what's your status?" Gro asked. "Will you make it until emergency rescue arrives?"

For several seconds there was no response, then, "I... I don't know. One of our air tanks seems to be malfunctioning."

"Let me go," Cade demanded, yanking his arm free of Isk's grasp.

In response, Isk lifted him from the chair. "No! I'm not losing my farm for them. You belong to me. You will do as I command."

Cade wanted to scream. He was so sick of Isk. The slaver had done nothing to help them throughout this race. He'd taken the lion's share of their food supply. And the constant physical and verbal abuse—

Then Gro tackled Isk. They all fell to the hull in a heap. Isk let Cade go as he struggled to break free. Gro shoved the slaver down, pinning him. Isk had a little bit of size advantage, but Gro had the leverage, and Cade jumped over to assist, grabbing one of Isk's arms. Isk wriggled and fought, bucking them and cursing. It was all Cade could do to keep Isk's arm pinned down.

A moment later, Gro had a pair of handcuffs in one hand, which he slapped on Isk's left wrist. "Give me his other arm."

"Where did you get those?" Cade asked, as they forced Isk over onto his belly so they could cuff him behind his back.

"Kept the one Ansa used on me. With everything that's been going on, I thought we might need it."

With Isk restrained, they grabbed him beneath his shoulders and dragged him to the back of the sub.

"You're going to pay for this," Isk snarled at them, casting Cade a look that would've given him pause back on the farm. No more.

While Isk hurled curses at them, Cade hurried back to his chair and guided their sub down beside the other. "What do we do?" While he wanted to help, he didn't know any practical means of aiding the other racers.

"We don't have the equipment to remove whatever is prohibiting them from ejection," Gro replied, hopping down into their own escape pod and removing a pair of diving suits from a compartment. He offered one to Cade, who joined him in the pod.

Cade started to slip the suit on. "What then? How do we get them out?"

"We can't," Gro replied. "But they don't need to get out. They just need air."

"So we take them some of ours," Cade said, following Gro's reasoning.

"Exactly. They have a bad air tank in their escape pod, we have spares."

Once they were in their suits, Gro closed their escape pod hatch and separated from the sub. He guided it around and set it down near the other team's pod, which was jammed three quarters of the way out by a boulder-sized piece of metal.

"That's why they can't fully eject," Gro said through the suits' built-in comm system. "Did you see the hole in the other side of the sub? I bet that's the missing piece."

"You're right. We won't move that out of the way."

Gro activated the pressure seal on the escape pod exit and opened the hatch. The seal allowed them to leave, but kept water or pretty much anything else from coming back in.

Cade climbed out, feeling a momentary shock of cold from the water, before the suit's heater's kicked in. They weren't powerful enough to completely warm him, but enough to keep him from going numb. He took in his surroundings, as much as he could see in the darkness this far down. Mostly sand, rocks, and some sea plants. A part of him feared the Eelsin Dragers might attack again, materializing out of the darkness. Or something worse.

A shiver ran up his spine. He jumped when Gro tapped him on the shoulder and waved him over. Cade swam after as friend, but kept a lookout for threats. Long, reed-like plants covered most of the ocean floor. Cade wondered what might be lurking down under them.

Gro opened a panel in the side of their escape pod, revealing an air tank. It took him a few minutes, while Cade nervously studied their surroundings, to disconnect the tank.

"Help me with this." Gro grunted as he pulled the tank free. "It's heavy."

Cade grabbed the handle, grunting from the effort. It weighed them down, dropping them to the sea floor. They were forced to walk through the reeds toward the other escape pod, dragging it along, which kicked up dust that made it even harder to see. With each step, Cade searched for movement, anxious that something would grab his feet and pull him down, and from there…but they managed to haul the tank to the other escape pod without incident.

While Gro set about opening the panels to identify which air tank was malfunctioning, Cade kicked his feet up so he was floating above the reeds, giving him a small measure of comfort.

"We are working on replacing your bad air tank with one of our spares. Should have it in place before long," Gro announced over comm.

"Thank you!"

"Thanks!"

"You're a lifesaver!"

Cade nodded. "We found a piece of your ship wedged against your escape pod. We can't move it. You'll have to wait for emergency rescue to get out, but with our spare air tank you should be fine."

"Understood," the earlier hoarse voice replied.

Gro slapped Cade on the arm and waved him over. He'd managed to locate and remove the bad air tank. Now they grabbed their spare, rotated it sideways to align with the escape pod, and raised it up into the open slot. Gro re-attached it.

"We've got it in place," Gro said. "How's your air readings?"

"It's seeing the new tank," the hoarse voice replied. "I think we're good now."

"Great. We're going to go back to our ship, but we'll stay until help arrives just in case."

"We owe you, big time."

Cade and Gro swam back to their escape pod, and removed their suits once they were back inside. Cade was relieved to have gotten back safely. He leaned back against a wall, resting, while Gro guided them back to their sub. He hoped he'd never have to do that again.

When they reattached, they climbed back up to find Isk sitting in Cade's chair, trying to steer the sub with his face, hands still handcuffed behind his back. He swore at them when they entered.

"I locked all the screens before I left," Gro said. "Without my passcode, it's not moving."

"I'll kill you both," Isk screamed, gills flaring. "You've cost me everything."

They grabbed him by the arms again, hauling him from the chair. He tried to lunge at Cade, snapping with his jaws. Cade lurched back, avoiding the bite, then hauled back and punched him. Isk's head reeled back.

"You'll never do anything to me again," Cade growled, and they dumped Isk at the back of the sub once more. If he managed to get out of this, he'd make sure Space City investigated how widespread slavery was on Araxia. He hoped it was uncommon, but found himself reluctant to ask Gro about it.

"What now?" Gro asked.

"Wait on emergency rescue, I guess."

It took four hours for crews to arrive, ten subs in all. And Cade was thrilled to see them. All ten were enormous subs with lights that cut through the darkness like lighthouses. One angled toward them. When it was close, it sent them a direct message.

"Identify yourselves," a voice ordered. The tone was stern, with an air of authority.

"We're sub twenty-three," Gro replied. "We were competing in the Tefnot."

"Are you in need of medical assistance?"

"No," Gro replied. "But our companion sub is. They can't eject their escape pod. We stopped to help. Wanted to make sure they were all right until you arrived."

"So nothing is wrong with your ship?"

"No. We just didn't feel right continuing on when fellow racers needed our help."

"Commendable of you," the voice said. "Well, I guess that makes you the winners then."

Cade blinked.

Gro gaped, pausing for a moment. "Sir, can you repeat that?"

"I said, you're the winners of the Tefnot."

"But how can that be?" Gro asked. "Two other subs continued on toward Amadii ahead of us."

"They didn't make it far before they were attacked by the Eelsin Dragers. You're the last working sub in the race. We've been listening to the race broadcast on our way. Everyone thought all the ships were out. A lot of fans and bettors were pissed. All you have to do is proceed to Amadii. We've got things now."

Gro turned to him, a stunned look on his face. Cade imagined he wore the same expression. They had won the Tefnot? It didn't seem possible.

"Congratulations," the voice on the comm channel said. "I've radioed back to Amadii, and they've confirmed that you are the only remaining sub in the race. You are the winners."

Gro jumped up and down, screaming. "We won the Tefnot! We won!"

Cade pumped his hands into the air, elation welling up inside him. They'd actually done it. They'd won the Tefnot!

Then he remembered the other sub they'd encountered back in the maze of Coventina.

"There's one other crew that needs rescuing, back in the maze," Cade said. "Wanted to make sure they aren't missed."

For a moment there was no response, then the captain of the other ship spoke. "That is confirmed. We have their coordinates and one of the rescue subs is in route. Now get going! Congratulations again."

Cade didn't have to be told twice. He activated the engines and began ascent.

Chapter 9

It took them three hours to reach Amadii. As they debarked—first uncuffing Isk, unfortunately—Cade had considered using the momentary spotlight to request help in freeing Aidan, but Teze had intercepted them, warning them that any public accusations would have repercussions. Teze had herded them through acceptance of a trophy and the winner's earnings, ensuring they never had an opportunity to speak with anyone alone.

Now, as Teze led them back toward Laza's mansion, three armed bodyguards ringing them, Cade wondered if paying Laza the winner's earnings would earn them their freedom. The Murgin couldn't just let them go without fallout from Space City. Would Laza take the money and enslave them anyway? Or simply dispose of them?

And where was Ansa? He had been surprised that she wasn't waiting for them at the finish line to collect her share of the earnings.

He didn't have time to ponder her further before Teze led them back to Laza's mansion. In the middle of the room, Aidan sat, hands chained behind his back, surrounded by Laza and a dozen Murgin guards. Aidan's red-rimmed eyes had bags. His shoulder-length blonde hair was tangled. And he reeked like he'd been locked up in a hot cell since before the weeklong race.

Cade mustered up a false bravado. "Let us go. We won the race. I have your money."

Laza wore a pleased expression as Teze handed him the bank data chip with the winner's earnings. "You did. I don't know how, but I was cheering for you."

Of course you did, you wanted the money, Cade thought.

Isk stepped forward, chest puffed out, and seized Cade's arm. "I believe that takes care of my farm debt. Now, if you'll excuse me, I'm a week behind on work. My slave and I need to get to it."

Cade yanked free. "I'm not your slave anymore."

But Laza simply nodded at Isk. The nod was like another blow. Cade had anticipated that Laza wouldn't simply let him walk, but to end up back where he started. To have won the race and it mean nothing. And this time without the hope that Gro or Aidan were out there looking for him. Instead, they'd be enslaved as well. Thanks to him.

He wanted to run to Aidan and fight to free him. Or to apologize and beg for forgiveness for having put him through this torture. Gro as well. Would this be his life from now on? A series of rock bottoms, showing him that things could always get worse.

Canisters clanged off the floor, interrupting his thoughts. Gas from the canisters sprayed outward, filling up the room. Shouts of shock and anger turned to coughing fits. Laza barked orders to his guards, shouting at them to keep him and Teze safe, as well as repel the intruders.

Within seconds, the gray gas had filled the room, making it impossible to see more than a couple feet in any direction. Cade stumbled toward Aidan's silhouette, aware of movement all around him, but all he wanted to do was get to his brother.

Someone slammed into Cade's back, knocking him to the floor. He gasped, rigid with shock. He tried to fight, to free himself and crawl toward Aidan, all the while coughing from the gas. His arms were wrenched behind his back and chained. He was left lying there.

So he wormed his way toward his brother. "Aidan, are you all right?"

His brother grunted noncommittally.

The most Cade could manage was to roll to a sitting position beside his brother. He coughed fitfully. Was the gas lethal? He tried to hold his breath, but couldn't stop coughing, already feeling short of air. His lungs burned with the effort.

Several figures with gas masks fought with the Murgin guards. Well, fought wasn't really the right term since the guards were mostly doubled over or fleeing, except those already sprawled unconscious on the floor.

A giant gust, as from an enormous fan, swept through the room, driving away the gas. By the time the smoke cleared, Laza, Teze, and a number of the guards lay disabled and restrained around the room. One of the intruders approached Cade and removed their gas mask.

Ansa stood over Cade, smiling. "You've really got the damsel in distress thing down."

He could do no more than cough, trying to clear out his lungs, but he managed a glare. Here she was again. A third time.

"Guess you're here for your money?"

She reached out and rubbed his chin as if he was a cute puppy. "Once Gro told me Aidan had been taken by Laza, I knew you'd need my help."

He wanted to remind her that they wouldn't be in this position if it wasn't for her, but she'd already shifted responsibility back to him.

She turned her attention to Aidan. "You look terrible. I didn't know you'd take losing me so hard."

Aidan's eyes blinked slowly, uncomprehendingly, his chin slumped to his chest. So Anza turned her attention to Laza, strolling over.

"Untie me," the Murgin demanded. "How dare you!"

She reached into Laza's shirt pocket and removed the bank chip.

"You'll regret this girl," Laza spat.

She didn't respond, instead turning back to Cade and exaggeratedly slipping the chip into a pocket in her gray jacket. "I'll just take this for my troubles, damsel." Then she motioned to her compatriots and started toward the entrance. As she passed by Cade's back, she knelt and uncuffed him. "This should make us even. Try to look out for yourself going forward, huh?"

Cade rubbed his wrists, but said nothing. What else was there to say? At least she had set them free. Instead, he freed Gro and together they hauled Aidan to the Space City Embassy. They'd be back for Laza, Isk, Teze, and the rest.

And one day he'd catch up with Ansa, too.

THE END

Space City Outbreak

Following is a sample from the third book in the SPACE CITY series, SPACE CITY OUTBREAK:

Chapter 1

Neil as Team Captain: Day One

Yellow sand dunes yielded to a wall of giant red sequoias. Neil stood on the line demarcating the desert and forest, heat baking the left side of his face while a cool breeze caressed his thick curly hair around his right ear. The sequoias were tall enough that they should cast shadows over the first row of sand dunes. Instead, the shadows ended at a line parallel to Neil's left foot, so that they looked headless.

"This is as great as your flying Venice sim," Neil said, sidestepping into the desert and bumping Nico Colombo as he did. The wind vanished and the heat from the sun toasted his bare skin; sensors in his silver Space City suit activated a cooling feature that kept him from burning up.

Anand and Devika Singh, twin brother and sister, trudged up a dune in search of the next base—the second of three that Neil requested Nico set up. Anand's bald head glistened with sweat and he looked to have gained more weight over the summer. As team captain, Neil would have to talk with Anand about slimming down a bit. Team grades at the Space City Preparatory Academy were more significant in year two, and he wouldn't keep up if he didn't get in better shape. Devika, by contrast, ran stairs in the Games stadium every day.

Jiro Takeda and Eris Zeigler hunted around the sequoias, in case one of the trees served as a secret entrance to the base. As the best shooter in their year, Eris' assignment to their team was a major coup as far as Neil was concerned. And Jiro, with his short, spindly frame made a great scout.

Rounding out the team, Dirk Fischer and Trini Flores floated around the crowns of the sequoias, dodging the occasional impossibly obese turkey with hummingbird wings; you could get away with defying physics in virtual worlds. But instead of hunting for the second base, the pair debated the merits of the new treaty between Space City and the Ukka on Letos; nevertheless, both were skilled Games players, making them ideal teammates for the increased field exams they'd encounter in year two.

Neil had been a little surprised when he'd learned the pair would be on his team. After all, Dirk was in his final year at the Academy, while Trini was in her third. But for some classes, the Academy mixed the second through fourth year students together a little more. It was going to take Neil a little time to get used to handing out orders to older students. That's why he had asked Nico to create the sim for them. Neil wanted to get a jump on the new year by leading the team through a series of tasks, so he could get used to giving orders, and so they'd get comfortable working together. Nico wasn't on the team, but his virtual settings were so stunning that Neil couldn't pass on one for their excursion.

Studying the map on his wrist-comp again, Neil strode across the dividing line from the desert into the forest. He shivered from the noticeable change in temperature, like exiting a hot tub and jumping straight into a pool. The base should be close by. They were inside the base perimeter, shown as a red circle on his wrist-comp map, but Nico had disguised it well.

Anand and Devika started shouting, drawing Neil's attention. Had they found the base entrance? But the twins raced down a sand dune, waving at them to run. Seconds later, a horde of small brown toads topped the dune behind the siblings, as well as every other dune in the area. A biblical plague descending upon them.

Neil tensed, unsettled by the sheer number of toads headed their way, but unsure how seriously to take the threat. After all, they were *toads*. "Nico, what danger level did you put the sim on?"

"It's not fun without a little danger." Nico scratched at the birthmark on the left side of his neck. "And their spikes are poisonous."

He started to dash into the forest. Neil grabbed a handful of Nico's suit and pulled him up short.

"What're you saying?" Neil asked. "Is the poison lethal? Did you set the sim to match reality?"

That had been a nasty surprise during Nico's Venice sim. The Malsain—an alien race possessing greenish-yellow scales, a forked tongue, and a stench that could make you lose your lunch from the day before, and everything else you'd eaten since then—had developed a high danger setting for the sims to mimic real life. Dangers faced could cause as much physical harm as if they were in the real world. To Neil, that was insane. The Malsain, on the other hand, turned up their collective scaled noses at sims that did anything less than perfectly mimic the real world and the dangers it posed. For some reason, thrill seekers onboard Space City had embraced the high danger setting. Nico was apparently one of those thrill seekers.

That's why Neil had told Nico, repeatedly, not to do that for this excursion.

"It won't kill anyone, but it'll probably hurt pretty badly," Nico mumbled with a guilty expression. "The spikes shouldn't pierce our suits."

"And if they get skin instead of suits?"

"You *may* want to die." Nico tugged free of Neil's grasp and took off.

They must be in the medium danger setting then. On low, there was no real threat in a sim. It was all an elaborate ruse. You could see, touch, smell, even taste, but it was an illusion. The sim tricked your mind into believing things were real. It was primarily used for first-years. For medium danger, the Academy wanted students to take threats more seriously, so they could feel varying levels of pain.

And while Nico had followed his instructions, he hadn't taken it easy on them.

As Neil turned back to check the twin's progress, his mouth went dry as the swarm of toads grew exponentially, new ones cresting the closest sand dunes every second. Why hadn't he clarified the threats with Nico before they entered the sim? As a team captain, he should've known everything before they'd started, same as if he were leading the group on a mission to a real planet. If this had been a class, the instructors would've been docking his leadership scores heavily right about now.

He retreated past the first line of sequoias where Jiro and Eris pointed at the oncoming toads, prepared to lay down cover fire for the twins.

"Poisonous? Really?" Eris demanded, casting a glare at Nico.

He chuckled, eyes darting back and forth between Eris and the toads, as if he were unsure who he should be more afraid of.

"Dirk, Arielle, can you help us out?" Neil called over his tradutor—the language translator and comm device was standard equipment for all exploration.

"Devika, sure. I'm on it," Dirk answered.

"I'll get Devika," Arielle corrected as she flew past Dirk toward the twins. "You get Anand."

"Oookay. I guess I'll get Anand." Dirk followed her.

"Nico, where's shelter?" Neil asked. They couldn't deal with all the toads headed their way. Watching them, he felt a little like a cricket about to get swarmed by multiple ant colonies. His instincts to run were almost overpowering.

"There's a grove to the East." Nico shifted his feet, clearly ready to get moving. "The toads won't enter it."

Arielle guided her scooter down alongside Devika, who refused to leave Anand until Dirk had rescued him. Dirk drew up next to Anand, so he could jump aboard. But when Dirk tried to lift off, the scooter rose no more than two feet off the ground.

"Nico, you should embargo Anand's candy supply for a while," Dirk complained.

Dirk and Anand had a good twenty yards on the toads, but the horde was gaining ground. Neil blinked once, activating his new Academy-issued contacts. The thought-controlled contacts could change their vision in a number of useful and surprising ways. He wanted to zoom in for a better look, and the contacts gave him a close up. Their backs were covered with little needles, much like a porcupine, but there was a greenish sheen to them. The poison Nico had mentioned?

It made his skin crawl. An image came unbidden of those needles piercing his skin over his entire body. He shivered and forced the vision away. He debated asking Nico to identify the toxin, but at this point the knowledge wouldn't do him much good.

Once the scooters were within range, Neil ordered the rest of the team to clear out the nearest toads to give their teammates breathing room. There were so many toads bunched together that they barely had to aim to score a hit. But for every one they shot, countless more remained. At ten yards out, Neil tossed a light grenade over the scooters, sending a mass of toads flying in all directions.

The toads had reached the forest and swarmed around and past the trees the way invaders stormed broken castle gates.

"All right, to the grove." Neil waved for everyone to get moving.

Unlike the toad army pursuing them, Neil and the team were hindered by the massive sequoias. He felt like a slalom skier as he detoured around them; despite the trees, they managed to stay ahead of the toads.

A nip of his ear caused him to duck in surprise. He swatted over his head, half afraid one of the toads had caught him. Instead, a pudgy turkey with a sharp beak dive bombed him, pecking at his ears. Others joined in, attacking the entire team. The turkeys also attacked the toads, swallowing them whole.

Neil pointed the fingers of his right hand at the closest turkey and fired a laser straight into its beak. It squawked and veered away.

"Almost there," Nico called over the tradutor. "A little south of where we started."

Neil modified his course, stumbling as his foot hit a root poking up from the ground. He just maintained his balance.

Up ahead loomed a sequoia with a massive hole in the center, so that it served as a tunnel. Through it, he could make out what had to be the grove. Amber, maroon, and purple leaves adorned aspen trees that huddled together like monks at prayer.

Arielle and Devika reached the grove first. Arielle landed the scooter and they both hopped off. Jiro and Eris weren't far behind. Neil reached the path heading through the sequoia, his lungs burning. He paused to check on Anand and Dirk. At that moment several of the turkeys attacked the pair and their scooter ploughed into the ground, sending both boys toppling over the handlebars. The toads swarmed over their legs and torsos and covered the turkeys.

Neil ran back to help, afraid to shoot lest he hit one of them. To his relief, both boys sprang back to their feet, shedding the toads. But the turkeys were gone. The boys ran, eyes wild. Neil tried to cover them, but it was like fighting off a tidal wave with a water pistol. Nevertheless, it was enough for Anand and Dirk to stay ahead.

It took all Neil's willpower to stand pat and wait for the pair to catch up. He feared being covered by the toads himself, unable to fight free as poison was injected into his body from a thousand glistening needles. His skin itched but he stood his ground until Anand and Dirk reached him, the toads close.

"Are you ok?" Neil asked as he directed them toward the grove and took off.

"Yes," Anand replied as they ran. "Don't think they pierced our suits."

A thump against Neil's back sent a chill through him. He'd been hit; he was sure of it. But there was no follow-on sting. "Faster," he ordered, not liking the panicked tone in his voice.

Up ahead, Nico beamed from the safety of the grove. Neil wondered why he'd thought Nico's sims were a good idea. Between this and the invisible Pandirus in the flying Venice sim, Nico was clearly unbalanced.

Panting, Neil leapt between two trunks into the grove. He kept running until he reached a small pond. Anand and Dirk followed a couple of steps behind him. The others watched the toads, which had ground to a halt beyond the perimeter. None entered the grove. They moved around the sides, as if to surround the place; lay siege to it. That was fine with him.

Neil turned around and shot Nico in the back, lighting up his suit target.

"What?" Nico asked.

Neil glared at him. "Are we safe?"

Nico stabbed a finger at the toads outside the grove. "They're programmed not to enter. The trees might as well be fortress walls."

Anand moved over to the edge of the grove, inspecting the toads, which hopped more urgently at his proximity. "Too bad these aren't real. Can you imagine one in Sergeant Terror's chair before she sat on it?" When Eris and Trini gave him horrified looks, he quickly amended. "I'd have an antidote on hand. A joke only. I don't want to hurt her."

"I can imagine her giving you detention in which you have to walk barefoot across a bed of hot coals because of it," Devika replied sweetly.

Chest heaving in an effort to catch his breath, Neil plopped to the ground beside the small pool. The blue-green water was clear all the way to the sandy bottom. Neil rose to his knees and shuffled closer. The air smelled damp, as if it would soon rain. He dipped his hands down into the pool and drew up the ice-cold water. When he took a drink, it tasted refreshing, but upon swallowing, he found it disappeared upon reaching his throat. He snorted in annoyance.

Sim. Of course.

It would be the same if he tried to eat anything. He'd get the taste—the sim could deceive his senses—but it wouldn't fill him. Thankfully, he wasn't parched. If he had been, he might've killed Nico over it.

"Neil!" Arielle shouted.

Neil twisted back to see her pointing beyond him, her eyes wide. In the middle of the pond, a round bubble the size of a carving pumpkin had emerged on the surface. It glided toward him. Six others joined it.

He jumped to his feet and retreated a few paces, shoulders tensing. "What are they?"

Nico hurried over to join him. "They're harmless. Touch one."

Neil shook his head. "Not a chance."

"It's okay," Nico said. "I promise, you've nothing to worry about. Check them out."

Everyone crowded around, though no one stepped into the water. The bubbles, now nearly as tall as Neil, paused at the pool's edge.

"Come on guys, someone has to have a spine," Nico huffed.

Since the bubbles had stopped moving, Neil leaned in a little closer to inspect one. It wasn't quite a bubble. Rather a sphere of water. Neil reached cautiously with a finger and tapped it. The bubble burst, dousing him.

As Neil wiped his face, the sounds of several water balloons bursting filled his ears. All of the bubbles had exploded, dousing everyone except Nico, who laughed so hard he cried. Neil shook his hands and arms, trying to remove the excess water… and not strangle Nico.

"You're a skunk sack," Jiro complained.

More water bubbles expanded out of the water. Everyone retreated.

"What are they?" Dirk asked.

"Aqua bombers," Nico replied, chest puffed out.

"Are they real?" Arielle took a couple of steps closer to examine one, but kept her arms tucked at her sides.

"As real as anything in a sim," Nico said.

Arielle rolled her eyes. "I meant, are they based off actual aliens?"

"Oh." Nico shrugged. "Could be. I don't know all the aliens in the universe."

Neil had to hand it to Nico. He was extremely creative in the handling of his sims. Crazy, but creative.

Anand and Devika grabbed Nico's arms, having snuck up behind him.

"What are you doing?" Nico tried to pull away.

"Let's go Space Ace." The twins dragged him to the pool and tossed him, causing the aqua bombers to all burst a second time. Nico lurched up from beneath the water, while the team hooted and hollered.

An alarm went off. Dirk checked the wrist-comp velcroed to his left arm. "We better get going, if we're going to get to the Space City Games Cup."

Neil glanced at his own wrist-comp. Three hours until the start of the championship match. He'd really wanted to complete all three bases, but it had taken them forever to find the first and travel from there to the second. Now he'd need to hurry to make it home. He'd been looking forward to the cup for weeks, ever since Grandpa had informed him they had tickets. He should've worked with Nico on better parameters for their tasks within his setting, rather than giving him cart blanche on everything.

"Nico, it's time to wrap this up," Neil said.

"I can't wait for our Games season to start," Eris said as Nico ended the sim, leaving them all back inside the large round cages in the clean room-like facility that comprised the sim training facility.

Neil couldn't either. After losing the Academy Games championship to Riagan last year, he'd waited all summer for revenge. He'd already circled their first match with the Taurus.

Opening the door to his large metal cage, Neil realized he was dry again. Mere seconds ago he'd been drenched. Amazing what the sim could fool the body into thinking was real.

His wrist-comp beeped at him, indicating a new message from Riagan. Likely an excuse for why he'd missed their first team exercise. There was also a message from Maellyn sent yesterday, promising she'd be home tomorrow. She'd spent all summer on Niveum working to cure the Apidium monkeys from an outbreak. He'd only exchanged a few messages with her since she left. The Apidium seemed to be adjusting well, so she was thrilled. But he was anxious for her return.

Pulling up Riagan's message, Neil read. *Need you ASAP. Guiman has a task for us.*

A task? Right now? Better not take too long. He wasn't missing the Cup. Grandpa had promised they had great seats.

"Guys, I've got to meet Riagan." Neil started for the door.

"You two are thick as thieves," Jiro noted. "What have you been doing all summer?"

"Just some work for my grandpa," Neil lied. He hated lying, but there was no way anyone could know what he and Riagan were up to. It would put them all at risk.

This exciting new entry in the Space City series is available now.

About the Author

Jared Austin is a young adult science fiction author who lives in the Rocket City—Huntsville, Alabama. With Space City and the books in the series to follow, he hopes to show and inspire his daughter and son, as well as all of his readers, that science and technology are not dull subjects, but gateways to a brighter, exciting future.

If you would like to learn more about the series and future novels, visit: https://jareddanielaustin.com

Books in Series:
Space City
Escape
Space City Outbreak
Contact Not Found

Follow me on social media:
Facebook Author Page: www.facebook.com/jareddanielaustin
Instagram: jared_austin1981

Thank you for reading my book! If you enjoyed it, please consider leaving a review. Even just a few words would help others decide if the book is right for them. Best regards and thank you in advance!

www.ingramcontent.com/pod-product-compliance
Lightning Source LLC
Chambersburg PA
CBHW071256190726
48292CB00007B/2554